MR. MARSHALL'S METHOD

JESSA YORK

"I don't know what lies around the bend, but I'm going to believe that the best does."

L.M. Montgomery

ALSO BY JESSA YORK

Mr. Marshall's Method

Ebook

Cover Design by More Than Words Graphic Design

Proofing by Emily Kirkpatrick

❀ Created with Vellum

1

Holly

"Fuck me hard and then some," Ivy said, peering over my shoulder as I shoved more junk inside my locker, praying it would shut this time.

"Thanks for the offer, chickie, but I'll refrain if that's okay?"

"Is he a student or a teacher?" Paige said, slithering up on the other side of me. She gave my locker a body check to assist my efforts, eyes sticking off to the side.

"Teacher," Ivy said, running her fingers through the mess of blonde curls on her head, fluffing herself up like she was ready to pounce.

Turning around, I shook my head. "What are you guys...holy cow," I whispered as any breath I had in my lungs disappeared. The man these girls were talking about was hot. Take your breath away, strip your panties off kind of hot.

His dark hair was on the longer side of short. Just enough so I could run my fingers through it.

The man could be in film—he had just the right amount of rugged good looks mixed with boy next door charm.

They giggled at me while I attempted to recover. "Pick your jaw up, Holly," Paige said, tapping her finger under my chin. Her arms were full of books and assignments not due for weeks. I'd bet my life on it.

"I would have done my makeup if I'd known we were getting a new teacher," Ivy said, currently sporting an hour's worth of face fixing.

"Kensington's ticker went on the fritz last week," Alex said, moseying on up to us. "My mom said he'll be out for weeks if not months." His mom was the principal of our high school. Therefore, he was our inside scoop into any and all gossip on the students and teachers.

"The new guy's name is Mr. Marshall. Brand new to the system so we get to break him in," Alex said, giving his hips a thrust.

"I have a feeling my English mark is about to improve dramatically," Ivy said, shamelessly sticking her chest out before strutting off to introduce herself.

"You go, girl," Alex said in his high-pitched voice. Ivy's skirt was too short—her tight shirt, too low. Just like every day. The admin stopped calling her on dress code violations years ago. It did nothing anyway. The girl wore what the girl wanted to wear.

Which was interesting because we all had the same uniforms, but Ivy liked to get them—altered.

The last time Alex's mom sent her home for improper hemlines, Ivy's mom created such a shitstorm on social media the school ended up with a PR nightmare.

Thus, the reason little Miss Ivy got to prance around in her short skirts and gaping necklines. Not that any of these "boys" at school were her type anyway. She just liked to flaunt and tease the young hopefuls at Santa Lena's Academy for the brightest and best—and those with the deepest pockets who were lucky enough to snag a spot.

Her real sights were normally set on college guys. Not that I blamed her one bit. While some of the boys in my school could be nice, they just didn't—do it for me, if you know what I mean.

I'd always been attracted to men's bodies as opposed to pre-growth spurt. Of course, it wasn't only their physical selves that needed to catch up—their mental and emotional states were years behind us as well.

That was where I differed even more. In my mother's shining brilliance, she decided to hold me back a year before sending me to kindergarten. My birthday is in August, so mom decided to give me a leg up on my classmates.

This backfired drastically on her once I began puberty earlier than expected. Add on the extra year I was already ahead of the other kids--you can imagine the awkwardness.

Sporting a full C-cup in grade six was not something you wanted when most of your friends were still playing with dolls when nobody was looking. Those middle school years were filled with boys' stares, rude comments and unwanted, "accidental" touches.

Ivy flipped her hair back in the universally known love language of, "I'll do whatever the heck you want," as she laughed. Mr. Marshall nodded, smirked, then strode into his awaiting classroom.

"Burn," Alex yelled, quickly getting Ivy's attention. She saluted him with her pink-tipped middle finger before walking away.

"GOD DAMN IT." I heard a raspy voice say further behind the auditorium stage. It kind of freaked me out because other than myself, nobody was ever back here. Normally when I came during lunch to work on the drama set, I was all alone. Treading more carefully, I hugged my backpack closer to my stomach. The scent of decades of musty, dusty costumes and props filled my nose.

Passing the last curtain, I poked my head into one of the makeshift dressing rooms. It was the new teacher, shoulders hunched awkwardly over as he maniacally rubbed at his crotch. "What the..." I said out loud, not able to contain my confusion at what I saw. Was he getting—friendly with himself back here? My backpack dropped to the floor, creating a hollow, thudding sound.

His head jerked up, rag in hand, more than a little surprised to see me. My eyes couldn't help but travel down to his pants where a large, blue spot appeared beside his pocket. "Oh, I'm sorry. I didn't realize anyone else would be back here," I said, floundering with embarrassment. The white rag sported streaks of the same blue stain on his light brown pants.

"What happened?" I asked, retrieving my bag, walking into the room.

"I'm supposed to check on how the props are coming for the play. One of the projects tried to get up close and personal," he said, a sexy smile popping up on his way-to-handsome face.

"I don't blame it one bit," I said in a low voice, taking the time to get a good look at our newest faculty member. The sleeves of his button-down shirt were undone and rolled up to his elbows, displaying the finest arms I'd seen in my life. If his forearms were that muscular, what would the rest of him look like?

"Pardon?"

"I said, I'll help you out in a minute." A faint blush started somewhere around my breasts then traveled upwards. Bending down, I hid my face for second, opening a few zippers in my bag before finding what I was looking for. "Got it," I said, victorious, smiling as I stood.

"A marker?" he asked, not understanding my glee.

"It's one of those stain eraser pens. Here," I said, handing it over. His fingers touched mine when he grabbed it. A zing of hot electricity shot straight through me.

"Hmm, what do you do?" Not waiting for instructions, he uncapped the lid, rubbing the stain, making even more of a mess.

"No, no, no." I scolded him, snatching the pen out of his hand. "You're just making it worse." I was close enough now to smell his spicy aftershave. My body couldn't help swaying toward him for another sniff. Kneeling down in front of him, I ripped the rag out of his hand. "First, you're supposed get as much off as possible."

Dabbing the spot, I glanced up at him. His sparkling blue eyes bore into me, giving me a funny feeling in my stomach. "Then you have to push the applicator in, so the stuff comes out."

His eyes closed as another smile appeared on his face. Placing his hands on his hips, he said, "You don't say?" One dark, eyebrow cocked upwards while he looked back down at me.

"Trust me, I've done this a hundred times," tumbled out before I could stop it. I was mortified as a blush burned my cheeks. Scribbling harder now, trying not to think about what I'd just said, my other hand dropped the rag so I could get a better grip on his leg. Holy crap, his thigh was made of concrete or something. The heat radiating into my hand was nearly scorching. All on their own, my fingers flexed, confirming the fact that Mr. Marshall rarely missed a workout.

"Have you now?" he said suggestively, his tone making my cheeks even redder.

"I'm a bit of a klutz," I said, dabbing the ever-improving stain. "It looks better already, see?"

"Better, but still noticeable. I'll have to go home and change, thanks anyway," he said, reaching down for my hand, halting any further attempt.

As he pulled me up, we were face to face, his eyes falling to my mouth. My breath caught in my throat as I began to feel a bit dizzy. "No, really. Dry it with the hand dryer in the washroom and use this again," I said, swinging the stain remover in front of him as nonchalantly as I could while my heart thumped a crazy beat.

"That'll work?" he asked, eyes still stuck on my lips, hand continuing to grip my sweaty one. The skin on my hand tingled, sending a sensual warmth through me.

"Yep, trust me. It works." Sliding the pen into his pocket, his mischievous eyes darted up to mine.

"We haven't been properly introduced. I'm Evan," he said, shaking my hand. Well, more like holding it tighter.

"Holly." I choked out, sputtering a bit from a throat that had suddenly gone dry.

"Grape?" He cocked his head to the side.

Puzzled, I searched his face. "My name's Holly, not grape."

Leaning in, he smirked. "Your gum, is it grape?"

My jaw gaped open. We were so close he could smell the flavor of my gum. I swallowed loudly. "Uh, yeah, I think so."

His eyes flickered over my face as a slow, sexy smile crossed his face. "I like grape," he whispered into my ear, leaving goose bumps in his wake. I inhaled sharply, shocked at his insinuation. "What do you teach, Holly?" he asked, squeezing my hand a little more now, peering down at me. We were so close, his lips wouldn't have far to go if he were to kiss me.

"Teach?"

"Teach. Or are you just the resident laundry personnel?" He joked, his other hand moving to my lower back.

"I don't teach, I'm a student."

"What?" he said, shocked, the air leaving his lungs as though someone had punched him.

"I'm in grade twelve."

Eyebrows up, eyes practically bugging out, he immediately dropped my hand, taking a step back. "You're, you're—a student?"

Sad for the loss of his touch, I sighed. "Yeah."

"Fuck," he said, raking his hand through his hair. "I'm so sorry, Holly. Jesus, I thought you were a teacher." His eyes scanned me again. Shaking his head, he said, "You look a lot older than grade twelve. And where's your uniform?"

"I don't wear one when I'm working on the props. Things get messy back here," I said, glancing again at his stain.

"Damn, I'm really sorry."

"It's fine. Look," I said, grabbing onto his arm. It felt—manly. His eyes dropped down to my hand. "No harm, no foul. All I did was help you out with a wardrobe malfunction in the drama department. Happens all the time." My smile was genuine. Right now, I wanted nothing more than to relieve his anxiety. "Besides, even if something had happened—I'm no snitch."

With that, I picked up my backpack, turned around, heading back out to my project.

2

Evan

An hour later and still, all I could think about was Holly's hands on me. Every time I closed my eyes to shake her out of my head, I pictured her gazing up at me from her knees. I'd never had to concentrate so hard on keeping myself in check.

There was only so much Shakespeare I could recite on demand. The Bard never let me down when I was in a bind —like when sexy, cute, blondes began rubbing the front of my pants. How I managed to keep an erection at bay, I'd never know.

The bell rang, interrupting my train of thought. "Paraphrase the next chapter for homework, please." I instructed the class as they collected their books. Sounds of chair legs scraping the floor filled the air.

"Mr. Marshall?" I heard my voice called behind me. Turning around, I saw it was that same blonde who had been outwardly flirting with me this morning.

"Hi—Amber, is it?" I said, even though I remembered quite well what her name was.

Her forced giggle made me nauseous. "Ivy," she said, laughing like it was the funniest thing she'd ever heard. The way she flipped her long, curly hair told me I hadn't made myself clear with her earlier.

"Right, Ivy." I nodded, giving her a completely neutral look. This girl didn't need one ounce of encouragement.

"Umm, the assignment?" she said, twirling a strand of hair around her fingers while she gave her best attempt at sticking out her chest. Good grief.

"Yes?" I answered, crossing my arms in front of me, getting increasingly more annoyed.

"I'm not sure I exactly understand it?" She looked at me from under her long, mascaraed eyelashes.

Holly didn't wear a lot of makeup. She was more of a natural beauty—shit. My blood ran cold. I needed to stop thinking about her. "Look, Amber—I mean Ivy—I explained it thoroughly during class. Try your best at it tonight. We'll share in class tomorrow."

With that, I spun around, putting away the books I had used for this class, then opened the ones for the next. One more period, then home time.

"But do you think you could—"

"Time for your next class, the bell's about to ring," I said, not bothering to look up. Leave, little pest. Erasing the wipe off board like it was my soul purpose in life, I peered over my shoulder to see her rushing out the door.

One more hour. Then I could congratulate myself on my very first, full day of solo teaching. The fact that little Miss Stain Remover hadn't shown up in any of my classes filled me with relief. Last thing in this world I needed was to deal with her and those wide, almond shaped eyes staring at me for an hour every day.

The bell rang, signaling the beginning of class. "Okay, everyone. Take your seats please. My name is," I said, stopping the second my vision landed on her. Shit, so much for being home-free. Our eyes locked immediately—Holly's holding mine a willing hostage. Her delicate hand grasped a silky tendril, winding it seductively around her finger. "Mr. Marshall. I'm taking over for Mr. Kensington while he recuperates."

A wave of heat shot through me as I watched. Dragging my gaze away from her, I cleared my throat attempting to remember what exactly I was doing here.

Scooping up a stack of freshly photocopied handouts, I strolled down the aisle handing out papers to the students as I went. A few more steps and I'd be at Holly's desk. Her long legs came into view first—that skirt seemed very short as my eyes lingered over the expanse of smooth, tanned skin. My gaze whipped to hers as I held my breath.

"This contains the course outline for the next month." I inhaled, deeply. "If Mr. Kensington is gone longer..." The paper I passed to Holly somehow slipped through her hand. Bending down, I reached for it just as she leaned over. Our heads collided with a crack.

At this angle, I could see directly down her shirt, those breasts that I'd ogled earlier, now in full view. My breath caught in my throat. "I'm so sorry," I said, standing up once she was safely out of harm's way. "Are you all right?" Her fingers traced a red mark on her forehead.

"Yeah, fine. Sorry, I shouldn't have..."

"No, it was completely my fault, I didn't see you." That was a lie. Every fiber of my being knew exactly where she was. Heat curled down my spine as she adjusted her shirt, glimpsing up at me with the most captivating eyes I'd ever seen.

A small smile appeared on her face. "Thanks," she said, pulling the course paper out of my hand. Deciding to stop standing there like an idiot, making even more of a scene than I already was, I continued my way around the classroom.

Discussing exams, papers, grading, etc. took up a large part of our first class. Luckily for me—but unfortunately for Mr. Kensington—they'd only been in class a couple of weeks before he had a heart attack. That meant there was still time to mold the first part of the semester how I wanted it, yet still fit in with what was already taught.

Complaints about the upcoming Shakespeare sections made me smirk to myself. Not many kids liked those compulsory aspects of English classes. To me, though, that was my favorite part. Reading, deciphering, then absorbing his words gave me a certain—high, if you will.

As I said, my opinion wasn't exactly popular. Certainly not to a bunch of seventeen-year olds. "We use many of Shakespeare's own words today, in our everyday language. Can anyone give me an example?" I asked, knowing full well I'd look out into a sea of lowered eyes and uncomfortable glances.

To my surprise, one hand went up. Quirking my head to the side, I asked, "Yes?" More than curious to hear this answer. My heart rate quickened—almost nervous for her.

Holly's sharp eyes examined me as she straightened herself in the desk. "Wild-goose chase."

A smile the size of London crossed my face along with a sudden burst of pride. She had beauty and brains. "Very good." Scanning the rest of the class, it appeared just as I'd expected.

"How about, "Eaten out of house and home"? I'm sure you've heard your parents say that." The students began talking to each other.

"Bet you hear that every day, Wyatt," a kid with spikey, blonde hair said, kicking the desk in front of him—which likely held Wyatt. I didn't doubt his accusation one bit. The student in question was at least a head taller than his classmates. And that was with everyone sitting down.

"Whatever, jerk," Wyatt said, swatting his log of an arm behind him, swooping a few papers as he went. The class laughed at their exchange.

"Anyone else have anything to add?" I leaned back on my desk, taking my glasses off for a brief second to rub the bridge of my nose.

"Green eyed monster. That's in Othello." Holly announced, not waiting for me to call on her.

"Brown-noser," the girl beside her said, giving her a sly smile while Holly just rolled her eyes.

The sound of the bell surprised me for the first time today. Reluctantly, I shoved my glasses back on. "Review your notes on what Mr. Kensington gave you on "Romeo and Juliet". We'll continue with it tomorrow. More groans of protest followed my instructions.

As everyone filed out with the usual roughhousing by the boys and cliquey magnetism of the girls according to their social strata, one student lagged behind, slowly filling her backpack. I wiped a sheen of sweat from my brow as I arranged my books, notes, pens and laptop into my bag, waiting until she was closer to my desk.

Gliding up the aisle, her skirt swayed enticingly, drawing my eyes again. Snapping my vision up to her face, I nodded toward her. "I was very impressed with your answers," I said, digging around in my pocket for what I was looking for.

"Oh, that was easy. I love Shakespeare. It's a bit of a hobby for me," she said, a beautiful flush covering her skin, apparently embarrassed by her answer. That caused a desire deep inside of me to flicker to life. Every inch of my body craved her.

"You like Shakespeare?" I asked, a bit surprised as removed my glasses. God, I hated these things.

"Mmm hmm, always have." I wanted to hear her to explain in that breathy voice why she liked Shakespeare and what her favorite plays were. Maybe we shared similar views or—even better—perhaps we didn't. Damn, how I wished we could go out and talk endlessly about this. Closing my eyes, pinching the bridge of my nose, I took a deep breath.

She's your student. She's your student. I repeated in my head.

"I wanted to thank you for letting me borrow this," I said, handing her the stain remover pen.

Holly giggled, shaking her head. "That's fine, I have like three more in my locker. Just keep it." Hiking her backpack on her shoulder, she prepped to walk out.

Everything in me wanted to stop her. "No, really. I insist." Holding out the pen, she moved to grasp it, our hands touching during the exchange. A shock ran through my body at the sudden contact with her soft skin. Her mesmerizing eyes met mine, holding my gaze as our fingers stilled. Did she feel it, too?

"Umm, thanks." Was all she said before ripping it out of my hand, hurrying from the classroom. I watched her go, my stomach sinking as she left.

3

Holly

"Babe, we have watched this movie twice already tonight. Now, you know I love me some Audrey Hepburn but even my eyes are starting to cross," Alex said as he fell back on the nest of pillows he'd arranged on the floor of Ivy's room.

Ivy threw a stuffed giraffe at his head. "Hush, Holly likes it," she said, squeezing me in an awkward backward hug as I laid on my stomach on her bed.

"I know, I know, she was named after the beautiful heroine," he said, rolling his eyes as he threw his arms out.

"Oh, come on. I see you making eyes at George Peppard," I said, fluttering my lashes at him.

Alex simultaneously stood and snapped his fingers. "That man is all class. Let me tell you."

"They don't make actors like that anymore." I sighed, dragging the pillow with me as I sat up.

"Mr. Marshall has that same debonair look about him," Alex said, dramatically falling back down on the pillows, his hand over his face as though he were fainting.

"Mark my words—I will have that man." Ivy pointed her finger at Alex.

My stomach tightened at her words. I could feel my heart pounding in my ears. The thought of Ivy having Mr. Marshall made me feel sick.

"Get in line, sistah. Get—in—line," Alex repeated as he reached his long arm over to grab more chips from the bowl beside him.

Paige stood up from her place on the oversized chair, stretching and yawning. "I should go."

Ivy shot her eyes over, glaring at poor Paige. "Sit down, the night is young," she said, slowly pointing her finger toward the chair.

Sighing, Paige said, "I've got work to do." Then bent down to pick up her bag.

"Drop it, missy," Ivy said, shaking her head. "You agreed to a movie night with us and you're staying."

"We've watched two movies already. Besides, I need to get this novel assignment finished—"

Ivy rolled her eyes. "The assignment that's not due until next month?"

I giggled as Paige's face dropped, a look of defeat crossing it. "One more movie and then we can stop for a study break?" I suggested with a smile.

"Fine," Paige said, giving up with a loud exhale as she sat back down, bag in her lap.

"I can't believe we're in senior year already, can you?" I asked, attempting to change the subject.

Ivy smiled ear to ear as she rubbed the palms of her hands together. "Senior class trip, the drama production—"

Alex cut her off. "Prom," he screamed, jumping up clapping his hands maniacally. These two thought about prom far too often. For me, it was just another event that I didn't have the money for.

Ivy gasped, covering her mouth with both hands. They gazed at each other like they were in on a secret I wasn't privy to. "I almost forgot," Ivy squealed, flying off the bed and dashing off to her closet.

I shot Alex a puzzled look. In a soft voice he said, "Keep an open mind, sister friend. Promise?" His eyebrow raised in a, "You better listen or else" warning. Oh boy. Whatever conspiracy they'd dreamed up made my stomach twist and my palms sweaty.

Before I could pump him for answers, Ivy zoomed out with her arms full of dresses. "Oopff," she exclaimed as the dresses went sailing onto her canopied bed. "There," she said, out of breath, fixing her ponytail. "Which one do you guys like?" Her eyes snapped to me as she tilted her head in that cute way she had about her.

Moseying up for a closer look, I chose one immediately. "You look killer in red," I said, grabbing the long, silky, deep colored dress. It shimmered in the light making it even more glamorous.

Ivy shifted to the side. "I already picked mine, silly. Which one do you like?"

My breath caught in my throat. "What do you mean?"

"She means, pick a damn dress already and try it on." Alex reached around me, snatching a pink dress. "Pink is definitely your color." He draped it over my shoulder, careful with the hanger. Pushing me toward the closet, he said, "Make it snappy, we haven't got all night." He turned to Paige, "You, too. Get a move on."

"My mom's making mine." Paige huffed, leaning her head on her hand, elbow resting on the arm of the chair.

"Oh, I'm sure it'll be great," Alex said, trying to recover even though we all knew it would probably not look great. Paige's mom was single. Her dad was around but not a lot—he mostly spent his time taking care of his new wife and their three kids.

They were better off than I was. That didn't mean life wasn't tight for them, though. Paige's dad was often too busy to send a maintenance check. Meanwhile, her mom worked as a maid.

"It'll suck but mom's intent on sewing it for me. She's so excited, too. I don't want to hurt her feelings."

A pang of jealousy stabbed through my stomach. Paige's mom loved her so much and was involved in everything she did. It drove Paige crazy, of course. What I wouldn't give for a mother like that.

"Honey, don't you worry. I'll do your makeup so well that it won't matter if you're wearing a paper bag," Alex commiserated with her. "Now you," he said, pointing at me. "Try that on."

Still confused, I tried to question their motives. "But—"

"That's right, get that curvy butt of yours into this immediately," Alex said with glee. One more quick nudge from his hand got me into Ivy's closet.

Admittedly, her closet was probably as big as our entire trailer. Not to mention nicer. Rack after rack of clothing, cubbies bursting with shoes, it was every teenage girl's dream.

Hanging the dress up while I removed my clothes, I couldn't help but ogle it. The halter neckline would leave my shoulders bare. A zing of excitement ran through my body at how daring that would look.

Two minutes later, I emerged from the closet, dramatically leaning against my hand as I struck a pose for them.

"No way," Alex whispered, one hand to his throat, the other on his hip.

"It's perfect on you," Ivy screeched, rushing up to me. "You have to pick this one. I mean—try on the others but this is the one." Her fingers straightened the long skirt.

Paige squealed, "You look like a movie star." She'd dumped her schoolwork to come get a closer look.

My heart stopped as my stomach did a strange flippy thing. "Ivy, I can't afford it. Unless I quit paying the electric bill for the next year," I said, giving her a sweet smile.

She breathed out a gentle sigh. "It's on me, you know that."

"I couldn't," I stated, shaking my head. "It's too much."

"You have no choice. We need you with us at prom before you go jetting off to some Ivy league school, leaving us behind." Alex gave me a pouty face, his hands together in a praying position. "Please?"

"It's too expensive."

"Hush, Ivy's dad makes that much in a minute I bet."

"More." Ivy shrugged and they both laughed. "Whatever you don't take I'm just donating anyway. You might as well take it."

She was always so generous with her clothes—giving Paige and I things she claimed were just taking up space. "Are you sure? I feel bad," I said to Ivy, moving a step closer. She cracked a grin, pulling me in for a hug.

"Girl, it would be a crime not to wear that. It fits you like a glove," Alex said, retreating to his spot on the floor. Digging through the cabinet under the TV, he pulled out a DVD case. "Patrick Swayze and I'll be waiting for you when you're done." He cackled, cracking open the container.

4

Holly

Beep, beep, beep. I heard the familiar, annoying sound. "No way," I whimpered, searching the covers for my phone. Finally locating it, I shut the noise off. Laying back down was all I wanted to do. Instead, bleary-eyed, I plopped my legs over the side of the bed, feeling the soft rug under my feet.

The fun fur ran through my toes as I moved them gently. Sighing, I stood to turn on my light, glimpsing at the alarm clock on my tiny dresser. Four-thirty. Yawning, I ran a brush through my hair before twisting it up into a neat bun at the back of my head.

Gazing into the cracked mirror, thoughts of everything I had to do today came flooding into my brain. I closed my eyes as feelings of anxiousness flooded through my body. It was like this every morning. And every morning, I allowed myself a few moments of self-pity before shaking that off and getting on with my day.

~

"THREE SUNNY SIDE UP, ON WHITE," I yelled through the narrow window to the kitchen on my way to grab the pot of coffee.

"Gotcha, Dolly." Len snickered from the back. His nickname for me always made me laugh, even at six o'clock in the morning.

"Coffee?" I asked, pouring and swaying through the breakfast rush of business people on their way to work. Why they all couldn't just cook their own eggs at home, I didn't understand.

The sharp sound of ringing caught my attention. Looking up, I saw Len hitting the bell with his long handled, silver spatula. Yay. More orders to deliver.

"Hey, toots, hit me up before you go," a familiar voice sounded from the table to my left.

Ahh, Mr. Over-Entitled was back again. "You bet," I said politely, even though all I wanted to do was smack him over the head.

"Whoa, baby, leave some room for cream and sugar, will ya?" he said, pulling the cup as I poured, causing me to spill a bit.

"Sorry about that," I told him, yanking out the small rag I kept in my apron. "My fault." Resisting the urge to roll my eyes, I quickly mopped up the puddle of coffee.

"It's okay, beautiful. I like the view," he said, leering at my behind, making his other three friends at the table laugh. "Bring me a muffin next time you come by."

Flushing a bit, I nodded, then rushed off to grab my next set of orders.

~

"CAN'T you stay a few more minutes?" Dave begged as I filled out the timesheet in a hurry.

"I'll be late for school, I'm sorry," I said to my boss. Glancing down at my phone, I knew I'd likely be a few minutes late as it was. If the buses were running on time, I probably just missed the one I was supposed to take. "See you later," I called on my way out.

Raindrops hit my face as I stepped outside. Just my luck. Shoving my bag over top of my head, I ran for the bus stop. The very empty bus stop.

"Shit, shit, shit, shit," I shouted stamping my feet as I realized that I'd be waiting there at least another fifteen minutes in the rain. Throwing my bag down on the ground I looked up into the sky, and yelled, "Really? Like you haven't thrown enough shit at me? Now you're going to add rain?" I stood there letting the water rush over my face, milliseconds away from bursting into tears. Suddenly, a loud horn sounded, scaring the crap out of me.

Clutching my hands to my heart I opened my eyes wide to see a dark Jeep directly in front of me. I picked up my bag as the passenger window rolled down.

"You okay?" Mr. Marshall asked, quirking his eyebrow up.

"Umm, not exactly." Stunned, I stood as still as a statue, rain dripping down my eyelashes, making it difficult to see.

"Need a ride?" he asked looking me up and down.

"No, I'm fine thanks."

Mr. Marshall turned his head and looked out the front window chuckling. "I think you're less than fine. Get in the Jeep, Holly, I'll drive us to school." His eyes found mine and a sexy little smile crossed his face.

I peered down the street, hoping to see my bus driving

up. No such luck. In fact, I couldn't see much through the sheets of rain that were now falling down from the sky.

Weighing my options, I quickly understood there were none. I would be stupid to pass up a free ride to school in this weather. Slinging my bag over my shoulder, I opened the Jeep's door.

The spicy smell of his cologne surrounded me as I jumped inside. I shut my eyes, inhaling deeply while I reminded myself that this man was my teacher.

"I don't think you're supposed to give rides to students," I said, attempting to dry my face off on my sleeve. Realizing that my sleeve was even wetter than my skin was, I stopped the pointless action.

"So, I should just leave you out in the rain? That would be safer?" he said, glancing over at me quickly before watching for an opening to get back on the road. Traffic was crazy at this time of day. Add in the bad weather, and it turned into a virtual nightmare.

"I think there are rules about faculty driving students around."

He smiled again looking over at me. "You going to tell anyone?" He took his right hand off the wheel and reached behind us moving his body closer to me, causing his shoulder to bump mine.

"No," I said emphatically, shaking my head wondering what he was doing.

"Good, use this. It's clean," he said, tossing a gray towel in my lap. I picked it up, taking a quick sniff. It did indeed smell wonderful.

Mr. Marshall started laughing so hard his body shook as he pulled back into traffic. "Believe me now?" he asked still chuckling.

I couldn't have been any more obvious. "No, I believed

you. It's just a habit. I love the smell of fresh laundry." Undoing my hair, I let it down my shoulder as I used the towel to sop up as much water as possible.

Once again, his eyes checked me out, making me feel even more self-conscious. "Just getting off work?" he asked his eyebrows coming close together as he nodded, staring at my diner uniform.

"I work the early shift at the diner some days."

We stopped at a light and he turned to me. "You have a shift before school?"

His attention on made me uncomfortable causing me to squirm a bit in my seat. "Yeah, today I did," I said offhandedly like it was no big deal.

"How many days a week exactly?" His probing gaze not letting me go.

"As many as they need me for," I answered back quickly, using the towel on my chest and neck.

"And how many days a week would that be?" he asked pushing on the gas after the light changed.

"Most of them," I said, slightly annoyed to be found out.

"What?" he said as though he didn't believe me. The only thing I did was shrug.

"What time do you start?"

Sighing, I decided to just tell the truth. "Five."

"Five o'clock in the morning?" his voice rose with surprise.

"Yep, I'm at the school on scholarship." I explained in as few words as humanly possible.

His eyes shifted, then he nodded and continued driving. "That must be tough."

That was an understatement. This man had no idea about my life or how hard things were. "It's okay, really. I'm grateful that I even have a job."

"And you don't have a car?"

Peeling off my sweater, I began drying my arms. "If I had a car would I be standing outside at a bus stop?"

"Good point," he said turning onto a street that was just a few blocks from the school.

"Can you pull into the donut shop, please?" I asked, pointing to the right side of the road.

"Why? You hungry?" he said, taking his foot off the gas.

"No, I ate at work. I have to change into my uniform before I go into the school. I'd hoped I would make it to the bus on time if I didn't change first." Boy was I wrong.

He pulled into the strip mall parking lot, right up to the doors. The rain was still just as fierce. When I tried to return his towel, he refused, saying, "Keep it. You'll probably still need it."

Tucking it into my bag, I prepared to jump out. "Thanks for the ride, Mr. Marshall."

Those dark eyes of his, scanned my face. "You're welcome."

Evan

SHE'S YOUR STUDENT. She's your student. She's your student. I repeated again on a constant loop. Christ, having her sitting beside me like it was a wet T-shirt competition wasn't exactly helpful. The lace of her bra showed right through the thin material of her light-colored uniform.

Pinching the bridge of my nose, I tried like hell to get that image of her out of my mind. And what the hell was she doing working at a diner at five o'clock every morning? Then off to a full day of school?

As I continued through the drive though, I turned off the heat in the vehicle—blasting the fan to cool myself.

It didn't help.

~

SIPPING ON MY COFFEE, I kept watch on the donut store door. Well aware of the issues I could be getting into, I decided against propriety and waited for her anyway.

Finally, I spotted her blonde locks and school uniform. Honking the horn made her jump about a foot in the air. Her head snapped toward me, an incredulous look on her face that made me laugh. She quickly switched direction, stomping up to my window.

"You really need to stop doing that before you give me a heart attack," she said, standing back a few feet under the cover of the store awnings.

"Your heart is young, I'm sure it can take all kinds of exertions," I blurted out before I realized what I'd said. Images of her breathless, underneath me flooded my brain. She's your student. She's your student.

Her eyes narrowed on me. "What do you want? I have to run," she said, jerking her head in the direction of the school.

"I'll drive you there. Get in." She looked all around, hugging her bag to her body. Her indecision was driving me crazy. "Holly, get in the Jeep," I ordered. "I'm not letting you get soaked again."

She gave up, sprinting to my Jeep. "What if someone sees?" she said in a huff, jumping inside then pulling hard on the seat belt to buckle up.

"Then I guess they'll see a teacher giving a wet rat of a student a ride to school," I said snidely. Placing my arm on the back of her seat, I slowly reversed with extra care and attention in this weather.

She thwacked me on the arm. "I'm not a wet rat." I caught a whiff of her soft, floral perfume. A powdery, clean smell. It caused me to take a few extra moments to back up just so I could inhale her scent.

My damn eyes may have lingered on her bare leg where her school skirt hiked up a bit. She's your student. She's your...shit, when I looked up, her eyes were on me. Holly caught me looking. Clearing my throat, I put the Jeep into drive.

"What's your first class?" I asked, trying to get my mind on something else.

"Bio," she said, exhaling hard.

"You don't like biology?" I asked, signaling to turn down the road the school was on.

"Not really."

"I was a bio wiz kid. If you ever need help—" I said before she cut me off.

"That's nice of you. I do well in it, I just don't really like it. I find it boring."

Of course, she does well in bio. She likely does well in every class if she's here on a scholarship. They don't hand those things out to just anyone. You'd have to be exceptional for the academy to accept you.

"What subjects do you like?" I asked, waiting behind a group of cars as they stopped for a few pedestrians blindly crossing the street in the storm.

"English and Art mostly," she said, wiping some of the condensation off the inside of her window with her light-pink polished finger.

My heart beat faster when she said, English. She could just be saying it because that's what I taught. On some level,

I didn't quite believe Holly was the type to bullshit or brown-nose her way through life.

"I'll drop you off behind the school?" I asked, slowing to turn into the parking lot. This would be the best way not to get noticed.

"Yeah, that's cool, thanks." Holly slipped an elastic off her wrist, gathering her hair together on the back of her head. Those movements caused her breasts to jut out in a very alluring manner, enticing my eyes to snap over for a quick peek.

Once we were at a safe enough distance, I stopped near the benches. It was dry there because of the overhang from the roof.

"Thanks, Mr. Marshall. And seriously, I won't say a word. I promise," she said, looking at me with a sweet, genuine smile before opening the door to hurry out.

She's your student. She's your student. She's your student.

Closing my eyes, I tried yet again to stop thinking about Holly Anderson.

5

Evan

"It really just makes sense, Evan. I mean you do teach English. Romeo and Juliet is on your docket at the moment. The leap to drama isn't out of your wheel-house, I'm sure," my boss lectured me. Apparently, the drama teacher's wife had their baby early. Too early. He was going to be gone for a while.

Now, Principal McGreggor needed a fill in for that teacher as well. "I've never directed a drama production before. Honestly, I wouldn't even know where to start."

"I was told you acted in plays?"

Damn, she caught me. "Acting and directing are totally different things."

"We hold three major drama plays here each year. It's a fine oiled machine. Most of the regulars are involved already. The cast has been chosen so you don't even have to go through the torture of auditions. All you've got to do is be there to direct and act as a go-between."

Looking out the window, I saw the sun finally peeking

out from behind the morning's storm clouds. If Principal McGreggor was asking me to help, they were obviously hard up. Plus, it's not like I had any seniority to say, no, and pass it off to the next sorry teacher.

I was the sorry teacher. "If you think I can do this, I'll try my best," I said, rubbing the back of my neck. Doubt and uncertainty were my new best friends.

My boss smiled a knowing grin. "You'll do just fine, don't worry." Then she opened her laptop signaling the end of our chat.

Great, I'd somehow gone from overseeing the set displays and costumes to directing the whole fucking shebang. Walking out of her office, I felt like a load of bricks had been dumped on me. Without even thinking, my feet headed straight for the drama department.

Opening the giant doors with a loud screech, I walked to the back where the light was on. Sure enough, there was Holly, wearing tight, black yoga pants and a loose, pink top. Her hair was up in a messy topknot, a few lazy tendrils escaping down her face.

"How's it going?" I asked, leaning up against the wall.

Her head turned fully to me. "Good. You don't have to worry about me. I've been in charge of the sets before." Her hand held a large paintbrush, full of the same blue paint that had accosted me the other day.

"Not worried about the set," I lied, because I had no idea if Holly knew what she was doing or not. Not to mention the fact that the large, blue board in front of her looked very— blue. Just like yesterday. No change at all. "Apparently, Mr. Rodriguez's wife had their baby this morning."

"Oh that's," Holly started out all cheery, then her face dropped. "Way too early. Is everyone all right?" she asked, voice and face full of concern.

"So far so good. He's taking time off starting now."

"Good for him. Gosh, I hope everything turns out," she said, staring at the ground. "Who's going to direct the play now?" she asked, gazing up at me.

I didn't answer, just lifted my eyebrow. "No way," she said, beginning to giggle. The sound of her laugh lightened my day.

Nodding, I said, "Uh huh, lucky me."

"Have you ever directed before?" she asked as her eyes studied me.

"Nope."

More giggling. In fact, she laughed so hard, the paint brush dropped to the brown paper that was covering the floor. Blue paint splattered in a neat effect, splaying out like the sun's rays. "Oh shoot," she said, bending over to pick it up. Her round, shapely behind on full display.

She's your student. She's you student.

"This is all, very nice," I said, creeping closer to her. "It's extremely—blue."

She burst out laughing. "It's blue, now. Later, it'll be less blue."

I raised my eyebrow at her in disbelief. "I'll take your word for it."

"You'll eat your words, Mr. Marshall. Just remember that. Great works take time to create." She looked me over again then turned back to making more stuff—blue.

Holly

"DID YOU HEAR?" someone screamed behind me, causing me to drop my brush again, splattering paint all over my pant leg.

Spinning around, I said, "You scared the crap out of me."

"Mr. Marshall," Ivy squealed, bouncing around. "He's our new drama director."

"Oh really? Why's that?" I responded, not wanting to let on that I already knew.

"Mr. Rodriguez's wife had their baby and our hot teacher gets to take over for him." She skipped over to me grabbing onto my shoulders, jumping. "Can you believe it? Getting into his pants is going to be even easier than I originally thought." A chill ran down my spine at the thought of Ivy getting anywhere near Evan's pants.

Gently removing her fingers from my shoulder blades, I backed up snagging my brush again. "Why exactly do you want to get into his pants? He's a little old, even for you." I turned back around, dipping my brush into the paint as I felt a sudden rush of butterflies invade my stomach.

"Are you blind?" she asked, then began counting off on her fingers. "He's hot. He's not that much older than us. Did I mention he's hot?"

"Yeah you may have mentioned it. What you didn't mention was the fact that he is our teacher."

"So?"

"What do mean so? Typically, we shouldn't use high school faculty as a dating pool."

"Oh, who cares? He's maybe only a year or two older than the guys I normally date anyway. Can you stand how hot he is when he takes off his nerd glasses and rubs between his eyebrows?"

Ivy was not wrong, Mr. Marshall was entirely too sexy when he took off his glasses. Actually, he was equally as hot with them on. "He's your teacher. He's off-limits. Besides you have at least three college guys on the line right now as we speak. That's not enough for you?" I tried not to growl as I plastered on a fake smile.

She shrugged, flipping her hair. "They mean nothing to me. Anyway, I'm pretty sure Mr. Marshall is into me."

For some reason that statement tied my stomach in a knot. "Why would you say that?" I asked turning back around to finish painting.

"Just the way he looks at me when I talk to him. Give me a week. I'm telling you he's definitely interested. Who could resist all this?"

I twisted my head back around to see Ivy doing a sexy dance that made me snort. "You're crazy."

Ivy did one last suggestive shimmy before she strode out the door.

After she left, I tried to get rid of the sense of dread that came over me. I wasn't sure if the feeling was fear that Ivy would make a fool out of herself or fear that she would succeed in her endeavor.

Evan

WHAT A MESS. Well-oiled machine my ass. This was more like a cluster fuck if you asked me. However, it was now my cluster fuck, and I needed to get things under control. The kids and their bags, sweaters, papers and various other para-phernalia spread out over the entirety of the auditorium.

Fingers to my lips, I did a shrill whistle before I spoke, "All right everyone quiet down please. I am sure you have all heard by now, Mr. Rodriguez and his wife just had their baby and I'll be taking over his duties. I'm not going to lie—I honestly have no idea what to do here. You guys are going to have to help me."

"I know, how about we start on the first page," a short girl with even shorter hair suggested as she pushed glasses that were way too big for her face back up.

"You don't just—start—Belinda," a know-it-all sneered at her. "Don't you know anything?" she said, completely disgusted. Everyone began taking sides, arguing their points amongst themselves.

It was even louder than it had been before. Raising my voice, I said, "What I need you to do is gather into groups based on your duties or roles and choose a representative. This will be someone who will report to me and come to me with questions or concerns. For example, we'll need a group consisting of cast members, a group consisting of stage-hands, lighting, sound, etc. You get the point."

"Do that for me now, please. I'll give you five minutes to assemble and choose a rep," I said, dismissing them with my hands. For a moment or two everyone stood looking rather shell-shocked. Then the born leaders began to take control.

Searching around the theater, I saw Holly walking off to the side of the stage by herself. I knew I should stay where I was—both in mind and body.

Something inside of me made that impossible. Something about her drew me in. Before I knew it, my feet carried me to her. Those light blue eyes looked up at me. "I didn't take you for a loner, Miss Anderson."

She cast her eyes to the ground for a second before gazing back at me. "Hmm, you'd be surprised," she said, fidgeting with her skirt.

"Really though, why aren't you in a group?" I asked, bending down on my haunches so I was closer to her now.

"I am in a group."

"By yourself?"

"Yep."

"You're serious?" I said, frowning at the genuine expression on her face. She had skin that would make Snow White jealous—a perfect complexion. And not because of powders and creams and other shit that chicks put on their faces. Holly was a natural beauty.

"Set design isn't high on most peoples' lists."

"You can do this yourself?" I asked, having more serious doubts about our designer's fetish with blue.

Holly, laughed, throwing her head back like I'd said the funniest thing in the world. "Yeah, it's pretty easy to slap a bunch of blue paint on stuff. I should be finished in an hour or so," she said, giggling again.

The sound of her laughter squeezed at my heart like nothing ever had before. Now that I'd heard it, I wanted to hear it more. No matter what I had to do. Clearing my throat, I said, "I'm pretty good at painting. If you need help, let me know."

That set her off again. So much so that she doubled over, unable to catch her breath. When she finally controlled herself, wiping under her eyes she said, "I don't think it's me who's going to need help."

Staring into her eyes, it didn't feel like I was speaking to a high school senior. At all. "You're probably correct on that assumption. If you were me, how exactly would you run this operation?"

She looked me over. If I wasn't mistaken, I'm pretty sure there was pity in her eyes. "You're off to a good start. But—"

"But?"

"Yes, but. You're going to need more structure. I'll bring you the handouts that Mr. Rodriguez usually gives us at the beginning of each production."

"When?"

"Tomorrow morning?"

"What about tonight? Can you scan and email them to me?"

Her hands twisted together as she hmm'd and haw'd. "I don't have a scanner."

Although I thought it was odd for anyone to not have some kind of scanner in this day and age, I offered a compromise. "No problem. Can you just take pictures of the pages and email them to me?"

Holly took a deep breath. "I have a shift right after this, and I won't be home until late."

Wait a minute—she had to work again? "What? You just worked this morning. What time do you work tonight?"

"In about an hour. Usually, I'm off by nine or ten. It really depends on how busy it is."

"You're nearly working full time hours and going to school? When do you have time to study?"

"I fit it in."

She's your student. She's your student. She's your student.

"Tomorrow's fine, Miss Anderson. Thanks," I said, trying to smile even though my heart bled for her. If my assumptions were true, her homelife was probably less than fun.

With that, I ended our conversation and called over the chosen representatives. Then I pretended like I knew what I was doing.

6

Evan

There she was, five o'clock in the God damn morning unlocking the tiny diner's door. I yawned again, fiercely. My body shook from lack of sleep. How did Holly do this every day?

Lights flickered on reluctantly, like they also were too tired to wake at this ungodly hour. A few minutes after the lights went on, a man of larger stature walked up to the door and swung it open. He wore white pants and shirt. I'd bet he was the cook.

Still, I kept an eye on him. Holly waved to the man as he entered then marched his way to the right. It was still dark out, so the inside of the diner shone like a real-life diorama.

She moved around quickly, my tired eyes sometimes losing her as she went from table to table, setting up for the day. Ten minutes later, the first customers began filtering in. I waited until six o'clock before I left the comfort of my Jeep.

By then the place was humming. A bell announced my

entry as I pulled the door open, looking around for Holly. Her eyes immediately caught me. Surprise showed on her face before she composed herself, walking up to me.

"You're up early," she said with a sweet smile.

"I guess," I said, not really knowing what else to say.

"Table for one?" she asked, tilting her head toward door probably to see if I was with anyone.

"Just me."

She grabbed a menu from the stack on the counter. "Follow me." She smirked, her eyes cast down for a second. I didn't mean for it to happen, but my vison fell to her swaying hips as she walked in front of me. It was mesmerizing, like some kind of marvelous, sexy pendulum.

I was so hypnotized that I nearly bumped into her when she stopped at a table. "Oh shit, sorry," I said, grabbing onto her arms so I didn't push her over.

"Ooff," she said, before letting out a laugh. "No, I shouldn't have stopped so quickly. My fault." She twisted out of my hands.

"I wasn't watching where I was going, it was completely my fault." I apologized again. What I really should have apologized for was being a creeper.

"No problem, have a seat," she said cheerlily, sliding the menu on the table.

I sighed getting into my chair. "Thanks, Holly." I picked up the menu. Basic diner foods: pancakes, sausages, fruit, cereal, toast.

"Coffee?" she asked, back already with a steaming pot.

"Please. And keep it coming."

She smiled, flipping over the cup before filling it. "I'll be back in a few minutes," she said then rushed off to pour coffee for dreary patrons.

Before I knew it, she was back, order pad in one hand, pen in the other. "Ready?" she asked in such an—awake voice, she actually startled me.

"Uhh, the toast and eggs special, please," I said, yawning as I handed back the menu. She nodded, then spun around before I had time to blink.

Drugs. She must be on drugs or something to do this every day. Pulling my phone out, I checked my social media. Hmm, apparently everybody I knew was still sleeping. Lucky bastards.

Out of nowhere, a pretty, pink binder slapped onto the table, jarring me out of scrolling on my phone. Peering up, I saw Holly grinning down at me. "I didn't forget. That's the binder with all of Mr. Rodriguez's handouts. I made some notes as well. You know, what worked, what didn't work, what we should change to make things more efficient."

Grabbing the binder, I pulled it closer, then opened it. Christ, there were dozens of pages in here. I had assumed it would be some three-paged deal. "Thanks, this is a great start." She just smiled, then zoomed off to seat more customers who'd just walked in.

I'd only flipped through a few pages by the time she came back with my breakfast and more coffee. "Anything else for you at the moment?" she asked, staring down at the open binder.

"Your notes are incredible. I have a few questions when you have a minute."

She looked around at the full tables. "I'll try and sneak back over."

Holly's observations on what worked and what didn't were a thing of beauty. Going over the details she had on the pages would help out a ton. This certainly was over and above what I thought she'd be giving me.

"Okay, I might have a minute now." Holly crept up beside me. "I'm just going to pretend that you're ordering more food so nobody gets pissed off," she said, grabbing her pad of paper and pen.

I nodded and played along. "When you said that Mr. Rodriguez should ask the actors for their opinion of the characters, what did you mean?"

"One year, for "As you Like It", he tried telling everyone how they would play their part, but it didn't work out very well. That's why I noted it. It was better when he met first with everyone in a group and then individually to iron out interpretations."

"Hmm, smart. And what about assimilating the crew?"

She briefly explained why she'd added that as well as a few other things to her notes. "Sorry, I have to make my rounds again," she apologized for nothing as she shoved her pad and pen back into her apron. Off she went, seating customers, serving food, and filling cups.

It was never-ending hell.

I sat there forever, reading page after page, slowly making my own plan of action for today's drama meeting. Holly's brilliance lifted much of the hesitation I had for taking over this play. It was still going to be a lot of work but having a plan now, put me at ease.

The bell over the door clanged again. In walked a much older gentleman. Holly smiled at him as she stood behind the counter, filling out something on a clipboard. As they talked, she shook her head sadly at him, then set the clipboard down. They conversed for a minute longer before she hefted her big bag over her shoulder, ready to leave.

Gathering up the binder as quickly as I could, I raced out of there right behind her. "Holly," I called to her. She turned around, surprised to see me out there.

"I have to catch my bus," she shouted back to me.

My hand reached out to snag her to a stop. "I'll drive you. I'm here anyway," I said, knowing that I was venturing into dangerous territory. Again. "Go change, then we don't have to stop."

"It's fine, really. The bus is coming right now," she said, trying to jerk away from me.

"Holly, that's ridiculous when I'm right here. Come on, I'll drive you," I coaxed.

She looked conflicted as her eyes traveled from me to the bus that was pulling up. "Are you sure?"

My head nodded. My brain shouted a loud, "No".

"I guess I'll go change," she whispered, glancing down at my hand on her arm. Immediately, I let go.

"Holly," I called to her as she ran back to the diner.

"What?"

"I'm parked across the street." I nodded in the general direction.

~

"IF I WERE YOU?" she asked, a hint of humor in her voice. "I'd tell them to get buddies and then they can run their lines off with each other."

"Huh, that's not a bad idea," I said, raising my eyebrows at her. "You're good at this."

Holly shook her head. "No, I've just been around the drama department longer than you have, Mr. Marshall."

"Evan," I blurted out.

"What?"

"You can call me Evan when we aren't in school. Nobody's around to hear you."

"Yeah, but it's a respect thing. It'd be too weird calling a teacher by their first name." She frowned at me, twisting her body toward me.

"It's my name, Holly. It's not weird. And really," I said, turning my head to look down the street before I made a right turn. "I'm not exactly that much older than you." I'd checked out her file yesterday. Curiosity got the better of me. "If you think about it, you calling me, Mr., is more odd."

"How old are you?" she asked in a low whisper.

"Just turned twenty-two." And she was eighteen—legal in every state. My hands grasped the steering wheel a little firmer.

"You look older than that," she said, her gaze washing over me like soft silk.

Laughing, I turned my face to hers. "Do I need some work done on my crow's feet?"

That made her burst out laughing. "Yes, I didn't want to draw attention to them but a touch of Botox," she said, placing her fingers near my temple, "right here would do wonders to erase the years."

I couldn't help but smile. "Who do you use?" I shot back, grabbing her hand. Instead of pulling it out of my grip like I thought she'd do, Holly squeezed my hand back.

"I never divulge my beauty secrets," she said in a fake, Russian accent. At least I think it was supposed to be Russian.

Realizing I was still essentially holding her hand, I quickly set it down on her knee—my fingers grazing her thigh as I did so. A sudden wave of desire flowed through me.

"Drop me here and I'll walk the rest of the way. I've got more than enough time today," she said, pointing to the side of the road.

For a second, I considered protesting. She was right,

though. This was by far the safest option. As I came to a stop, she picked up her bag. "Thanks for the ride. Again."

7

Holly

"But I need someone to run my lines with, Holls," Ivy begged me again for the millionth time, stealing another fry from my plate.

"I work at night sometimes. How can I possibly help you? Alex or Paige can do it," I suggested, giving her two perfectly good options.

"Ugh, they're terrible actors. I need someone half-decent."

I rolled my eyes at her backhanded compliment. "Thanks, I strive to be half decent in everything I do," I snarked back, pulling my plate closer to me in an exaggerated way.

"Oh don't get all butt hurt. You know what I mean. You're just more—artsy than they are. It's incredibly difficult to go all in with lines when the person you're practicing with is awful."

The problem was, I completely understood what she

was talking about. Paige and Alex sucked at acting. They'd come out to support their friends in the play—Alex also assisted backstage with makeup. As for helping with anything else, they were hopeless.

Sighing, I picked up a fry. "I'll do my best, but you should really have a back-up buddy to help you."

Ivy gave me a naughty smirk, waggling her eyebrows. "I intend to have Mr. Marshall back me up."

Normally, I would have joked around about her rude comment. This time it felt different. I mean, I know I was an idiot for even thinking it or feeling it. After the last couple of days interacting with Evan—Mr. Marshall, it almost, kind of felt like he was my friend.

"What's your problem?" Ivy kicked me under the table, giving me a nasty look.

"Nothing, just tired."

"Skip out on work tonight then. Run lines with me instead."

Exhaling loudly, I said, "You know I can't do that." This was like banging my head against a brick wall. Trying to explain to my very rich friend why I needed to work was pointless. To her, money grew on trees.

"I'll pay your rent for the next two months if you quit and help me instead."

That thought made me laugh. Not out of merriment, though. "And then where am I going to live in sixty-two days?"

Ivy squealed in her exaggerated way, bouncing in her chair, "You can move in with me. My parents would love that." She clapped her hands, bringing more attention to our table.

"Your parents are barely there."

"It's not my fault they like L.A. better. Besides, they'd love to have you keep me company."

"Right, my mom could bring her sleeping bag." I snorted at the thought of us showing up at Ivy's mansion.

"Babe, you know I love you, right?" she asked, dramatically covering my hand with hers.

"Yeah, of course."

"No way in Hell can your mom move in. Like ever."

My eyes started to water a bit. "Gotcha. I'll go unpack," I said sarcastically even though her words stung a bit.

"Is she, you know, still drinking?" Ivy whispered, eyes wide.

Barely opening my mouth, I said, "Yep."

The familiar look of pity filled her face. "Did she at least find a job yet?" Ivy asked, taking her hand back and stealing another fry.

"Umm, not really," I said, taking a slurp of my drink as I shrugged, not wanting to talk about this. My mother's drinking and unemployability were my least favorite topics.

"Not really? Oh my God, did she get fired again?"

"Fired is a relative term." I gazed down, picking at my nail while I blushed a bit.

"In relation to termination of employment, did she get canned?"

"Difficult to get canned if you don't show up for your first day of work." I huffed out as I confessed my mother's latest cardinal job sin.

"Oh, for fuck sakes," Ivy said, arms up in the air.

"Who are we fucking?" Alex asked, straddling the bench I currently sat on.

"Holly's mom screwed up again." Ivy stared at Alex without blinking.

"Is it Tuesday already?" he asked sarcastically, hands

askew by his shoulders, mouth open wide for extra emphasis.

"I need Holly to run lines with me but she's always busy working because her mom's a deadbeat."

"Umm, am I chopped liver? I can run lines with you anytime," Alex announced.

"No offense, but Holly's a way better actor," Ivy whined, fluttering her long lashes.

"That's because she knows all the damn words to all the stupid plays by heart like some Shakespearean prodigy," Alex complained. "How can anyone compete with that?"

"I don't know all the words," I said, shaking my head.

"Fine," Alex said, banging the palms of his hands on the table for emphasis. "You, Holly Anderson, only know ninety-nine percent of the words to every painfully boring play ever written."

Shoving my shoulder into his chest, I offered him a fry. "I like plays. You know every shade of eyeshadow, lip gloss, and nail polish."

"Damn right I do. And I'm telling you we need to get rid of this baby soft pink for something more dynamic." He picked up my hand, examining the current shade I sported on my nails. "Like vivacious red," Alex screamed so excitedly, most people stopped to look over at us again. "I just happen to have some in my locker." The funny expression on his face made me laugh so hard. The only thing that made Alex happier than applying makeup to himself was using it on others.

"I have to work tonight," I told him, rubbing his arm for the kind gesture.

"That's it. I'm hooking up your house to my mom's truck and having it towed to Oregon. Your mom won't even notice," he said.

I felt slightly offended, but these guys weren't trying to put me down on purpose. "That's the nicest thing anyone's ever said to me." I joked, hugging him tight.

"For real, sister. Anytime you're done with that woman, say the frickin' word and I'll come pack your shit up. Actually, just leave it all there and we can go on a shopping spree."

His kind words brought tears to my eyes that I refused to let fall.

Evan

IT WAS DEFINITELY Holly's voice reciting the role of Romeo in the balcony scene. The voice with no emotion or feeling reading Juliet's much shorter lines was Ivy. How she'd won this role baffled me. If Ivy was the best pick for Juliet that told of the scarcity of talent at the school.

Originally, I'd come here to ask for Holly's advice on something. Now it was five minutes later and I was still standing like some stalker outside the door. Time to make myself known. Slowly, I walked into the open doorway. Neither of them looked my way.

Ivy was too busy with her head down, reading from a script while Holly balanced on a ladder painting that same huge board—blue. I opened my mouth to speak when I suddenly realized that Holly wasn't reading from a script. She knew these words by heart.

"I have night's cloak to hide me from their eyes, And, but thou love me, let them find me here; My life were better ended by their hate Than death prorogued, wanting of thy love," Holly said as though she were performing on a stage.

I was dumbstruck. Awestruck. How did an eighteen year

old high school senior know Romeo and Juliet, verbatim? Standing there for another few moments, Holly finally glanced over when she descended the ladder.

"Didn't see you there, Mr. Marshall," she said calmly, going to fill up her paint can. Her gorgeous, shining, blonde hair was tied back in a neat ponytail today.

"We're just going over lines," Ivy said, shooting me her usual fuck-me eyes. This was getting tiring.

"That's great," I said, my gaze naturally gravitating to Holly.

"My mom said she'd even hire me a professional acting coach," Ivy added. The girl was going to need more than that to help her out. I smiled back at her briefly. "Want any food, Holls? I'm going to eat before drama practice." Ivy stood up, brushing the dust off her skirt.

"Nah, I have to leave in ten minutes anyway. Thanks, though," Holly said before climbing the ladder, armed with more blue.

I moved to the side as Ivy passed me with another, I want you so bad look. Good grief. "More blue?" I asked, surveying the project that looked exactly the same as it did yesterday.

"More blue, Mr. Marshall," she said, pausing to smirk at me.

The brown paper crinkled under me as I sat on the cold floor. We stayed silent for a while as I gazed up at her, watching every move she made. I felt like I could stay here for hours doing nothing more than observing her and watching the paint dry.

Suddenly, our positions made me snicker. Holly looked down at me, a quizzical look on her face. Clearing my throat, I said, "But soft, what light through yonder window breaks? It is the east and Juliet is the sun! Arise, fair sun, and kill the envious moon," I started, then finished Romeo's line. She giggled a bit, a shy smile on her face before she turned fully, peering at me. After a brief hesitation, she began reciting, right on cue. Line after line we exchanged, Holly getting into her role just as much as I was in mine.

"Art tho not Romeo, and a Montague?"

"Neither, dear love, if either thee dislike," I said, rising from my place on the floor, hopelessly compelled to her beauty and playfulness. A small, delicious hum warmed my body. Our eyes locked together as I began to climb the other side of the ladder. Holly laughed a bit. Instead of saying her next line, her gaze lingered over my face as I got closer, desire burning inside of me.

An indescribable force drew me in as my pulse sped up. There was nothing in the world I wanted more than to be next to her. Her skin flushed darker with each step I took. A slow smile crossed my face as the corner of her mouth quirked up. Everything in me wanted to kiss that grin off her face.

Finally, our faces were so near, I could feel her sweet, cinnamon laced breath on my cheek. "How cam'st thou hither, tell me, and wherefore—" she said before being interrupted by the echoing sound of students entering the hallway. Damn but they had poor timing. I stepped down unsteadily from the ladder that had served as my lattice, inwardly cursing our interruption.

When I reached the floor, I took a few steps back, clearing my throat. "How exactly does a high school senior know Shakespeare by heart?" I asked, my voice sounding deeper than usual as I crossed my arms in front of me.

Holly turned back to her blue paint. "The balcony scene from Romeo and Juliet is one of the most famous scenes in literature. I'm sure a lot people know it," she said like it was no big deal.

"Mmm, hmm. It's highly unusual for someone of your age and stage of life to know that scene."

"You know it," she shot back at me, making me grin.

"I do."

"Why do you know it?"

"Firstly, I love literature. Majored in it."

"And secondly?" she asked rather sheepishly.

"Secondly." I chuckled. "Secondly, playing Romeo in school plays got me a certain amount of—attention."

"From girls?" she asked, pointing her paint brush at me. I shrugged my shoulder a bit. "Basically, what you're saying is you played Romeo to get laid?"

"It helped."

Holly shook her head as she let out a hoot. "Good to know. Glad The Baird was there to assist."

"You didn't answer my question, yet. Why do you know all the words?"

She sighed then made her way down the ladder with her paint, the ladder squeaking as she did so. "Nanny—my grandmother—used to play Shakespeare on her old record player. She was straight from England and never lost her love for home—or Shakespeare."

"Your grandmother passed away?"

"Yeah, a while ago."

"I'm sorry."

"Thanks. I still miss her a ton. She's the one who taught me how to read and write. I even copied her English accent for a while. Drove my mom crazy," she said, sticking her brush in the sink while covering the paint can with plastic.

"That's a beautiful story," I said, swallowing over the

lump in my throat, thinking about how she'd had—then lost such a close relationship.

Holly didn't answer. She just kept on washing her brush. I slowly plodded over to her, feeling almost nervous. Resting my hip on the large, white sink, I stood there, watching her. The blue paint circled the bottom of the porcelain sink before falling to its doom.

Much like our current conversation. "I'm sorry, I didn't mean to upset you," I said in a low voice. Stretching out my hand, I pulled the brush from hers. She let me have it, willingly, then shifted to the side to give me room.

"I'm not upset. It just—brings back memories."

"You guys were close. It must be difficult to lose someone you loved so much." Squeezing out the last of the water from the brush, I tapped it a few times on the side of sink. "You were lucky to have that kind of relationship with her. Even if it was for short time."

"She practically raised me," she said, grabbing the brush out of my hand and placing it bristles up in a glass jar to dry.

My heart sunk at her admission. Shit. If her grandma raised her, where the hell was her mom?

"Mr. Marshall, Carlos wants to use the red filter for the lighting. I told him this is Romeo and Juliet, not Dracula," a student with a nasally voice barged in, complaining. "Can you please come talk some sense into him?"

"Uh, sure, umm," I started, trying like hell to remember the student's name.

"Angela," Holly whispered to me, her back still turned.

"I'll be right there, Angela." Angela, seemingly vindicated, spun around and ran out the door. Feeling uneasy about leaving right in the middle of our conversation, I struggled to think of what to say to Holly. "Look, I'm sorry. I didn't mean for things to get so—heavy." My finger grazed her arm briefly.

"Not a problem. Thanks for washing up. I have to go. See you tomorrow," she said, glancing at me quickly before scooping up her bag and leaving me alone to ponder how unfair life was.

8

Holly

The deep, rhythmic bass of the music filled my ears as I tried my best to duck out of our teacher's sight. What were the chances we'd run into Mr. Marshall at a bar?

"Come onnn," Ivy whined in the middle of the club. Her double D's nearly spilling out of her skimpy blue dress. Those spaghetti straps weren't going to hold on forever. "He's a cool teacher. No way would he rat us out," she said, begging me again to let us stay.

"Dude, he works with my mom. We need to get down on our knees and pray that he didn't see us," Alex said, trying his best to hide behind me.

"Oh, I'll get down on my knees for him any day," Ivy said, licking her lips in a seductive manner.

Rolling my eyes, I said, "We have to go, Alex is right."

"Fiiine, you win. We'll find somewhere else to go," she said, grabbing onto my arm.

"Yo, my sistahhh." Xavier Lewis interrupted us, giving

me a big hug. He must've stumbled in when we weren't looking. "How's ya guys?"

"Not quite as good as you from the smell of things," I said, pushing him away roughly. His body banged up against the opposite wall. "I'm sorry," I said, rushing forward to make sure he was okay. "I didn't think I pushed you that hard."

"You didn't," Ivy said in her annoyed voice. "He's loaded."

Ivy and I shared a look of concern. "Who are you here with?" I turned back to Xavier, hands on his shoulders, attempting to keep him still.

"Owen's comin'" he slurred, gesturing toward the doors.

Sure enough, Owen stumbled his big, stupid self through the doors right at that moment. "Oh, you guys. How'd you even get here? Do not tell me you drove or I'll beat you," I threatened, shoving his shoulders even more.

"Billy dropped us off, chillax," he said as his noxious breath nearly made me gag.

"Friends," Owen said, tripping his way down to us.

"We're leaving. Now," I said to Ivy and Alex.

"We just got here, babe," Owen said, draping his arm around me like we were best friends. Or potential lovers. Neither of which we actually were.

"And now you're leaving," I said, putting my arm around his waist as I grabbed Xavier's hand and pulled. "This way. Time to go."

"You guys are a disaster," Ivy said, clomping behind me in her heels—that were at least two inches taller than mine. "Come on, buddy, this way," Alex said, taking command of Xavier for me. It was a relief to only have one drunk to take care of.

"They aren't getting in my car like that. What if they get sick?" Ivy said once we got out the doors.

"What are we supposed to do? Leave them here?" I asked Ivy, shaking my head. "They live right near you. Plus, you have a convertible, just leave the top down." She didn't come up with another argument, so we continued on to the parking lot.

After getting the two drunkards seated and buckled, Ivy said, "And where are you supposed to fit?" Her arm motioning at the tiny car built for four.

I sighed, admitting defeat. "I'll stay back," Alex offered, like the good friend he was.

"That makes no sense. You live in the same neighborhood as they do," I said, resigned to my fate.

"I'll come back and get you," Ivy offered.

"It's a forty-five minute drive. Both ways." Closing my eyes, I thought about what to do. "I'll catch the bus."

"You're not taking the bus," Ivy snapped at me as she angrily dug in her purse. Opening her wallet, she pulled out a card. "Use this. You can take a cab," she said, shoving a credit card in my hand.

"That's nice of you," I said, gazing down at the shimmering gold card. The flashing lights from the bar's sign reflecting off its perfectly smooth surface. "But I can't accept," I said, handing it back to her.

"Take the card or I'll—oh, just stop being so proud and use it. Unless you want to sit on Owen's lap?" she asked, opening her eyes up wide.

"Woohoo, yeah baby, come to papa," Owen said, pumping his hands up in the air.

Even though he was being an ass, I giggled slightly. "Shit."

"Yeah, shit," she said, curling my fingers around the

credit card. "Promise me you'll use it." The look of worry etched on her face somehow warmed my heart.

"I'll use it," I said, giving her a quick hug before spinning around to Alex. "Take care of them and make sure she doesn't leave them on the side of the road," I told him, wrapping my arms around his shoulders.

"Anything for you, Holls," he said into my ear.

After they drove off—the drunk boys singing a boy band song from the nineties—I hurried out of the parking lot. Looking down the street, I considered hailing a cab. A bus would take twice as long but I also wouldn't have to worry about paying—or more like, not paying—Ivy back for the fare.

Truthfully, cab fare would be a drop in the bucket of what that girl would put on this card in a week. My friend loved to shop with her daddy's money.

The ethical war battled inside me—pride winning again.

Not many people took the bus at this time of night. It was just me, waiting. An uneasiness came over me like an invisible, itchy blanket making my skin crawl. Spinning around, I saw a man slowly making his way in my direction.

Mentally, I calculated how long it would take me to run in these heels back to the club.

Too long.

"Whatcha doin' out here on your own, beautiful?" he asked, his tone smarmy, shirt undone too far down his chest. The gold necklaces around his neck swayed from side to side as he shimmied closer. I had a faraway thought wondering if the hair on his chest ever got tangled up with all that jewelry.

Backing up as he advanced, I said, "Just waiting for my boyfriend to pull up with the car." My heart pounded away, fear coursing through my veins.

"Yeah? I don't see no boyfriend," he said, his arms out to the side in an exaggerated way while looking both ways down the street.

"We parked further down and he didn't want to make me walk," I said, trying like hell keep my voice steady. Assholes like this smelled fear.

"I'll drive ya, come wiff me," he said, stepping closer.

"No, really. He'll be here any minute," I said, escaping around the bus stop bench. A cold shiver ran up my spine. I shouldn't be here.

"Ohh, you wanna play hard to get? I like that game," he said, a sneer crossing his face. He lunged around the bench as I took off in the direction of the club. Even drunk, he was faster than me. His fingers dug into my arm. "Caught ya," he bellowed as he pulled hard on my arm, causing a shooting pain in my shoulder.

"Ow, let go," I yelled, attempting to wrench my arm away from him. It didn't work. Instead, he yanked me into his sweaty body. The stench of body odor was overwhelming. "I said, let me—"

"What the fuck?" I heard a man say directly behind me. It was enough of a shock that smarmy guy's grip loosened for a split second. I took the opportunity to escape, although not without injury.

"Whassup, buddy? Just talkin' to my girl here. It's all cool," smarmy guy said, with a smile.

"Your girl? She's my girlfriend and I'd like to know what the hell you're doing with your slimy hands all over her," Mr. Marshall said, hands on his hips, legs spread slightly. My heart thudded louder as panic seized my chest.

"Heyyy, not my fault the girl came onto me. She likes me better I guess," smarmy guy said, before he grabbed for me again. Anticipating his move this time, I got away. Barely. I shrank back as I trembled, willing my knees to stop shaking.

"I see you're a slow learner," Mr. Marshall said, pushing smarmy guy's shoulders, sending him stumbling back. You'd think the jerk would get the hint and take off but instead, he recovered his footing looking even more angry than before.

"She's mine," the jackass said again, bolting toward Mr. Marshall. My body stiffened, a small squeak exiting my mouth as I watched helplessly.

Evan was done. He pushed the guy harder this time, causing him to fall back on his ass. "You need to leave," he told the jerk. But up he got again.

"She's mine." This time smarmy swung a punch. Evan easily evaded it before offering his own right back. The drunk lurched back, holding his cheek. He gazed up at each of us as though deciding what to do next.

Luckily, tail between his legs, he took a few unsteady steps backward, then turned around to hightail it out of there.

"You okay?" Evan said, coming at me like a freight train.

Instead of answering, I opened my mouth, then closed it. Too shocked and scared to speak just yet.

"Jesus, come here," he said, pulling me into him. I melted into his warm body easier than I should have, his spicy cologne filling my senses. God, he felt good. He squeezed me even tighter.

"I'm fine, he just scared the crap out of me. Thanks for helping," I said into his perfect neck as I used every bit of restraint I could to not kiss it.

"Spotted you guys when you walked in. What are you doing here anyway?"

Pushing back a bit, I gazed up into his eyes. "It's far enough from home that nobody we know comes here."

Evan chuckled. "Uh huh, that's why I suggested this place, too." He smiled sadly down at me. "Now tell me why your friends took off on you?" he asked, his comforting hands moving to my shoulders, stroking me gently. It felt so good, I wanted to stay here forever.

"Owen and Xavier showed up. Inebriated. Ivy brought her convertible so there was only room for four."

His eyes closed. "They left you behind to take the bus? At this time of night?"

"I volunteered. All of them live in the same neighborhood anyway. It just made sense for me to stay back."

"Yeah, makes perfect sense to leave your friend alone with a bunch of drunks," he said sarcastically. "Are you all right?" he asked, stepping back, then grasping one of my hands in his. He gently turned my arm around as his fingers grazed the red marks still visible on there. "Does it hurt?" His eyes were so kind, his voice so soothing, I wanted to float away on it.

"Not really," I said, too hopped up on adrenaline and distracted by Evan's actions to feel any pain.

Dropping that arm, he picked up my other one, investigating it just like the first. My breath caught at the feel of his rough fingers on my soft flesh.

"These will likely bruise," he said, flinching sympathetically while his fingers circled the bigger marks. Watching his movements on my skin made me dizzy.

"I'm fine now. Thanks for intervening when you did," I said so low it was almost a whisper. Grudgingly, I pulled my arm out of his hold. I didn't know how much more of his touch I could take.

"I'll take you home. Come inside for a minute. I have to tell my friends I'm going and I don't want to leave you out here alone," he said, reaching for my hand.

Before I knew what was happening, Evan guided me back in the club. When we stepped further into the entryway, he said, "Wait here for me. Don't move." With that, he squeezed my hand one more time then strode off to find his friends.

He walked with a smooth confidence I wish I possessed. My eyes dropped to his fine behind. I couldn't help it. His tight jeans accentuated his attributes very nicely. Very, very nicely.

"Holy shit, did you see that hot guy," a girl not much older than me blurted out to her friend as they passed by.

The other girl laughed. "Girlfriend, he is way out of your league." Her friend pushed her playfully in the shoulder.

Looking up, I could see Evan talking with some guys at a small table. They were all grabbing their phones and throwing down what I assumed was tip money on the table. As they made their way in my direction, I was careful to not make eye contact. I even turned around completely, pretending to be very interested in the sign on the wall.

"Heaven is missing an angel tonight," a guy behind me said. "Would you look at that perfect, heart-shaped ass?"

"Down boy," Evan said. Briefly, I glanced behind me for a quick look. He was walking out with his friends. My heart sunk for a moment, scared he was going to leave me behind, too. "You know what? I think I forgot my phone. You guys go on ahead, I'll meet you there."

They exchanged nods and see you laters.

Phew. I breathed a sigh of relief. He wasn't going to skip out on me.

"Sorry about my friend," Evan said into my ear. As I turned around, our cheeks brushed together lightly. The stubble on his face scratched my skin. "Shit, sorry," he said, frowning, placing his fingers under my chin as his thumb softly grazed my check.

My heart nearly stopped. The feel of his touch on my skin electrified me. "It's fine," I said, instinctively grazing his hand with my fingers. "I don't break that easily," I murmured. Our eyes met and something changed in that moment. A few beads of sweat fell down his temple, his breathing accelerated. I could smell his manly, musky scent now magnified from the altercation. I don't know exactly what transpired in the seconds or minutes we stared at each other like that. All I knew was after that, things were different.

"I should go," I said reluctantly, breaking the spell. "It figures, you know?"

"What does?"

"This is the first night out I've had in weeks and look what happens."

"You don't get to cut loose very often, do you?"

"Practically never."

"Do you dance, Miss Anderson?" Evan asked, grabbing my hand again, stepping closer to me.

"Like a champ."

He laughed so hard he threw his head back, exposing that neck I was so close with just minutes before. "Show me," he said, picking up my other hand then walking backward. The devilish look on his face stole my breath away.

"What if someone sees?" I asked nervously, turning my head this way and that, looking for recognizable faces.

"Nobody we know is here," he said with a mischievous look on his face as he turned around. Dropping one hand, he tugged me along more quickly. An excitement ran through my body. Was I really going to dance with my teacher?

Maneuvering through the crowd of people, we stopped in the middle of the dance floor. Surrounded by gyrating, jumping dancers, Evan let go of my hand and started to move his body to the beat. That cocky, sexy smile came out again.

I couldn't help it—I burst out laughing then joined him. His eyes dropped from my face to my chest, then back to my eyes. That smirk got wider. Even though he wasn't touching me, I could feel his eyes traveling the length of me, lingering on my curves.

Stepping closer, he gently placed his hands on my waist as though he was testing out the waters. The heat from his skin burned sensuously into mine. A small ache in my lower belly intensified into a throb I couldn't ignore.

Evan pulled me tightly to him and I realized the music had changed. He picked up my hands, dropping them on his hard, muscular, shoulders. I could feel a slight dampness seeping through his shirt. My breasts pressed deliciously into his chest as his hand on my lower back pushed me further into him.

I inhaled a deep breath as his thick arousal made itself known against my belly. Just thinking about what was under those jeans gave me immediate palpitations. Slowly dragging my hand from his shoulder down his sharp pectorals caused my knees to wobble.

Would I survive this? Being this close to him made my head swim with thoughts and ideas you shouldn't have about your teacher. "We shouldn't be doing this," I said in a voice too soft for him to hear.

He dipped his head, his scruff once more gently scraping my cheek, sending a wave of heat over me. "What?" he asked, his breath hot on my neck causing goose bumps to form.

"I said we probably shouldn't be doing this." Oh God, inhaling his musky, spicy scent while staring at his beautiful neck was too much. My fingers tensed into his shirt, again feeling the taught muscles there.

"Probably not," he said into my ear, his lips lightly touching my skin as he spoke. I'd heard what he said, loud and clear. But neither of us made a move to part.

Quite the opposite happened. We swayed to the slow song for what felt like hours. Eventually, my head rested on his chest, feeling the steady beat of his heart against my ear. His hand slowly dragged over the expanse of my back as we continued to move with each other. The friction making my body sizzle.

"What do you say we get out of here?"

9

Holly

Did he just suggest leaving? Of course, he did. He was dancing with his student whom he felt sorry for. Now he was done. Disappointment washed over me with its cruel vengeance. Did I really allow myself to believe I had a shot with him?

I tried my best not to let Evan see how crushed I was. "Okay, I just need the ladies' room before we leave," I said into his ear. My nose touched his dark, damp hair and I inhaled his scent one last time before starting toward the bathroom.

Maneuvering through the crowd of people was no easy task, especially as the next song changed to a faster one again.

"If you're out before me, wait here," Evan said, wrapping his hand around my upper arm. I turned around, seeing him point to the wall between the bathroom doors.

"Yes, sir." I grinned and saluted him before disappearing into the washroom. Oddly enough, it was empty. I had to close my eyes tightly for a minute. I'd misinterpreted Evan's intentions tonight. Right at this moment, I was feeling like quite the fool.

The man was being kind. Nothing more. How could I be so stupid?

After washing my hands, I held a paper towel under the cold water for a few seconds. Squeezing it out, I pressed it to my cheeks. No matter how hard I tried, I couldn't for the life of me change the funky mood I now found myself in.

He's your teacher, you idiot. No matter how hard you crushed on him, he had better things to do than hang around a silly student who lived on the wrong side of the tracks.

Taking a deep breath, I blinked my watery eyes, threw out the soggy paper, then plastered an "I'm perfectly fine" look on my face. After all these years, I was getting pretty good at that.

Stepping out into the hallway, I couldn't see Evan yet so I stood against the wall to wait for him. My eyes started to fill again as thoughts of how unfair the universe was invaded my mind. Really, I couldn't be surprised. This was the story of my pathetic life.

"What's wrong?" Evan said, rushing right up to me, putting his index finger underneath my jaw then tipping it up. He examined my face. "Something happen?"

Feeling his warm breath on my face made me want to dive into him. The stubble on his face was more visible in this lighting. My hand itched to reach out and feel it.

"No, just tired. I've been yawning," I lied, putting on a smile for him. Not sure if he bought it or not but he stared at me for a few more seconds before letting it go. His hand grasped mine then he slowly led us outside.

The cool air hit my body with a shock. An instant shiver

traveled through me. Evan stopped, pulling me over to the side. "Here." Before I knew it, he'd taken off his jacket then placed it around my shoulders. Tilting my head down, I took a quick sniff as I shoved my hands into the sleeves. I couldn't help myself.

Gazing up at him, he had a half-smirk on his face. "What?" I asked, knowing full well he'd seen what I'd done. A slight blush rose up on my face.

His eyes scanned me one more time. "Nothing, let's go." He grabbed my hand again, pulling me more quickly to the parking lot. We walked for a couple of minutes, neither of us saying a word until we stood in front of a motorcycle.

"Is this yours?" My eyes went wide with surprise.

"Yep," he said, letting go of my hand as he picked up the helmet. Adjusting the straps first, he walked over to me, putting it on my head. It was heavier than I thought it would be. "It needs to be tight but not too tight." The feel of his fingers on my neck as he did up the buckle gave me more goose bumps.

"Still cold?" he asked, obviously feeling me shiver again. Only this time it wasn't from the weather. Stepping closer to me, his hands rubbed up and down my arms.

I stood there, mesmerized by the smell of his jacket, the motion of his hands and the proximity of his body.

"I'm good," I said, my eyes looking up into his. If he leaned down just a little bit, our lips would touch. That thought alone caused my lower belly to tighten and that dull ache started again. As I took a breath, I exhaled loudly, stepping away. "Do I get on first?" I asked, turning to face the bike. Dragging my fingers on the cool, leather seat, I remembered I was wearing a dress.

"Uhh, I can't ride this," I said, frowning up at Evan.

"No? How come?" he asked, striding over then straddling the motorcycle in one quick move. He shot me another grin. "Get on."

Anxiety shot through me. "I'm wearing a dress," I said, pulling down the short hemline. It was pointless. No matter how hard I tried, I'd never be able to stretch this material.

Evan laughed, his entire body shaking. "Just get on. Nobody will be able to see anything. You'll be behind me."

Creeping up to him, I unsuccessfully tried to lift my leg, nearly falling over in the process. Luckily he grabbed ahold of my arm. "Whoa, careful," he said, peering down at my legs.

I looked down, noticing part of my white, lacy panties were showing. "Shit," I said, fixing myself too late.

"Hands on my shoulders," he said, laying my right hand on his right shoulder, pressing down.

Again, the heat radiating through his shirt made my knees weak. There was no getting out of this, I just had to do it. Placing my other hand on his opposite shoulder, I swung my leg around, hoping nobody was around to see the show as my dress rose hopelessly up.

Evan started up the motorcycle. Immediately, it began to vibrate my bottom. I felt the motion acutely, not having much between me and the bike. Being pressed up to Evan's back, my legs tight to his felt so—forbidden. But also so right.

He used his hands to capture mine then pull them around his waist. In the process, my entire body was now virtually crushed into his. Including my crotch. Only the thin material of my panties now separated me from Mr. Marshall's jeans. The thought made me clench deeply inside myself—a slow, methodical throb beginning for him. My skin heated as a new desire coursed through my veins.

His head turned around briefly enough to say, "Hold on,

don't let go," grasping my hands together on his stomach—
his very hard stomach. Clench. My heart skittered being this
close to Evan, his manly smell clouding what was left of my
brain.

Finally, he took off out of the parking lot. As we turned
left, I realized I hadn't told him where I lived. I opened my
mouth to speak just as he accelerated onto the street. There
was no way he'd be able to hear me over the roar of the
engine. Maybe he had looked at my student information
and memorized my address?

At this point, I didn't care. Being this close to Mr.
Marshall was its own personal Heaven and Hell. It was so
wrong but felt so right.

The wind rushed past us even faster as he sped up. His
hand covered mine as if to ask if I was all right. Without
thinking, my body pressed even further into his. He let go of
my hands, pressing on the gas again.

I couldn't help but laugh out loud. Being so close to
Evan, having the wind whip mercilessly over us, feeling so
—free. Not a care in the world. Joy bubbled up inside of me
and I felt light for the first time in a long time.

In fact, I was so into the ride I completely lost sight of
where he was taking me until he turned left into the parking
lot of the beach. A big smile crossed my face. I hadn't been
here in ages.

Evan had his pick of spots in the completely abandoned
lot. A few lights above made it possible to see in the otherwise dark, black night. After he turned off the bike, the
sound of crashing waves filled my ears. Another smile filled
my face as I closed my eyes, breathing in the salty air.

"You asleep?" he asked, shifting around in his seat.

My eyes popped open as I startled a bit. "No." I giggled
softly, looking into his dark eyes. "I haven't been here in

forever. Just enjoying it." A fresh energy filled my body as I fell into his gaze.

"We can enjoy the actual beach if you get off," he said, raising his eyebrows, chuckling.

"That sounds like a great idea."

10

Holly

My legs felt a bit like jelly as we walked down to the water. Being so close to Mr. Marshall—Evan, was like being in some sort of dream that I didn't want to wake up from. And now, smelling the salty, fresh ocean air deep in my lungs and feeling the cool, wet sand between my toes—my spirits lifted in ways I couldn't explain.

When we neared the ocean's edge, I dumped my shoes and Evan's coat carelessly behind me, rushing to the water's edge. Immediately I sunk in a few inches like quicksand relieving me of all my cares. Joy bubbled up in me, ready to explode.

The constant slosh, slosh, slosh soothed the angry, tired beast I tried to hide from everyone on a daily basis. It was exhausting. Just then, the vibrant moon peeked out from behind the clouds to say a hello.

Cautiously entering the cool water one step at a time, I stopped once I was up to my knees, enjoying the ocean's refreshing touch. The waves hit me even higher, surprising me as it splashed further up my thighs. Staring up at the moon again, I wondered when the last time was that I took a moment to really appreciate its brilliance. Life was always so busy—such a struggle minute by minute—that I rarely had free time to do things like this.

Taking in another soul-cleansing breath, I closed my eyes to let all of this soak in.

Looking back, I saw Evan still at the edge of the water. "Come in, it's beautiful."

"It sure is," he said, staring right at me. My stomach flipped and squeezed watching him, completely still, not taking his eyes off me. Clearing his throat, he widened his stance. "I left my bathing suit at home," he said dryly, making me laugh.

"Too bad. Didn't think you were a chicken," I said in a sing song voice, stepping forward a bit more as I bent over to stick my hands in the water. A rogue wave hit me higher on a very sensitive area. I inhaled loudly. "Ohhhh."

Beside me, I saw a flash of a person running directly into the ocean—in his underwear? Turning around to check for Evan, I quickly surmised it was him in the water. Holy cow. Mr. Marshall in his very tight briefs mere feet from me. My heart sped up watching him dive into the water once he was in up to his waist.

Did he really just strip down to his unmentionables and jump in the ocean? Right in front of me? When he came up for air, I yelled, "You're crazy," to him, cupping my hands on my mouth.

"Couldn't let you have all the fun," he responded from a distance. His voice breathy and carefree.

I'm not sure if it was the shroud of night, the excitement of being back on the beach after all this time or just getting caught up in a moment. Whatever it was, Evan's playfulness and willingness to throw caution to the wind gave me the courage to say, "What the hell?" as I unzipped my dress, pulling it over my head before I tossed it in the general direction of my shoes.

The cool breeze brought goose bumps to cover my body. Wrapping my arms around my breasts to hide myself a bit from his eyes I slowly ventured further in. Every step I took warmed my skin after the initial shock of it.

"Just rip off the Band-Aid, woman," Evan yelled to me.

What exactly did I have to lose now? We were alone out here and he did remove his clothes first, after all. My lacy bra and panties weren't much coverage but on our beaches there were many women who wore a lot more revealing things I guess.

With that logic, I ran screaming into the waves. I was almost positive I heard Evan shouting with laughter as I continued my daring entry into the dark, black sea. Once the shock of it wore off, I dipped my head back, wetting the rest of my hair as I swam toward him, the water trickling off me as I glided though its warm caress.

Slightly out of breath, I paused to tread when I got near enough. His focus jumped from my lips to my eyes and back. He drifted closer—so close I thought he'd kiss me. My breathing ceased as I waited for his lips to meet mine. Instead, he suddenly sunk down with a loud, whoosh, creating a surge of waves in his midst.

Coming up for air, his lips parted in a devilish grin, water dripping down his handsome face. The dark shadows the moonlight created accentuated the commanding, chiseled features on his face. A tightness in my lower belly intensified.

"Follow me," he said, diving off in a powerful stroke

leaving me in his wake. I trailed behind him, moonlight on our shoulders, the water invigorating me with each stroke I took. Evan checked for me frequently—making sure I was close—slowing down whenever I fell behind. His kindness made my heart burst with happiness.

After a while, he flipped, floating silently on his back. The water coursed over his rippled abs with each swell of the ocean's call, tugging again at that tight sensation inside of me. Unable to stop myself, I eyed the large bulge in his underwear. Swallowing with a dry throat, I closed my eyelids, gently drifting on my back.

Aware that my wet, lace covered breasts would be visible only a few feet from his eyes—if he decided to look—made my nipples harden at the thought. Unadulterated lust flowed through me as all pretension of modesty flew out. A wonderful throb began between my legs at the thought of Evan gazing at my chest, seeing my curves that craved his touch.

I squeezed my legs together, attempting to quell the desire as I imagined first his hands traveling over me—then his mouth. It was my turn to sink into the water, hoping to douse the flames inside me.

Rising back up, I tried again to float, my breathing even, eyes closed, allowing all the shit I had to do tomorrow and the next day and the next to gently exit my mind. Nothing mattered except being here. Now.

That odd feeling you get when someone's watching you, crept over me. Turning my head, I saw Evan treading beside me, water droplets falling down his face. His black hair slicked back in a way that made my hands itch to reach out and feel it between my fingers.

Righting myself, I treaded face to face with him. "Thank you for bringing me here. You have no idea how much I needed this," I said, my voice cracking a bit with emotion. My eyes began to fill with tears all on their own free will. It surprised me because I never allowed myself to go down the dangerous path of self-pity—except for a minute a day, first thing in the morning.

I knew firsthand what a poor me attitude did to a person.

He swam closer, his fingers resting on the side of my face as he wiped under my eyes with his thumbs. My heart stuttered at his tender touch and the look of heartbreaking concern on his face. "Shh, don't cry. I brought you here to make you happy, not sad."

Sniffling, I said, "I am happy." More tears fell in contradiction to my words.

"Then why are you crying?" he asked in a voice so deep I wanted to fall into it and never climb out. His hands cradled my head as his eyes darted over my face.

As I opened my eyes, I inhaled deeply, attempting to calm myself. Evan made it so easy to open up to him. I spent my days shutting this part of myself down so people wouldn't know how horrible I felt. "Because I can't remember the last time I felt this way." My vision clouded while I openly cried, mortified at how I was acting. A physical pain surrounded my heart, wringing it without care.

"Holly," he said, firmly, demanding my attention as his hold became more insistent.

I looked at him, his face so fierce it almost scared me. "You have no idea how wrong that is. Someone like you should feel like this every day." My heart skipped a beat at his kind words.

Sniffling, I answered back, "It's just not in the cards for me." A sense of dread weighed down on me like a hundred bricks. I'd never get out of the mess I was in—the life I was born to. A stab of remorse shot through me.

"That's not true," he said, his eyes boring into mine. "You deserve so much more." His vision darted down to my mouth, making me wish he'd kiss my waiting lips.

"I've never met anyone like you before," his voice rasped before he leaned over, touching his mouth to mine. I sighed as his tongue searched and found mine, a new kind of excitement zinging across my skin.

His hands dug deep into my hair as he claimed my mouth, causing a new desire to spark inside of me as he groaned loudly down my throat. I found it difficult to keep up to his enthusiastic kissing, but I did my best.

Evan inched back a bit before giving me one last lingering kiss that shattered everything I'd ever believed about longing and passion. I wasn't completely innocent— there'd been boys in my life. Awkward, front seat fumblings —groping, sloppy, messy kisses.

But this? Kissing Evan? It wasn't even in the same universe. This was hot, heavy, forbidden hunger—we both knew the consequences of our actions if anyone found out.

We panted for a minute, our breath mingling, unsure of what to do next. I closed my eyes for a moment as my heart rate slowed. Looking blindly into the sky, I found the moon sneaking behind a cloud. Was this all a dream?

I could feel Evan's penetrating gaze searching my face for answers to the questions I didn't want to think about. Not right now. Not ever. We waited in silence, neither of us quite ready to break the spell. I let out a breath I hadn't realized I'd been holding, my lips swollen and numb yet still tingling from our kiss.

Nothing in my life thus far had taught me what to do after your English teacher kissed you in the moonlight. So, I did the only thing I knew. "Race you," I said with a huge smile on my face.

Evan's mouth twitched. "On five, four—"

Needless to say, I didn't wait for his countdown. Laughing as I swam made it difficult but not impossible. Feeling like my lungs and heart might burst at any moment, I slowed down to catch my breath. Spinning to my back, I saw Evan was directly behind me.

As soon as I'd slowed, so did he. "I didn't take you for a cheater, Miss Anderson," he said in a very formal manner, making me giggle.

Splashing him with my hand, I said, "Am I in trouble now?" My heart leaped, feeling mischievous and daring.

Twisting his head to the side from the onslaught of water, he chuckled. Looking at me, wiping his face with one hand, he said, "I'd say I'm the one in trouble." His eyes looked at me tentatively, worry etched in his expression. My heart dropped to my stomach and stayed there, jabbing with anxiety.

I slowly made my way closer to him. Setting my hands on his shoulders, feeling the scorching heat emanating from his bare, wet skin, and meaning every word, I said, "No, you're not."

His dark eyes reflected the moonlight back to me as his expression sobered. "Yeah, I really am, Holly." Again, my pulse raced as his strong hands found my waist, pulling me into his body. "Big trouble." His jaw tightened—a vein popping out on his neck. The feel of his fingers seizing into my skin made me feel like I was trapped—willingly of course.

Something inside of me needed to show him I was okay with whatever we were doing—even though I really had no concept of exactly what that was. My fingertips grazed the stubble on his face then moved up into the hair I'd been so curious about. "Mmm," I moaned, running my hand through his soft, wet waves.

He didn't do anything, other than scan my face and allow me the freedom to do as I pleased. Trailing a finger from his temple, down to his mouth, I touched the pad of my index finger on his soft, smooth, still wet lips—the lips that were nearly devouring me a minute ago. I wanted him to do more than just kiss me. A lot more.

I felt completely unguarded as I memorized the small dip in his top lip and the slight roughness to the bottom one. His searing gaze cut into me like a knife, opening up a sensual part of me I didn't know existed. My stomach tightened as I thought about how badly I wanted this man.

Yielding, I pressed myself close, my breasts tight against his chest. The friction we created rubbing my nipples in the most divine way, sending shocks to my pussy. Sighing, I kissed him gently, tasting the salty sea water. His hands dropped to my behind, shoving me more forcefully to him. A rush of water rose up between us, hitting our faces for a brief moment.

My heart thumped faster as I melted further into him. His slippery skin made it nearly impossible to maintain a hold on his sculpted frame. My core throbbed with need for him.

Maneuvering my legs around his waist, he set on a devastating frenzy on my mouth. If I was hungry—he was ravenous. Somehow, he managed to keep us afloat as my hands explored his back, feeling the tight, lean muscles under my fingertips.

Eventually, he laid back, gliding through the water with me on his chest. I held onto his shoulders as he pulled us through the jet black sea. "You're a good swimmer," I said, still holding on while he towed me.

A bit out of breath, he answered back, "I love the water. You're not so bad yourself."

I kicked my feet but it was clear who was doing the lion's share of work here. The power Evan had in his strokes surprised me—it also turned me on even more. He flipped over quickly, grabbing my arms to put them on his shoulders.

We swam like that for a while, the moon up above us, reflecting in the vast, dark water. Coming to a stop where he was able to touch the bottom, he swiveled around, moving me from his back to his front once again, my legs wrapped around him.

"It's like being in a different world out here. Like nothing else matters," I said, my fingers playing with his hair, feeling the water drip down my hands. My flesh tingled everywhere we touched, a longing for more whispered through me, but I was unsure how to ask.

Evan replied by crushing his mouth to mine. We were used to each other by now, so I responded just as enthusiastically. His tongue fighting with mine, dueling for control I was too willing to give. He tasted of desperation as though these were our final moments on Earth. His hungry mouth kissed down my neck, licking, sucking, nipping. Even in this cool water, I melted with the fire of his touch.

I bent my head back as his lips found my nipple over top of my bra. With only the lace between us, his hot mouth on me felt beyond incredible. When he added his tongue, I was sure I'd lose my mind. My heart nearly stopped as he flicked the hard nub, shooting waves of delicious heat down to my core.

My thighs tightened around him, my hands grasping his

head. That ache between my legs was now an entity of its own, needing more. "Evan, I need you," I whimpered while he moved to my other breast, leaving his fingers behind to continue playing.

The shocks that shot through me were relentless. I'd do anything to relieve this ache. "Please, I want you," I whispered into his hair, kissing his head. He stopped what he was doing then kissed my lips with more determination than before. He stole my breath as his tongue plunged so deep in my mouth I could barely breathe—his grip tensing even harder on me.

Sighing, I clutched onto him for dear life, letting him do as he pleased.

My hands touched his feverish skin everywhere I could. Finally, I tore my lips from his and kissed down his perfect neck. He tasted divine. Alternately kissing and licking his skin, I couldn't help but press myself closer.

His hands roamed my back, stopping on the closure of my bra. In one second, it went slack. I backed up, both of us scrambling to get rid of it, pulling it forcefully off my arms as though it was a matter of life or death.

Skin on skin, our chests finally touched without the confines of anything between us. Moaning into his mouth, I hunted for his tongue. Once I found it, I drew it into my mouth, grazing it slightly with my teeth. That brought out a guttural moan from Evan that I'd never heard from anyone before.

"We should stop," he said before taking over the kiss, his hands heading straight for my breasts.

"Probably," I replied, smiling as his hands caressed my nipples into hard peaks. "But I want you, so much."

He ceased his kisses and his touches, leaning his forehead onto mine. "You have no idea how much I want you, too," he said, lightly shaking his head side to side.

My hand brazenly traveled down his chest to his abs then even further down until I felt his hardness. "Mmm," he said, taking my mouth again. I continued touching him for a moment before slipping my hand inside his tight underwear.

Gasping at the feel of him, I gripped his hard, veiny length then began stroking him at a slow, steady pace. His hips thrust up into my hand asking for more. The thing was, I didn't know what else to do. This was about as far as I'd ever gone.

All I was certain of was that I needed him. All of him. However that came.

"Please?" I asked one more time before he conceded, placing his hands on my behind, walking out of the water to where our clothes sat. With my legs still around him, he bent down to his knees then spread out his jacket on the beach.

Lowering us down on the sand, I sighed. This is what I wanted. Me underneath Evan. His warm, wet body above mine. I could feel his cock, hard and hot against my stomach as he kissed my neck. "Yes," I moaned as his hand cupped my breast and his mouth covered my nipple, sucking harder this time. As though they were somehow connected, my pussy contracted at his attentions.

Evan's hand moved from my breast, down my stomach to find my core. When his hand dove inside my panties I knew this was going to be the night. I wouldn't be leaving this beach a virgin. An excited thrill surrounded me thinking how perfect and unexpected this all was.

"You're so wet for me," he said, laying on his side, his fingers doing amazing things I'd never felt before.

"That feels good," I said, kissing his lips lightly.

His finger found my entrance, slowly going further and further inside me. My hips pushed up against his hand, craving more contact, more movement—more of something I didn't really understand. When his thumb brushed over my clit, I gasped out loud, my fingers digging into his arm.

"You okay?" he asked, stilling.

"Very okay." Placing my hand on his, I encouraged him to start again. "Keep going."

Touching his lips to mine again as he gently restarted his movements. "More, Evan," I said breathlessly into his ear. His hand yanked hard on the lacy material of my panties, pulling them down. Once he removed my underwear completely, I spread my legs open, encouraging him with my hands to lay on top of me.

He reached over me, looking for something in our discarded clothing. Pulling out what looked like his wallet, he opened it. A crinkling sound came next and I knew what he was doing. After he was fully covered, he laid on me. "Are you sure about this? Is this what you really want?"

My hands went to the sides of his face. "I need you, please? I've never done this before," I told him in barely a whisper.

"Holly," he said, motioning like he was going to move off of me.

My heart panicked at the thought of him leaving. "I want you to be my first." My legs and arms tightened around him attempting to hold him where he was.

"Are you sure?"

I nodded, then answered, "Yes." I'd never wanted anything more in my life.

He reached down between us, lining himself up with me. "Relax, I'll go slow," he said, his lips touching my cheek.

The bright moon was directly in my sight, surrounded by a million stars. It was like being in some kind of dream.

The fullness he created as he pushed inside of me took my breath away. I'd never felt like this before. After a few moments, Evan worked his way back and forth in a slow, torturous motion. When he was fully inside of me, my legs relaxed. Raising my hips up, I bucked him to let him know I was all right.

Withdrawing slightly, he pushed back in with such restraint my heart nearly burst. Evan treated me with such care and concern, it brought tears to my eyes. "Oh no, am I hurting you?" he asked, his face filled with regret.

Smiling, I said, "No, you're being so sweet." Pulling him down, I kissed him.

He wiped away my tears, kissing one eyelid then the other. His movements sped up after that, creating a sensual fire that quickly drove me insane. Evan lifted up on his arms, powering into me faster now. "You are so beautiful," he said, dipping down to me for a second to kiss me, then going back to quicken his pace even further.

Tingling started, just like when I touched myself at home alone in my bed. Only this time it was with Evan inside of me. The sensations he created shocked me, I didn't know what to do so I held onto him for dear life as every muscle in my body tensed.

"Are you coming?" Evan asked as I wrapped myself around him, not breathing, unable to answer back. He kept thrusting into me, filling me up so completely I felt dizzy. "Let go, I've got you," he said in a strained voice, surrounding me in his safe cocoon.

Flashes burst behind my eyelids as I cried out. "Oh, yes, ohh," I said grasping at Evan's back, looking for purchase so I didn't fall away. My entire body pulsed with the force of my orgasm, his movements making it go on and on like I was floating away, never wanting to return.

"Fuck," he said, stilling inside of me as he gasped over and over again. His chest expanding and deflating with such force I worried if he was okay. Moving in and out of me a few more times, he withdrew, rolling over onto his back.

"Come here," he said, pulling me with him onto his chest as he tried to even his breathing. His hand rubbed my back while I settled into his sweaty body. Playing with his slight spattering of chest hair, my heartbeat finally returned to normal. "Holly?"

Reluctantly lifting my head, I rose up resting my chin on his chest. "Mmm hmm?"

His arm bent behind his head, propping it up. "You okay?"

"I'm way better than okay," I said, tapping my finger on his hard pectoral muscles.

"Yeah?" he asked, his eyes scanning my face.

"Yeah," I said, moving up to touch my lips to his.

11

Evan

Seven o'clock in the morning and I was already planning a nap in my Jeep at lunch. How did Holly work these crazy hours and keep up her grades? Stretching one more time in the Jeep, I swung open my door, making my way to the diner.

The entire weekend my mind was a flurry of wondering if she was going to report me. Would I walk into school and be shown the door? Did Holly hate me now that we'd slept together? She made no attempt at exchanging numbers when I dropped her off at her house—or trailer, I should say.

By the time we got to her place it was late. Really late. Because of how loud my bike was, she'd wanted me to leave her at the entrance to the park but I wouldn't listen. Instead, I parked and we walked to her driveway.

I'd dragged her into me for one last kiss. In fact, I swear I could still feel her body touching mine. It was so perfect.

Ding, ding, went the bell above the door as I sauntered

inside. Her eyes met mine instantly, like a magnet. She finished pouring a few cups of coffee then made her way to me. "For one?" she asked politely as if we'd never met.

"Please," I answered back, both relieved and disappointed she didn't run into my arms.

"Follow me," she said, coffee pot in one hand, menu in the other. She sat me at the same spot as last time. Flipping over the cup on the table, she emptied the pot into it. "Do you need a moment? Or do you know what you want?"

My eyes traveled the length of her, remembering what was underneath that uniform. I knew exactly what I wanted. Her sweet body squirming beneath mine on the beach, under the moonlight and the stars.

"Uh, just give me a minute, please."

"I'll be back," she said before spinning around to take more orders and remove plates. I needed to get my head on straight. Every time I was around her, my brain clouded— only wanting one thing. My palms were sweating profusely now, and I wondered if the rest of my body was as well.

Once I remembered how to read, I decided on the special. Taking a few deep breaths, I steadied myself for Holly's return. When she finally made her way back to me, she said, "What would you like to eat?"

Now, I have no idea if she said it in a provocative voice or not, but hearing her say that made me think of certain things we hadn't gotten around to that night on the beach. Things I would very much like to do right now.

"I'll have the special," I practically croaked as she giggled to herself.

"Sounds good," she said, stuffing her order pad into her apron. Hesitating for a moment, like she wanted to say more, she gave up and walked back to the kitchen.

I relaxed against the back of the seat. Part of me knew it

would be weird, seeing her in the daylight after our night together. This was more awkward than I'd imagined. My heart was beating like crazy and my brain couldn't remember any of the prepared speeches I was going to make to her.

Closing my eyes, I tried to think about what to say. Blank. Nothing came to mind.

"Tired?" she asked, startling me a bit as she filled up my untouched cup.

That familiar floral scent I knew so well wafted toward me. "A bit. I don't know how you manage to get up so early every day," I said, pouring sugar into my cup.

"You do what you have to do," she said in a chipper voice. "I'll be right back with your order."

I watched her hips sway as she walked away from me. She had this job because she needed the money. A concept so foreign to me it wasn't even funny. Never in my life did I have to work even half as hard as Holly.

When she came back with my order, I thanked her. "You're welcome. Just call if you need anything else."

As she moseyed away, a man stopped her, gesturing with his hands, then taking an obvious look right at Holly's behind. What the fuck? A second later, his hand touched her ass and stayed there. Oh, I did not think so.

Instead of helping her, the other men at the table laughed. Screw this. Pushing away from the table I rose up, storming over to them. "Excuse me, I think the lady would appreciate it if you removed your hands and left," I said, nodding toward the door.

"I think the lady would appreciate me keeping my hands on her and staying. Right, toots?" he said, squeezing her ass.

That was it. I saw red as I pushed between Holly and the

asshole. "I asked you to take your hands off her and leave. Not saying it again."

"Why? You'll get your turn after," he spouted back, his buddies laughing again.

Reaching down, I grabbed the front of his shirt, pulling him up. "Let's go. Now."

"Hey, hey, hey, I was just jokin' around. You and your tie need to settle down, boy," he said, moving back a bit. "The girl flirts with me every morning. We got a thing, ya get me?"

"I get that you aren't welcome in here again. And if I see your stupid face, I'll call the cops." Shoving him with my fist still in his shirt, he stumbled before straightening himself up.

"Yeah, we'll see who's allowed back in here after I speak with the manager," he said in a loud voice, looking around the restaurant. "And I got witnesses, too." His hand went into the air to accentuate his point. Yanking his coat from the back of his chair, he stomped out first, followed by his motley crew.

"You okay?" I asked Holly, putting my hand on her arm.

"Fine, thank you," she said, avoiding my gaze as she picked up the money the men had thrown haphazardly on the table. Her lips were pressed into a tight line. The other patrons had quieted, their eyes and ears focused on us.

Not knowing what else to do, I went back to my seat. Pushing my food around, unable to eat with the sick feeling in my stomach, I wondered how often ignorant men put their hands on Holly. No matter what that jerk said, she wasn't flirting with him at all.

Someone slid into the chair opposite me. "Thanks." Holly leaned her elbows on the table. "You didn't have to do that, but I'm glad you were here."

"That happen often?" I asked, staring into her sparking

blue eyes, remembering how she looked up at me in wonder right before she came hard on my cock. I shifted in my seat, taking a breath. She bit her lip for a second. Hesitation was never a good thing. Throwing down my fork, I said, "You need to quit working here. It's not safe."

She laughed briefly. "It happens but not every day. There are slimeballs everywhere, Evan. This diner isn't anything unusual. I've worked at lots of different places."

My hands clenched together, wanting to punch every asshole who'd ever touched Holly. Including myself. How could I have crossed the line with this innocent girl? "That's just not right."

"That's just how it is," she said, rising from her chair, a sad look on her face. "Anyway, thanks again for sticking up for me."

$\sim$

SITTING IN MY JEEP, I waited illegally in the bus zone. Holly ran out of the diner like it was on fire. Struggling with her bag as she simultaneously fixed her shoe, I chuckled at the sight before me. Man, she was cute.

Beeping my horn, she looked up at me. Her face changed from "how dare you" to something I couldn't read. Hiking her bag onto her shoulder, she marched to my vehicle. "I'm taking the bus."

"You're getting in. We need to talk."

"We don't need to talk. I'm getting on the bus. Now go before it pulls up," she said, motioning with her hand to where the bus would soon be arriving.

"Holly, get in the Jeep. You're not winning this. I'm not moving, so you'll be the reason I get a ticket if you don't hurry up."

"Gahh," she said, ripping open the passenger door then jumping in. "Why are you so stubborn?" she asked, arranging her bag on the floor before reaching for the seat belt.

"Habit," I responded as I shoulder checked before pulling out into traffic. Glancing down for a quick second I noticed she had already changed into her uniform. "We need to talk about—" I started, looking at her in the eyes.

"You have nothing to worry about." She sighed, staring out her window. "I told you I'm no snitch."

"I—we—I shouldn't have done what we—did. I'm your teacher and I crossed a line you're never ever supposed to cross with a student. It was wrong and it won't happen again." My stomach sunk saying those words because that was not how I felt at all. What I wanted to do was keep driving to the beach where we'd spend the day in the sun and the water. With me reapplying sunscreen to her beautiful skin several times. Then we could go back to my place and—

"I get it. I'm not some doe-eyed kid who doesn't understand how the world works. If there's one thing I know how to do it's keep my mouth shut." Her face turned to me. "I have no interest in getting you fired or gossiping to my friends. Don't worry."

The look on her face was so sincere it made me want to pull the Jeep over and kiss her. No matter how relieved her words made me, I was still deeply saddened by what she said. "Why are you good at keeping your mouth shut?"

She rolled her head on her shoulders. A movement someone her age shouldn't be doing to relieve stress. Something inside of me wanted to erase all of the anxiety in her life.

"I just am, Evan. It's just how things are." Holly exhaled

heavily, and I wished she'd trust me enough to share her burdens with me. But I needed to keep my distance. What happened that night on the beach could never happen again.

My hand reached over to touch her knee gently. "Tell me why," I asked as I turned right down a street close to the school.

Her eyes caught mine again and it frustrated me that she wouldn't share. "Drop me off here so nobody sees us," she said, waving her hand at a side street. Holly gathered her bag and took a quick look at her perfect face in the mirror in the visor.

I took the turn she advised but when I came to a stop, I grasped her arm so she couldn't leave. "Holly, stay for a minute so we can talk," I urged her, hoping she would listen.

"Everything's fine," she said, her eyes getting a bit teary. "Thanks for your help at the diner with that guy. I really appreciate it." Before I knew what happened she'd slipped from my hand and out the door.

12

Holly

Looking down at my phone, I saw the time. Eight thirty-six in the morning. Calculating in my head, I could cry in approximately—fourteen hours, give or take. I told myself I could do this.

However, my broken heart said something completely different.

It was silly and I knew it—to think a student and a teacher could have a relationship. The entire weekend, I went over and over that night in my mind. Being with him seemed so right. Like we fit.

After talking to him this morning, my hopes were finally dashed. He didn't want to continue anything with me. It was wrong—according to him he crossed a line. I suppose it didn't matter that I wanted him to cross that line.

Again, my heart squeezed, and my stomach hurt constantly. All I wanted to do was get under the covers and hide from the world. There was work and school and—my mother.

"Yo, girlfriend," Alex said with his funny little staccato voice that always made me laugh despite the fact all I wanted to do was cry.

I spun around to see him behind me strutting down the hall. What I wouldn't give to be as happy as he was. "Hi," I said, looking down at his bright sneakers.

"You okay after the club de-bac-le?" he asked, separating the last word into syllables.

"I already told you I was fine," I said, frowning at him. Alex was a good friend and he'd texted me while I was still with Evan that night to make sure I was safe.

"My dear, it took you forever to respond to my text. I thought someone had kidnapped you for the sole purpose of making a woman suit out of your gorgeous skin," he said, gently pinching my arm.

"No such luck. I went home, showered and didn't look at my phone," I semi lied to him again. I did eventually go home to shower but not until after my rendezvous with Mr. Marshall.

"I bet you were studying, you big geek," he said, wrapping his arms around me. "I'm sorry for dumping you. Do you really forgive us for being such asses?"

Hugging him back, I said, "All is forgiven." Holding him even tighter, I continued. "Besides, it's not your fault that Owen and Xavier showed up wasted. We didn't exactly have many options."

"Do not even get me started. I'm not on speaking terms with those two idiots."

"What's with all the touchy feeling stuff going on?" Ivy poked me in the back.

"I was re-apologizing to our girl for leaving her stranded," Alex said, pushing away from me, glaring at her.

"Don't make it sound like it was my fault those morons

showed up drunk," Ivy said, continuing on her way to our lockers.

"I almost forgot," I said, rummaging through my bag. "Here." I pulled out her credit card that she'd given me.

"Thanks, did it take long for you to find a cab?" Ivy asked, opening her locker.

"Nah, I got a ride right away," I said, a faint blush starting on my face. I was the worst liar ever. She looked at my face, frowning.

Scared that she'd call me out, I was grateful when Paige showed up, hip checking Alex. "Rumor has it that you guys saved Owen and Xavier's asses at the club on Friday night."

"We were bumping and grinding our brains out when I spotted the fine Mr. Marshall at the very same establishment," Alex said, raising his eyebrows up and down. "That's when we hightailed it out of there right into Owen and Xavier."

"Holy shit, Mr. Marshall saw you?" Paige asked, face full of surprise.

"We don't know if he saw us but we certainly saw him," Alex said, throwing his hands up in the air, dancing to his own beat.

"He wouldn't have narced on us," Ivy said, clearly disgusted. "We should have just stayed."

"Not wise, my sister friend." Alex grabbed Ivy's binder for her. "No need to poke the bear. Although," he said, placing his finger on the corner of his lips. "I'd poke a lot more than his bear." Alex broke out in hysterical laughter, nearly dropping Ivy's binder.

"Get in line," Ivy said, rescuing her schoolwork from the crazy man. "If anyone's getting poked, it's me. Watch and learn, people," she said, shaking out her hair before making a beeline right for Mr. Marshall whom she'd just spotted.

"Good grief, does she really think she has a chance with a teacher?" Paige asked, as I shoved things into my locker. "What do you even have in that bag?" she asked, frustrated at the door not shutting.

"The kitchen sink," Alex said, pushing us all out of the way so he could give it a try.

"I thought the saying was everything but the kitchen sink?" Paige asked.

"Yes, but Holly brought that, too," Alex said, laughing his face off, finally closing the door.

"Very funny," I said. What I didn't say was that they'd need to carry a lot of stuff around, too, if they were going to be gone until bedtime.

"Look how she's practically shoving her boobs right in his face," Paige said, scowling at the display Ivy was currently making for Mr. Marshall. At that exact moment, his eyes darted directly to mine. "Oh my gosh, he's looking at us. Do you think he heard me," Paige asked, swirling around so her back was now to them.

"Your voice does carry," I said to her, sliding my hand around her elbow. "You should have tried out for the drama production," I teased her.

"Do not even mention drama. Your bestie has been hounding us to run lines with her every second of the day," Alex said as his hands curled up into fists by his sides.

"And no offense, but how in the world did she even get the part? She's terrible," Paige whispered to us as we passed by Mr. Marshall, Ivy, and her very perky breasts.

"Terrible is too kind of a word," Alex said, barely moving his lips while he smiled at Mr. Marshall on our way past.

"Well, she needs more practice then," I replied.

"Girlie, she could practice until the next millennium and

I'd still prefer being eaten alive by red ants to watching her act."

"That's harsh, Alex," I said, snorting at his words. Truth be told, Ivy was a weak actor. I was fairly certain the only reason she got the part was because her parents had donated a load of money to the library renovation fund.

"Sometimes the truth hurts, my love," he said, skipping off magnanimously to his first class.

$\sim$

NORMALLY, painting relaxed me. Today it gave me too much time to think about and dissect everything that had happened since I'd met Evan. And not just the physical things that we'd done, but how we'd connected on another level. Or so I'd thought.

Dancing with him had been so much fun then when he'd pulled me close for the slow song, I felt like I was going to faint. It seemed like he was into it and having fun, too. At the beach, he really cut loose. Being with him felt like it did when I was with a good friend.

Until the kiss. That was his idea, wasn't it? Maybe I wasn't good enough at all the other stuff we'd done on the beach. He could have anyone he wanted. I'm sure he probably did have anyone he wanted. Why he'd gone all the way with me I didn't understand.

This morning he'd kicked that jerk out of the restaurant for touching me. It was like a scene from a movie how he'd pushed his table aside to get to me faster. That was twice now he'd helped. Just like back at the club when the drunk approached.

Nobody had ever stood up for me like that before.

Later when we were in his Jeep, his words cut into me

like a knife. I don't know what I expected him to say but not that. All that was left for me to do now was lick my wounds in private. And cry. In exactly—six hours.

"Congratulations, Miss Anderson. This looks substantially less blue today," Evan said, startling me.

I gazed up at him from the floor. "Thanks." Turning back to my work, I ignored him, wishing I could also ignore the feelings that bubbled up whenever I was around him.

"Hey, I'm just teasing. You know that, right?" he whispered, bumping his foot on mine.

"It'll be fine, Mr. Marshall. I'm on schedule to have it done on time, don't worry," I said, feeling like a hurt little kid. It wasn't easy for me to lie. Right now, my heart hurt, and my arms felt like lead. I wished he would just leave me alone.

"I see," he said to my back.

Switching brushes, I tried my best to ignore him, hoping he'd go. Hearing his footsteps get further away, I breathed a sigh of relief as I wiped a stray tear from my face. I was such a baby sometimes.

The slamming of a door had me twisting around out of surprise. "What are you doing?" I said nearly out of breath.

"Come here," Evan said, walking over to me with his hands out. Reluctantly, I reached up to him. He pulled me up, our bodies touching. His manly smell drove me crazy. As I looked up into his eyes, my hands clutched his even harder. Standing here this close to him was too much.

"What are you doing?" I asked, wanting him to lean down and kiss me.

"We need to talk," he said with more authority this time, sounding like he was pissed off at me. I found it sadly funny that he should be mad at me.

"No, we don't." I found my backbone somewhere,

pushing away from him, walking through a set of doors that led into the costume room.

He followed me, right on my heels. "Would you stop?" he said, anger in his voice.

Turning around on my heel, I said exactly what I wanted, "I get it. It was a mistake. It never should have happened." Chest heaving with anger, my head felt like it was going to explode. Why was he pushing this?

Striding over to me, he grabbed onto my upper arms, holding me close to him again. "Holly, you don't understand. The last thing I'd want you to think was that what we did was a mistake. It was by far the most beautiful, meaningful night of my life. What we did was—unforgettable. I meant everything I said and did. And I wouldn't trade it for anything."

His words made me cry. Tears flowing down my cheeks, I said, "It was my first time. I know I wasn't that good."

The expression on Evan's face changed in a snap. His brow furrowed as a deep frown crossed his face. In a soft voice he said, "Is that what you really think?" His eyes stayed on me, unblinking. "Fuck, I can't believe you would think that," he said, hugging me firmly. "You gave me a gift, Holly. A perfect, wonderful gift that I'll never, ever forget. It was incredible for me. I had hoped it was good for you, too," he said into my ear, stroking my hair with one hand, holding my waist with the other.

"I'm sorry if it wasn't what you expected. I really tried my best to go slow but—" He didn't finish his sentence.

"You didn't hurt me," I said into his warm, hard chest. How I wished I could stay here forever. Leaning back a bit, I said, "It was—beautiful."

He bent down, nearly touching my lips. "Under the moonlight, feeling you, touching you, kissing you," he said before touching his mouth to mine. Our tongues tangled together in a hot, passionate kiss. His hand held my head to his as his tongue probed into my mouth, like he was making love to it.

My legs felt weak, thinking about what else he could thrust inside of me like that. Moving my hands up his back to his head, I ran my fingers through his hair.

"Holly, are you in here?" I heard someone call from the other room.

13

Holly

"Shit," I said, practically jumping out of Evan's arms. Looking around, I whispered to him, "That's the only door out of here."

"I'll stay here until you give me the all clear," he said, fixing my hair then wiping under my eyes with his thumbs.

Running out, I saw it was Ivy. "Why were you in the costume room?" she said suspiciously, giving me the once over.

"I'm in charge of costumes, too," I said, shaking my head, taking my place back on the floor to continue painting.

"Why are you acting so weird? And your hair is screwed up," she said, narrowing her eyes on me.

"What's your problem? I was digging through boxes and racks of clothing." Picking up a brush, I painted a green leaf on what would eventually be a tall vine.

"Holly," she said, and I turned my head to her. "I need someone to run lines with me before drama practice starts," she said, waving her script in one hand.

"I have to leave for work in five minutes, sorry." Another lie. I was really racking them up today.

"Already? Why so early?"

"Someone has an appointment I think," I said, making up a few more lies.

"You work too much," she said, shaking her head. "I'm really worried about you." A crease formed as her eyebrows drew together.

Feeling guilty as hell, I spun around to face her. My stomach dropped. I couldn't tell her the truth and admit I was just making out with our English teacher so she needed to leave. Now. "It's okay, really."

"No, it's not," she said, her face holding so much concern for me, my heart ached at my deception.

"I'll help you tomorrow, I promise. Go ask Alex. He's probably out back."

"All right but you're coming over tomorrow for supper and to hang out." She gave me a sad smile before spinning around to leave.

I let out the breath I'd been holding and jumped up to save Evan. Gliding around the corner, I stopped short seeing Evan with a sword in his hand and donning a pirate skull mask. When he saw me, he assumed the fighter's pose, even cutting a "z" in the air.

That cracked me up. "Having fun?" I asked, eyebrows raised, stupid smile on my face.

"Actually, yes. It's been a while since I've played dress up." He swaggered up to me, making me laugh again. "Ever been kissed by a pirate?"

"Not lately."

"Then today's your lucky day." Literally sweeping me up in his arms, he dipped my body down, kissing my lips as I giggled in his arms.

"I think I'm in trouble, Holly," he said in between kisses. I didn't answer him because I agreed that we were both definitely in trouble.

~

"THE GREASE TRAPS need to be cleaned out again, Lenny," I said as I walked through the kitchen. "Those sinks aren't draining like they should." And I would know after doing an hour of dishes.

"I'll take a look, Holly. Have a good night," Lenny replied, continuing to scrape the grill.

"You, too," I smiled back at him as I searched around for my bus pass. "Ah, gotcha," I murmured to myself, pulling the card out. I didn't especially like working evenings. For one thing, it took away from my study time. For another, it was dark—really dark by the time I left.

Stop being a sissy, I coached myself. No matter what I did, thoughts of that drunk man outside of the club came flooding back, freaking me out even further. A horn honked from somewhere, making me jump. "Holly," someone called from across the street, waving an arm out the window.

It couldn't be. Could it? After my eyes adjusted, I saw that it was most definitely, Evan. What was he doing here at this time of night? My bus wasn't due for another ten or fifteen minutes, so I jaywalked across the street.

"Get in, I'll drive you home," Evan said. For roughly one second, I considered fighting him on me taking the bus instead. Then I gave in. I was exhausted.

Without a word, I circled his Jeep and got in, grateful for the door to door service. After I clicked my seat belt, I glanced over at him. "What?" I asked, unable to read his face.

"You got in."

"Are you going to drive or just sit here?"

He shook his head, starting the vehicle up. "You have time for ice cream or something?" he asked, watching for cars before pulling out.

Did he just ask me if I wanted ice cream? "I would, but I should probably go home and study."

"How long does the bus take you to get home?"

"Umm, I'd have to wait another fifteen minutes for it. The ride itself takes about a half hour depending on how many stops we make."

"It only takes ten minutes to get to your place. Therefore, with the minutes we're saving, you should have time to get ice cream," he said, glancing over me.

What exactly was he doing? "I suppose I understand your logic, Mr. Marshall."

He smiled at me then kept driving. When we pulled into the drive thru at the ice cream joint, he asked me, "What kind do you like?"

"Umm," I said a few times, reading over all the flavors. "Double Chocolate, I think." It was a tossup between that and Sinful Strawberry.

When he handed me my gigantic cone, I giggled. "This thing is huge."

He snorted, shaking his head as he took a lick of his strawberry cone. "What?" he asked, narrowing his eyes on me.

"I was going to get strawberry."

"Then why didn't you order it?"

"Because I also wanted chocolate."

He threw his head back, laughing. "Makes complete sense. You want some?" he asked in the most sensual way, his eyebrow cocked.

"Yeah," I said, feeling surprisingly brave right now. Holding out his cone to me, I took a long, slow, lick, as I held his eyes with mine.

"You're not helping matters," he growled in a deep, gravelly voice.

I leaned back into my seat, concentrating on my ice cream now. We drove for a bit, then Evan signaled left into the parking lot of the same beach we were at a few days ago. Again, it was completely empty.

Shifting into park, he shut the Jeep off then undid his belt. "Walk with me?" he asked, taking another lick of his ice cream. All I did was raise my eyebrows. He'd told me what we did on the beach would never happen again. "Just walk. I promise."

Knowing full well I should go right home instead of taking a stroll with this man, I went against my better judgement and opened the door.

Taking a deep breath, the ocean air filled my lungs making me smile. "All it takes is some sugar and the beach to make you happy?" Evan asked, holding a hand out for me.

"Yeah," I said, shooting him a grin as his warm hand enveloped mine, caressing it leisurely with his thumb. We walked in silence until we arrived at the edge of the water. I kicked off my shoes first relishing the feel of the sand on my feet.

Evan took his off next then we ventured into the water creeping up on the beach. The only sound I could hear besides our footsteps was the rhythmic crashing of the waves. Closing my eyes for a moment, I imagined a life where I could do this every day—with Evan.

It was a stupid, unrealistic fantasy—one of many that I'd allowed my brain to entertain the last few days. I was devastated this morning when Evan told me what we had done was wrong and it would never happen again.

The way he was treating me now seemed to suggest he'd changed his mind. "You good?" he asked, forcing me to open my eyes.

Turning my head to him, I saw his eyes focused on me. "Very good," I said, squeezing his hand, taking another lick of ice cream. His eyes narrowed on my cone. "Do you want some?" I asked, licking my lips.

"Absolutely," he said, pulling me flush against his body. Surprised and more than a little shocked, I looked up at him, mouth open. In an instant, his lips sank down to mine. The taste of sweet strawberry filled my mouth and I couldn't get enough.

He devoured me endlessly like he was never going to stop. His hand pulled me closer, deepening our kiss even more. After a few more breathless moments his kiss turned light and playful, teasing me as his tongue licked at my lips. "What are you doing?" I attempted to twist away from him, giggling at the same time.

"I have no idea," he said in such a serious voice I stopped moving.

Gazing into his conflicted face, his eyes wide as though he was struggling to figure out some kind of mystery, I sprang forward. He reacted immediately, taking over the kiss, pulling me tight to him. Standing there on the beach in Evan's arms I felt almost drugged as the longing for him inside of me spread. My nipples hardened, pressing against his hot, muscular chest. Through the thin material of our clothes I could feel his heart beating nearly as quickly as mine. Tearing my mouth from his I kissed down his neck, tasting just a hint of salt—his intoxicatingly spicy scent of desire overtaking me.

"I couldn't stop thinking about you all day," he whispered, making my heart race even more. "I don't think I can stay away from you, Holly."

"Then don't." I pushed back a bit so I could see his face.

"I'm your teacher," he groaned, touching his lips to my forehead.

"Not right now you're not," I said, lifting up on my toes to find his mouth again. Feeling a coolness on my skin, I lowered myself back down. "This ice cream is getting everywhere." I held out my arm, chocolate running down it.

Evan's face changed completely once he saw, pinning me with an almost feral look. Throwing his cone down on the ground he grabbed ahold of mine with one hand as he clutched my arm with his other. Slowly lowering his mouth, licking the chocolate off my skin as he refused to break contact with my eyes.

He moved his tongue down the delicate skin on the inside of my arm and across my pulse. It was by far the most erotic thing that had ever happened to me. Feeling Evan's hot tongue linger on my arm made me clench my thighs together, in a vain attempt to find some kind of relief. He stepped closer, kissing me again with the taste of delicious chocolate in his mouth.

He slowly withdrew his lips from mine before taking a mouthful of ice cream from my cone as he proceeded to tip it against my lips. I couldn't open my mouth fast enough as the cold liquid spilled down my chin.

Evan licked down my neck, bending me back slightly to gain better purchase. His tongue trailed down the sensitive part of my neck under my ear, drawing circles until I writhed in his arms. I shivered as he licked up the other side of my neck, tasting everywhere he could with his roaming tongue. Finally, he backed us up further onto dry land, still tormenting me with his actions.

Lowering me down on my back, his free hand went for the buttons on the front of my uniform. Fumbling, unable to open them fast enough, he said, "Open these." Fire shot through me at his demand, making me squirm as I thought about what he was going to do. My belly tightened and my breasts swelled as I undid my dress.

The back of his hand grazed my nipple. "Bra, too." Evan's sharp gaze penetrated mine, his jaw tight as his nostrils flared. Undoing the front closure, I shuddered as he stared at my naked breasts. "You are so beautiful," he whispered, right before tipping the cone above one nipple. I gasped as the chocolate spilled on my hot peak.

His tongue swirled, sweeping my nipple into his mouth. "Mmm," he said, sucking harder. He repeated the same process with my other breast, pouring the cold cream in circles this time. Immediately, his mouth began relishing every last drop, sparking more and more of a flame inside me. A hot, carnal shock shot directly to my clit, feeling like I may come just from his attention on my breasts.

Being bare to him—the light, warm breeze caressing my body—was a unique torture. I yearned for more of him. Fumbling, I wriggled out of my panties, unable to withstand much more.

Without a word, Evan moved between my legs, cone still in hand. Spreading my legs apart, he bent down before tilting the melted ice cream onto me. "Ohh," I said, bucking upwards. That's when his mouth found my core, stripping me of any insecurities I might have had.

He gently licked at my folds, keeping an eye on me as he went. After a few moments, his tongue slipped into me, tasting, thrusting, teasing. My hand covered my eyes as I surrendered to him fully. I writhed against his mouth, reveling in the feel of him.

Suddenly, he ceased his actions. I mewed a protest at the loss of his tongue. "Hold this," he said as he peered up at me for a brief moment handing me the cone. I couldn't fully comprehend what he was asking or why. Clumsily, I grabbed the cone realizing briefly what it was before I fell back into ecstasy as he added a finger inside of me, doing things to me I didn't know were even possible.

Evan touched places that made me tremble with need. When his tongue began flicking at that bundle of nerves, I knew I had no choice but to succumb to him. "Oh, Evan," I muttered as every muscle in my body flexed at the same time. He continued licking and rubbing as I shattered into a million pieces.

With continued swipes, his tongue urged more from me even while my legs quivered, and my body shook. When the last of the aftershocks left me, he sweetly kissed my thighs then my stomach, making his way back up. "You okay?" he asked, lying beside me, lightly running his fingers over my sated body.

"I'm great but I'm afraid the cone didn't survive." We both looked over at my hand where the remnants of the cone remained.

Evan chuckled. "You completely crushed it," he said, reaching over to remove a few broken pieces of cone from my palm.

"Had my mind on other things I guess," I said, smiling up at him.

"You're sticky in a lot of different places," he said, stroking my breasts playfully.

With as much sarcasm as I could muster, I said, "I wonder why?"

He shrugged. "I'm a messy eater I guess," he said, smug smile on his face.

That cracked me up. I laughed, my body shaking, still open to the world. "Are you going to—finish?" I asked, feeling a full body flush rising up.

"This was just for you," he said, standing with his hands out. I grabbed hold as he pulled me up. My legs were still a bit wobbly but somehow, I managed to stay upright. "Let's clean you up before I take you home." Then he proceeded to slide my uniform and bra down my arms, freeing me of any and all clothing.

"Only if you come with me," I said, grabbing hold of his hands. "Please?" I said, not waiting for his answer as I began lifting up his shirt. His arms rose, pulling the shirt off the rest of the way. Then his hands sat on my waist while I undid his button and zipper.

Pulling down on his jeans, the huge bulge in his underwear was impossible to deny. As I gazed up into his face, I held onto the sides of the material, setting the huge length of him free. My brain thought for a moment at the impossibility of all of that fitting inside of me.

I turned around, ready to splash into the waves. The water was cool but welcome on my overheated body, making me shiver a bit as I stepped in one foot at a time. Just like last time, Evan rocketed past me.

As he dove into the water, I laughed again watching his commanding form in the water. He truly was at home here. "Get a move on," he yelled, coming up for air.

"I'm chicken, I have to go slow," I said giggling, trying my best to hurry.

He swam quite a distance away from me then turned

back just as I got in deep enough to swim. Gliding my way to him, I savored the sensation of the water on my naked body.

We raced, kissed, and floated for a while until the threat of going back home crept over me. "We should probably go," I said, voice full of regret as I treaded water beside Evan.

"Or—we could stay out here forever." He grinned, the moonlight shining in his eyes making him look even more handsome if that were possible.

"I wouldn't want to fall asleep in my English class tomorrow," I said, circling around him. "My teacher's a real hard ass."

"While I agree he's got a hard ass, I think he'd still pass you anyway," he said, grabbing me as I swam by.

"Hmm, I can't disagree with you there," I said, finding his very toned behind with my hand and squeezing.

"I've had a great time with you," he whispered to me, placing a light kiss on my lips before putting my hands on his shoulders and towing me closer to the beach.

Once we could touch land again, I held onto his hand, slowing us down a bit. When the water was almost knee height for him, I pulled to a stop. His arms immediately went around me, hugging me tight. There truly was no better feeling than our two wet, naked bodies so close.

"I've never done this before, so I might be really bad. You'll have to teach me what to do," I said, kissing his neck, chest, and further down until I was on my knees in the water.

"Holly, no, I'm fine. You don't have to—"

"But I want to. Very badly. I'll need your help, though," I said, staring up at him. His cock began hardening of its own accord before I even touched it. Wrapping my hand around it, I steadied myself with my other hand on his thigh. Opening my mouth, I put the head in first, licking around it.

"Fuuuuck," Evan said, widening his stance, sighing. I sucked on it again then removed it from my mouth to run my tongue on the tip. "Take in as much as you can," he said, his hand on my head, guiding me forward as he held his manhood in the other hand.

I tasted the salty ocean but also his own special saltiness now leaking out a bit. Before my gag reflex kicked in, I stopped. "Now move your head back while you suck," he said, moaning as I quickly did what I was told. "Yeah, that's perfect."

Evan's groans told me I was pleasing him. Or at least I hoped I was. I'd never attempted to do this before, so I honestly had no idea what to do. "Add your hand in," he suggested, peering down at me, his eyes hooded. I placed my hand near his cock, not sure what he meant. "Like this," he said, closing my hand around him. "Now move it in time with your mouth."

It took me a few tries to get into a rhythm. Once I did, Evan's noises increased. "Fuck, that's so good. Mmm hmm, just like that." His words of encouragement were a big help, that was for sure. They were also a huge turn on. I started aching down below again, squeezing my thighs together, searching for relief. Taking back my hand that was on his thigh, I instead used it on myself. I moaned when I found the exact spot I needed while still keeping up my furious pace with Evan.

"Are you touching yourself?" he asked, almost completely winded. I nodded slightly. "Fuck, you are so hot. Yeah, that feels perfect, Holly. Just like that. Keep touching yourself, I want you to come with my cock in your mouth."

His dirty words made me hotter, causing my clit to swell up even more. A few more rough touches and I began shuddering as my pussy contracted violently. I moved back a bit, but Evan held me to him. "Keep me inside your mouth while you come."

Doing what he asked, I breathed heavily in and out of my nostrils as my orgasm finally left me. After I was done, I started back on him, just how he asked. Except faster and with more intent. I wanted him to feel as good I just did. Nothing would stop me in my quest.

His cock swelled so impossibly big inside my mouth I nearly couldn't accommodate him. "I'm going to come, back up," he warned, moving my head with his hand. But I didn't want to let him go. What I wanted was for him to finish. I gripped his behind with my hands, nails digging in a bit and kept going, sucking harder than before.

More of the salty taste came out of him until eventually he grabbed my head, stilling me. What I had been waiting for finally rushed down my throat in strong bursts as Evan cried out in the night. I sucked on him for a few more strokes after I felt the last throb of him in my mouth.

Letting go of him completely, I stood and took a few steps into shallower water and sat down to rinse out my mouth. Evan followed, splashing me as he threw himself down beside me. "You are amazing," he said, putting his arm around me.

"You're just saying that," I said, wiping the ocean water off my face.

In one quick movement, he picked me up, placing me on his lap facing him. "That was far and above the best head I've ever had in entire fucking life. Swear to God," he said, crossing his heart.

Seeing the content look on his face along with his actions filled my heart with warmth. "It was fun for me, too," I whispered against his lips.

"I noticed. And that," he said, pulling me closer so my

breasts touched his chest, "was what made it even more incredible. You feeling comfortable enough with me—trusting me enough to share that part of you is unbelievably sexy, I can't describe it." His eyes were so soft and genuine I leaned over to kiss him one last time before we'd have to leave this paradise and go back to real life.

14

Evan

"Son, you need to reconsider once this term is up for you."

"Going back to school is not what I want to do, I've told you that already," I said to my father for the umpteenth time in years.

"How is teaching going to help you get your foot in the political door, hmm?"

That was kind of the whole point. "I don't think politics is for me, you know that," I said, rubbing the bridge of my nose hoping for the intense pain to leave.

"It is. And if you'd have listened to me five years ago and taken law classes instead of education," he spat out like it was a distasteful word. "You wouldn't be in this predicament."

"I'm not in a predicament, Dad. It sometimes takes time to get a full-time teaching job," I told him, sitting down on my couch, switching the phone to my other ear.

"You're lucky that teacher had a heart attack and I could

get you into a decent school. Otherwise you'd be stuck in a public school right now," he said it like that would be the worst thing in the world. "Do you have any idea what goes on in the public school system? It's a bloody free for all."

Sighing, I leaned back against my couch. "It's not that bad. I would have gladly taken a position in any public school."

My dad coughed. "Son, listen to me. The public system is not where you belong. You weren't brought up like that." Here we go again—the lecture on my upbringing. "We have a higher station in life and we need to uphold that appearance." Yeah, we need to pretend to be something we aren't so you get voted back in. "If people see us taking menial jobs then they'll automatically assume we couldn't do any better."

"If you'd have become a lawyer like we told you to, you'd be set for life. Having to backtrack now and fix what you've done wrong is going to take valuable time away from building up your career. Just look at Emmit." Yeah, let's discuss my older, much more successful brother and all the ways he's perfect. "He followed our plan to the "T" and he's sailing along. The wedding is in August, by the way. Your mother will send you the details."

Yes, the royal wedding. The perfect merger of two political houses to create the ultimate bond. Too bad one member of the lucky betrothed was also very gay. I didn't know if my parents were really that stupid or if they just chose to ignore all the signs that my brother wasn't straight. More than likely the latter.

"Looking forward to it. I've got to go now, Dad. I'll talk with you next week," I said, pressing the giant X on my screen. "Fuck," I said out loud to no one. Placing the palms of my hands against my eyes, I tried my best to erase all the shit in my life that floated around endlessly in my brain.

The first thing to pop up, as usual, was Holly. Jesus, what the hell was I thinking? Starting an affair with my eighteen year old student was not something I'd planned on doing. She had somehow gotten under my skin to the point where she was all I thought about.

Not even sleep could stop my brain from replaying visions of her in my head. My brain kept telling me to stay away, this would only end in pain and heartache. But my heart and my body wanted her—no, craved her.

Just thinking about her on her knees, looking up at me with my cock in her mouth as she touched herself made me hard all over again. Remembering how I'd tasted her—how she'd responded—drove me crazy.

Something inside of me wanted to scoop her up out of her shitty trailer park and dead-end job and carry her away to a safe place where she'd never have to work that hard again. Somewhere she'd be happy and free just like she was with me on the beach.

Physically we sizzled, there was no doubt about that. Intellectually, she was my ultimate match. Yeah, I was older than her, but Holly was one of the smartest, most intriguing women I'd ever met.

My doorbell went off, bringing me back to real life. Standing up, I strode to the front door. "Jake, I didn't know you were showing up," I said, making room for him to come in.

"You've gone radio silent on us, buddy. What's going on? Hiding a hot little number in here somewhere?" he asked, hitting my shoulder on his way past me. His words made me wish that Holly was upstairs in my bed waiting for me.

"Busy with work, that's all," I explained away my

absence—which was only partially true. Indeed I was also spending time with a "hot little number" as well.

He walked into the kitchen, heading straight for the fridge as usual. "After you ditched us at that club, we assumed you found somewhere else to spend your time," he said, reaching his long arm in, pulling out an apple.

"Nah, I was tired. They've got me in charge of the drama production as well. I'm at the school a lot longer than I'd thought I'd be."

Jake nearly choked on his mouthful of apple. "How in the hell did they rope you into the drama production?" He laughed as he chewed.

"Long story but I've got the least seniority."

"But the most experience. You always did love acting in those stupid plays," he said, taking another huge bite out the poor apple. "I have to admit that I was jealous when you'd get into the lead actress' panties so easily, though. They always fell for your leading man bullshit."

I laughed at his words. "How could I help it if I was irresistible to the prettiest girls?"

"Uh huh. Anyway, Studly, what are you up to tonight? You still owe me a beer." Unable to come up with an excuse quick enough, he continued. "Okay, that settles it. I'll pick you up at eight."

∼

"YOU ARE SO FUNNY," Maria said, grabbing my arm, making sure to rub her breasts on it at the same time. She was hot. Her sleek, long hair shined with the lights of the bar we were currently in. I could feel the steady thump of the music vibrating through the floor.

"Evan has lots of fun stories he can tell you back at his house in The Heights," Jake said, emphasizing where I lived.

"Ohh, I'm up for that," Maria said into my ear as she pressed even closer. Jake waggled his eyebrows at me.

Holly

"THANK you so much for staying late, Holly," my boss said again. "I don't know what we'd do without you here." His glossy eyes tired and defeated.

I felt sorry for them. Trying to keep a small business like this going at their age must be difficult. "It's okay," I lied. The few breaks I'd had weren't enough for me to finish all the homework and studying I had to do for tomorrow—well, technically today. "Hopefully Millie will get out of the hospital soon."

His wife had taken a tumble down their steps at home and was currently in the emergency room under observation. "No broken bones," he said. Yeah, this time. It seemed like falling was a regular pastime with her now. I had an uneasy feeling some kind of health issue was to blame.

"You clean up the last of the tables and get home. Your mother is going to be mad that we made you work so late." Holding in my laughter at what he said, I smiled then went to clear the few tables that had just left. My mother wouldn't notice what time of day I came home.

Dumping the last of the dirty plates into the bin, I wiped off a table as I heard the bell ding at the front of the restaurant. Must be some late partygoers from the bar down the street. We made a lot of money off of the drunk and disorderly at this time of night because of our location.

Inwardly I groaned thinking of staying even a few more

minutes to seat them and take their orders. Looking up with a fake smile on my face, I headed to the counter for menus. What I didn't expect was the shock I was in for.

Two men and two women—obviously on a double date scenario—likely straight from the bar. The brunette hanging off Evan, giggling herself silly was gorgeous. All hair, legs, and fake boobs, she knew what she wanted. And that was Mr. Marshall in her bed.

Nausea overcame me with such a force I wanted to rush to the bathroom. Somehow, I was able to keep my cool. "Table for four?" I asked in a chirpy voice, pretending the sight in front of me didn't gut me to the core.

"Well, maybe three because I think Maria's going to spend the entire time in Evan's lap." Everyone laughed at the joke except Evan who was currently staring at me unblinking. Evidently, Maria decided this was a good time to sneak her hand up his shirt and stroke his chest. The very same chest that had been naked next to mine barely twenty-four hours ago.

Every muscle in my body tensed. "Follow me," I said, leading them to a clean table. Placing their menus down, I asked if they wanted anything to drink.

"I think we've all had enough to drink for tonight," the friend said, wreaking of alcohol. Again, they all laughed except for Evan. I could feel his stare burning into me as I took their drink orders, refusing to look Evan in the eye.

Marching away, I heard his friend say, "That waitress is smokin' hot."

His girl chided him. "Hey, you're here with me."

Even though the drinks were behind the counter, I walked around the corner, bracing myself against the cool, brick wall. Closing my eyes, choked with anger I convinced myself not to burst into tears until I was home.

My head pounded in pain, confused at what I had just witnessed.

Evan was a here with another woman. A tall, beautiful woman his age. My stomach churned at the thought of him touching her, kissing her—doing other things to her. Pushing off the wall, I went back to work. The quicker I finished with them, the sooner I could go home.

"How about we skip eating and just go back to your place right now," the brunette said into his ear loud enough for all of us to hear.

"Maria, you dirty girl," Evan's friend said, laughing again. Another wave of nausea hit me as I tasted bile rising up.

"Here you go," I said, putting their drinks on the table as my blood ran cold. "Are you folks ready?" I asked, pulling out my notepad from my apron. My fingers were numb. I didn't know how I was going to write.

"I'd say Maria's been primed and ready for a half hour already," his friend blurted out. The women giggled, not embarrassed in the least. I forced down the urge to heave as my stomach churned at the thought of Evan taking that woman home and—

"Jake, enough with the bad innuendos, buddy," Evan finally spoke up. "I'll have fries," he said to me. I still refused to look at him. I jotted down what the others wanted then quickly dashed straight to the kitchen.

"You okay, Holly?" Bert asked when I nearly ran into him.

"Yeah, fine. Just tired." I looked up at him, my knees more than a bit wobbly.

"I heard Dave call you a cab. Go home and get a few hours sleep, girl," he said, taking the order slip from me.

A small surge of relief ran through my body when I realized I was almost free. "I'll take this cardboard outside first, thanks." Gathering up the few empty boxes in my hands, I walked to the backdoor. The night was dark and the air around me felt heavy, hard to breathe. Chucking the boxes into the bin, I jumped when I saw someone else back there with me.

"It's not what you think," Evan came out of the shadows, startling me. Part of me was relieved it wasn't an axe murderer. The other part wasn't sure which was worse.

"My Nanny used to say, "If it walks like a duck and quacks like a duck, it's probably a duck"," I said to him, catching my breath as my mouth turned dry.

"Holly, there's no ducks here. I promise you that. Jake wanted to go out and—" he started before I cut him off.

"You don't owe me an explanation of how you spend your time, Mr. Marshall. I'm just some stupid teenager," I said as I glared at him, heat creeping into my cheeks.

He frowned back, mouth grim. As I strode passed him, he clutched my arm. "Would you just listen to me for a minute?" he asked, anger in his voice.

Shaking off his hand I kept walking. "There's nothing from you I need to hear. You should go back inside. I'm sure Maria needs someone's lap to sit on."

His hands stopped me by the wall in front of the stairs. Pushing me against the hard exterior of the building, he said, "The only person I want in my lap is you." The scent of whiskey was strong on his breath.

Tears started forming and I chastised myself for not being stronger. "She's gorgeous, Evan. I get it. Can't blame you for picking her over me," I said, sniffling as I looked to the side, avoiding his glare.

"You are the most beautiful woman I've ever seen," he

said, kissing me lightly on the cheek. Tears escaped when I closed my eyes.

Shaking my head, I told him, "Just go. This hurts too much." I gasped as a sob tore out of my throat.

"I can't tell my friends about you. Jake was suspicious of where I went after the club that night I saw you. I ditched them to be with you," he said, his hands on either side of my face. "He wanted to go out tonight and I didn't know what to say. I'm sorry, Holly. So, so, sorry. I honestly didn't think you'd be at work this late."

His admissions made sense but his apologies made me cry even harder. Still shaking my head, I said, "It won't work with us anyway. You should just leave with her."

Wiping the tears from my face, he leaned in. "I want you." His lips touched mine, gently at first then he plunged his tongue inside my mouth, searching with abandon for mine. When I finally gave in and kissed him back, he groaned loudly with need. Wrapping my arms around him, he completely overwhelmed me—physically and emotionally.

Heaving me up with his hands, I wrapped my legs around his waist as he imprisoned me against the wall. His hardness pulsed against my panties as I clung to him, wanting nothing more than for him to fill me.

"I want you so much," Evan said, inflaming my desire even further. His hand reached down between us feeling me. "Fuck, you're already wet for me," he whispered against my lips. Moving aside the thin material of my panties, he shoved a finger inside me.

"Uhh," I said, snapping my head back against the wall.

"You like that?" he murmured in my ear.

"Yes," I answered back nonsensically. The sensations he created rendered me helpless.

"How much?"

"So much, Evan. Give me more, please," I requested, his lips on my neck. He answered immediately, adding another finger to the mix.

The friction he created was magical yet maddening. Something was stopping me from tumbling over the edge. "Undo your buttons," he ordered. I quickly obeyed as I felt another rush of electricity between my legs.

I moaned again as he increased the speed of his hand. Shoving down the silky cup of my bra, he lowered his head to capture my nipple in his mouth.

"Mmm," he said, almost growling as he sucked on me, using his tongue to lick and sweep across the hard bud.

It was exactly what I needed to skyrocket over the top. "Ohhh," I said, surrendering to my primal desire for pleasure. An exquisite spasm finally started, pushing me mercilessly over the precipice. Satisfaction pulsed through my entire body as I clung hard to Evan.

"Yeah, give me that," he said, still milking every last pulse of my orgasm out of me with his fingers.

"Evan?" We heard a voice call from the top of the stairs. Our heads swung over to see who it was. "Jesus, man. Couldn't wait until you got home?" He chuckled, closing the door behind him.

15

Evan

"Not complaining about your choice, man, but you had a woman willing, ready, and able from the bar. What the fuck is up with taking that hot waitress out back?" Jake asked after we dropped the women off.

The cab was headed to our neighborhood now but not nearly as fast as I wanted it to go. "She's the one I met at the club that night. The reason I didn't follow you guys," I said, telling my friend a partial truth as I gazed out the window.

"I knew it," he said, punching me in the arm. "I told the guys you were off getting laid." He laughed for a second, then stared at me. "How old is she? She looks pretty young."

He was telling the truth. Without her hair and makeup done, Holly looked her age. "Young but not too young."

"What the fuck's that supposed to mean?"

"She's legal. Barely."

"Fuck, me. You could have any woman you wanted, and you choose jailbait?" he said in an admonishing tone.

"Shut up, she's not that young."

He looked me over, suspicious as hell. "If you think about it, she's young enough to be one of your students." My head snapped to his at his perceptive as hell senses. I must've looked guilty because he said, "No, man. No, no, no. She's not one of your students?" he whispered loudly. "What the fuck is wrong with you?" He jabbed me in the arm. "The press gets a hold of this and it'll mean disaster for your dad. You get that, right? Those vultures love a good scandal to take a political figure down."

"Nobody's going to find out."

"You think I wouldn't like to nail some of the talent that walks into my classes? But I don't, dude. Never will." He eyeballed me for a minute. "However, at least my students are university age—not fucking high school, man. You need to break this fling off. Now."

Holly

"Mom, I told you not to smoke in here," I yelled at my mother who was nearly passed out on the couch. "One flame and this whole trailer will cook us alive," I said, shaking her shoulders.

"Was waitin' fur yew," she mumbled out of her stupor nearly dropping her cigarette.

"I had to work late, Milly had another fall and she's in the hospital."

"Shhhurrr, I bet," she spat out at me, saliva hitting me in the face. As I put her arm around my shoulders to lift her up after she stubbed the cigarette out in the coffee can. "Out wiff some boy, more like it. You fink I don't see your wet hair when you come in here? Lookin' like a little slut," she bellowed, swinging her arm around.

"Let's get you to bed, it's late," I said, ignoring what she'd just called me even though it hurt like hell. She'd been saying things like that to me for years now.

"Yeah, fineee, don't admit sleepin' around like some little hussy." She stumbled, almost taking both of us down. Mom couldn't have been more than eighty pounds but at this point it was all dead weight.

"How's your side?"

"Hurts like a bitch. You should beee home lookin' affer me, not out wiff all those boys."

"I was at work, Mom, honest. I really wish you'd go to the doctor and let them look at it." Finally at the door to her room, we went inside. She dropped down on her bed. I helped put on her nightgown, looking down at her distended stomach. For someone so thin, her stomach was big.

By the time I laid her onto her back she'd already passed out.

When I walked out, I opened some windows in the living room and kitchen area to get rid of the stale smoke smell.

Opening the fridge, I noticed that she hadn't eaten the food I'd made ahead for her. Again. Always complaining that she wasn't hungry. If there was some way I could convince her to go to the doctor I'd do it. Shutting the door, I headed for the bathroom to shower.

As the warm water flowed over me, I picked up the soap, running it sensually over my body, everywhere that Evan had kissed and touched. It was like I could feel him doing it all over again. Tilting my head to the side, I smiled, remembering how he'd talked dirty to me. "You're so wet" danced through my head causing my nipples to bead up under the water.

When I soaped up down below, I was still tender from where his fingers played with me for so long.

What he'd told me about him wanting me and not that woman he'd come into the diner with seemed implausible. Any man would have gladly taken her home. He wanted me. He'd said it and apologized, making me listen even when I didn't want to hear it.

After I dried off, I grabbed my bag and dragged it and my sorry ass to my room. Pulling on my robe, I looked at the clock. One o'clock in the morning. Taking a deep breath, I calmed myself before opening up my biology textbook to get to work.

16

Evan

"**M**ercutio, we need you over here with Benvolis and Romeo for the orchard scene," I called for the second time with as much patience as I could muster. Four weeks of practice and it seemed like everyone was worse than when we'd started.

"Oh sorry, Mr. Marshall," he said, moseying up from a dark corner where he'd likely been making out with the girl who was playing Juliet's nurse. Apparently those two thought drama practice consisted of sticking their tongues in each other's mouths for as long as possible.

I rolled my eyes at Holly who was currently securing the first part of the backdrop to the ground. Don't ask me why the stage manager was helping her instead of managing the actual stage like he was supposed to be doing. My guess would be those yoga pants that Holly was wearing which showed off that perfect ass of hers.

Holly smiled briefly then went back to her work. I had to admit she was quite the artist. The vast blueness of her original artwork now made sense as she'd added vines, flowers, stars and a moon—the balcony was still a work in progress.

"Where do you want us to stand?" Our Benvolio inquired.

I was tempted to say, "Out in the street," but somehow, I behaved myself.

Three painful hours later, I was packing up to leave. The students had all left except for Holly. She was still busy with her electric screwdriver on the set. Grabbing my bag, I strolled over to her. "You've done enough for today, Miss Anderson," I said in a regular voice in case anyone was listening.

"One more screw," she said, smirking at me as she pulled the trigger once more.

Stepping closer to her, I whispered, "You don't have a shift now?" She shook her head. "Wanna come over?" I asked, wanting nothing more than to get into my hot tub with a naked Holly. She nodded.

"Meet you at the donut shop," she said in a low voice as she turned her back to me.

∾

WE'D GOTTEN good at hiding our affair over the last month. Holly's hours were difficult but somehow we made it work without anyone noticing. "Oops, look at that. I accidentally undid your bikini," I said, slyly watching the white strings go slack then fall down her chest.

"That was no accident," Holly said, climbing into my lap. Casually swiping the cups of her top down with my index finger, she sat exposed, nipples in perfect, hard peaks for me.

My hands touched her breasts, made slippery from the

bubbly, hot water we sat in. "It was, but now I suppose we should make the best of it," I said, leaning in for a kiss. Her arms went around my neck, settling into me with a sexy sigh.

She ground herself against my hard cock in an erotic, insistent way making it difficult to hold myself back. Trailing my lips down her neck, that flowery scent I'd grown to love filled my nose. Her skin was damp from the water but also from the heat of the hot tub causing a thin, sheen layer of perspiration on her luscious skin.

My tongue licked the salt from her shoulder as my fingers gently pinched her nipples. Holly moaned, pressing herself closer to me.

"So, this is where you've been spending all your time," a voice called from the side gate making Holly jump in my arms.

"It's just my friend," I said in a low voice, helping her tie up the bikini strings behind her neck. "Why don't you go upstairs and wait for me?" I suggested, kissing her lightly on the cheek. She made her way up the steps then into the house, holding her towel close.

"Remind me to never go in your hot tub again," Jake said with a devilish smirk on his face.

"You forgot to call first," I said, resting my arms on the edge.

"If you ever answered your phone I would have." He walked closer to me, staring down at the ground for a bit.

"Is there something you needed?"

"Yeah, we need to talk. Meet you inside," he said, picking up a towel and throwing it at me. Then he swaggered toward the house.

He was right, I'd been avoiding him and the rest of my friends in favor of any stolen moment I could spend with

Holly. Drying myself off, I headed to my house to face the music.

In my fridge as usual, I waited for him to make his choice. "There's chocolate cake on the top shelf if you want," I said, rubbing the towel on my head.

He peered over at me, narrowing his eyes. Grabbing a plastic container, he shut the door with his hip while opening it. "Homemade," he said, yanking the cutlery drawer open after chucking the lid on my counter. "Mmm, at least she can bake," he said through a mouthful of cake.

I didn't answer him even though what he'd assumed was correct—Holly had baked it. She loved my kitchen, taking so much joy in cooking "on a real stove" and baking with decent pans. Jake was also right—she was a great cook.

Striding to the fridge, I pulled out the milk, pouring him a glass then setting it beside him. Leaning my hip against the counter, I asked, "It was nice to see you, but this isn't exactly great timing." Trying to give him more than a hint that he needed to leave.

"It's never great timing, is it?" He looked up at me as he shoveled in more cake. "What the fuck do you think is going to result in you dating a student? I understand you saw a great piece of ass and wanted it. But, buddy, she's a teenager," he said, setting the cake down then picking up the glass of milk.

"That's not really any of your business."

Choking a bit as he drank, he coughed into his hand, clearing his throat. "It's going to be everyone's business pretty soon if you continue this bullshit. How long do you think it'll take the press to get wind of this?"

The crappy part of all this was that he spoke the truth. "Do you think I haven't thought about that? We're careful, nobody knows anything."

He laughed, taking another huge gulp. "Evan, Evan, Evan, you stupid fuck. Those assholes eat people like you for breakfast. If you're doing shit like this, it'll come out."

"She's eighteen."

"Ha, they have an entire industry based on barely legal, my friend. You really think that's what the papers are going to say when they skewer you and your dad on the front page? She may be legal but she's your fucking student, man," he said, slamming his glass down. I had no answer for him. This is stuff that ran through my head every day.

"One question before I take off." He looked me up and down. "She worth it?"

To that, I had a definite answer. "Absolutely."

Jake shook his head. "Think about it, bro. You're going to take down an entire dynasty because of some teenage pussy. Nothing is worth that." Patting me on the shoulder, he turned around and left.

Holly

I STOOD THERE, stock still, listening to every word that Evan's friend said. His dad could lose his political present and future because of me? My hands shook uncontrollably. There was no way that I wanted to be the reason for anyone's downfall or embarrassment.

If Evan's friend was right, and his dad was a prominent figure then the risk was too great. Linking Evan to his student—who also lived in a trailer park—was the last thing in the world their family needed.

There was only one thing to do.

Picking up my bag, I walked down the stairs after Jake left. Turning the corner, Evan stood in the middle of his kitchen, thumb and index finger pressing the bridge of his nose. He only did that when he was stressed or tired.

"I should go, it's getting late." My breath hitched as I tried my best not to cry. "Can you drive me, or should I take a cab?" I wandered up to him, a bit unsteady.

He glanced at me before opening his arms. "Come here."

"Really, I have homework to do. I need to leave."

"Holly, come here." He insisted, wiggling his fingers. Unable to refuse him, I dropped my bag and stepped into his body, his chest still covered with a few small droplets of water. "You hear any of that conversation?"

Nodding, I decided not to lie. Jake's voice was commanding, and it carried without much effort.

"He's my friend and he's pissed that I haven't been spending time with him lately," he said into my hair, squeezing me closer.

"I don't want anything bad to happen," I said against into his neck.

"Nothing bad is going to happen."

"What kind of politics is your dad involved in?"

Clearing his throat, he said, "Can we talk about that later? Look, we're careful and who knows how much longer I'll even be at that school."

Panic hit me directly in the stomach. Shoving away from him, I said, "You're leaving?"

"I'm only there until Mr. Kensington recovers. Then I'll be stuck trying to find another job."

"Right." Laying my head on his chest I savored this moment of just us, alone. My heart hurt thinking about what I was going to say next. "Maybe we should take a break until your term is done."

His body went stiff. "What?"

"It would be safer and the last thing I want is for you or

your family to get in trouble because of me."

Hands on my shoulders, he reassured me. "Nobody is going to find out."

"Jake said that the press might."

Exhaling deeply, he said, "He's concerned about me, that's all."

Shrugging, I looked into his eyes. "Evan, he seemed fairly certain we were going to get caught."

"Nobody will find out, stop worrying. Besides, Jake doesn't know you. He doesn't understand how things are between us—how much I care for you. Right now, all he thinks is that you're a fling." His eyes roamed my face.

"I'm not a fling?" I asked, my heart filled with hope and surprise because I really didn't know what I was.

A frown covered his face. "No, you're not a fucking fling. Do you think I'd risk everything for a lay?"

Shaking my head, I said, "I think you could get that anywhere. Still, maybe we should cool it for a while until you're at a different school or even the end of the year." Just the thought of not seeing Evan until the end of school made my stomach twist with sadness.

His jaw dropped. "The end of the year is eight months away." That seemed like an eternity to wait for us to be together. "Forget it, just stop. There's no way in Hell I'm giving you up. We'll figure this out, somehow."

Evan

It was still dark outside. Holly slept soundly in my arms all night, not moving a muscle. I however, hardly slept. Not because she was in my arms but because of what I'd read on her phone before she'd fallen asleep.

Holly had texted her mother, telling her she was sleeping over at a friend's house tonight. It was a Friday evening, so I hoped she wouldn't put up a fuss. We'd never spent an entire night together and I'd wanted to wake up with her in my arms.

After she finished texting, Holly snuggled into me, falling asleep almost instantly. Her phone was still in her hand, so I slipped it out ready to put it on the bedside table. When I looked at the screen, it was still in text mode—locked mode hadn't clicked in yet.

I knew I shouldn't read it. However, curiosity got the better of me. What I read make me sick.

Mom: You're at some boy's house, aren't you? Slutting around as usual.

Holly: No, I'm at a friend's. It's late and she's going to drive me to work in the morning. Make sure you try and eat something, okay?

Mom: Ain't hungry. Not that you care.

Holly: Of course, I care. Just try and eat something. There's casserole in the fridge you can warm up. Night.

If that wasn't bad enough, I scrolled up to see more of their conversations. Mostly stilted, Holly checking in from work or school reminding her mom of her schedule and instructing her to eat or call the doctor or both.

From the look of it, their relationship was a complete role reversal—Holly was the parent and her mom the troublesome teen.

Of course, from our discussions, I knew that her home-life wasn't the greatest. I'd dropped her off at her trailer, so I knew they weren't exactly rolling in money. Holly never mentioned a father and I hadn't pressed the matter. Yet.

To see how her mother treated her made my throat

tighten up. Holly didn't deserve that. Refraining from throwing her phone, I shut it down and put it away.

My parents were far from perfect. We fought and had our differences. There was never a time when they resorted to name calling. I knew they wanted the best for me even though our ideas of what that was differed greatly.

What Holly's mom was doing to her was out and out mental abuse. I'd never met someone who was as focused and hardworking as Holly. She brought home money that I assumed she used for them to live off of. Nothing about her screamed extravagance—not her clothes, hair, or makeup. Not to mention her lack of a car.

The guilt I felt about the discrepancies in our upbringings was fierce. Why I had what I did, while Holly barely scraped by confounded me. It made me want to give her the world.

The only problem was—the world couldn't know about us.

She stirred a bit next to me, her body likely knowing the alarm would go off in twenty minutes. Kissing her head, she stretched as she yawned loudly. "I didn't know where I was for a second." She wiggled her sweet ass against my crotch.

Smiling into the dark, I said, "Right where you should be." I gently thrust my now raging hard on against her backside.

Pressing further against me, she said, "Mmm, that feels good."

"Lift up your leg, honey," I asked, using my hand to assist. She did what I asked without any question. Plunging a finger into her, I found her more than ready for me.

"Mmm hmm," she muttered, tilting herself back for me. Removing my finger, I replaced it with my hungry cock.

"You always feel so fucking perfect," I said into her neck

as I slowly sunk into her. Surging up, she groaned a long, low mournful sound, encouraging me to go faster. My hand slid to her breast, playing with her nipple while she sighed.

"Kiss me," I demanded, needing her mouth. She turned her head as far as she could as I met her halfway. Her mouth was warm and needy just like her tight pussy. "You like that?" I asked, continuing to fuck her from behind.

"Yes," she said against my mouth, opening hers to let me in again. Sliding my hand down her stomach, I went in search of that one spot that drove her crazy. Once I started rubbing her, I felt her walls beginning to tighten on me. She was close.

Quickening my pace, I said, "Come hard for me, Holly. I want to feel you." That was all it took for her to let go and squeeze my cock until I couldn't hold out any longer. "Ahh, I'm going to come." Gasping, my orgasm surged out of me as Holly continued squeezing me with her own release.

Sliding my hand up to her stomach, I tried to soothe her as the last of our spasms left. "Why does it get better and better?" Holly said, snuggling up closer to me.

That made me laugh. "I think I'm going to take that as compliment," I said, kissing the side of her head, now damp with perspiration.

"You definitely should. Just when I think it can't possibly get any better, you surprise me with something new." She stretched her arm out as she yawned just in time for the alarm to go off.

"Can you call in sick?" I asked, palming her breast in my hand.

"I wish I could stay here all day."

"Then stay," I said, kissing her again, wishing not for the first time that our circumstances were much different than they actually were.

17

Holly

"When did you know that you wanted to teach?" I asked Evan as we laid on the blanket, looking up at the stars. The soothing sound of the waves in the background nearly lulled me to sleep. It had been another early morning, followed by another long day, which turned into a late night.

Story of my life.

Evan had picked me up from work bearing gifts of burgers and fries. We'd eaten, made out for a while and were presently laying on our backs, observing the dark sky.

He squeezed my hand. "Honestly?" he asked, briefly turning his head to me.

"Yeah."

"My dad wanted me to go into law. I knew I definitely didn't want that but time was running out to pick. I chose education because I really wasn't sure what else to do."

"You don't like teaching?"

Raising his shoulders up and down a few times, he said, "It's okay—but nothing like I thought it would be."

Rolling over to my side, head resting on my hand, I asked, "Then what do you, Evan Marshall, want to be when you grow up?"

He chuckled for a while before he turned to me. "I'm not completely sure. Stupid, right?"

"No, not at all. You're young. I read somewhere that people switch careers many times in their life."

His hand reached out to me, sweeping my hair behind my ear. "It's stupid to go to school for that many years when you're not sure it's exactly what you want to do for the rest of your life."

Smiling at him, I asked, "What would you have done instead? Say you had a time machine and could go back and do it all over again."

He gazed at me fondly. "Exactly the same thing because that's how I found you."

"You're so cheesy sometimes." I pushed him in the shoulder so he ended up on his back again. "Seriously, close your eyes. Don't even think about it. First thing that comes to your mind."

He shut his eyes as his forehead creased. "Ummm, ummm."

"Hurry up, you can't think about it."

"Travel around Europe?" he said, opening his eyes, staring right at me.

"What would you do there? Ravish all the sexy French girls?"

"Oui, oui," he said, making me snort as I slapped him playfully on the chest. His body shook from laughing, too.

"You aren't playing along. What would you do there?"

"I'd go to England and visit the places Shakespeare lived

in and wrote about. Watch endless, horrible plays, and eat food I've never heard of."

"I've always wanted to go to England. So many of the books I've read take place there. I'd love to see what it looks like in real life." Laying back down, I grabbed his hand again.

"You should go, Holly. For real. Go before you start university and get caught up in starting a life you don't know you want or not."

"Not everyone has that choice. I have responsibilities here. There's no way I can leave." A sudden hollowness entered my heart as I briefly considered his suggestion. There's nothing more I'd love to do than travel but there's only so far you can get with a student's bus pass and a few dollars in change.

"Is your mom any better?" he asked, turning to look at me as I answered.

"Worse. And she refuses to see a doctor," I said, my voice hitching a bit as my lower lip quivered.

Putting his arm out, he said, "Come here, honey." I skootched over, laying on his chest. "I'm so sorry. You have no idea how much I wish I could make life easier for you." His mouth touched the top of my head.

"You do make it easier for me."

"I complicate the hell out of your life."

"No, you make it fun." Resting my chin on my hands, I looked at him. It could be the way the moonlight hit his eyes, but they glistened.

"Holly Anderson, I think that's the nicest thing anyone has ever said to me."

Kissing his chest, I said, "It's true. I've never been this happy in my whole life."

He rolled over top of me. "You break my heart. Do you

know that? Do you realize how much I want you to be happy? Somedays that's all I can think about."

Tears fell down the sides of my face. "You're doing a great job," I whispered, pulling his head down to mine.

❧

"YOU COULD STAY over at my place," Evan said as we got into the Jeep.

"There's nothing more I want to do right now, trust me. But I have to get home and check on my mom."

He nodded in that cute, defeated way he had about him. "You didn't finish the game."

Tilting my head to the side, I asked, "What do you mean?"

"You never said what you wanted to do after high school."

"Ohhh. Well," I said, looking out my window. "That depends on if I get any scholarships or not." University cost a lot of money. Money I didn't have.

"Pie in the sky, you have all the money in the world. What would you do?" he asked, pulling out of the parking lot.

"Umm."

He laughed out loud. "You're cheating. You're not supposed to think about it remember?"

Giggling, I closed my eyes and waited for inspiration to hit. Blank. Nothing. All I saw was darkness. My eyes began to well up all on their own as a drowning sense of hopelessness and terror overcame me.

"Hey, hey, what's going on?" he said, holding onto my hand as he pulled the Jeep over to the side of the road.

Opening my eyes, I quickly shut them again as I sobbed.

"There was nothing there," I cried, putting my hands on my face. In no time, Evan had both of our belts off, hugging me.

"It's just a stupid game. You're exhausted as usual. I shouldn't have asked, I'm sorry for upsetting you," he said, rubbing my back.

"That's the point. It's just a dumb game. I should be able to come up with something." His hand held my head to his chest.

"You can do anything you want," he mumbled into my hair.

I did a weird laugh-cry with a hiccough as my hopes plummeted. "No, I can't. Don't you see that?" I drew away from him, wiping my eyes. "There's not much that I can do." Disappointment sagged through me as the reality of my life surrounded me.

"We will figure this out. I promise you." His hands went to my shoulders. "Holly." I looked at him through my tear-filled eyes. "You have options. I've never met anyone as smart, talented, and beautiful as you. Together, you and me will figure it out."

"You and I." I corrected him.

He threw his head back, chuckling. "Did you just correct the English major?"

"Maybe."

His eyes scanned my face for a minute. "Can you trust me on this one thing?"

I sniffed. "On what? You're poor grammar?"

Again, he chuckled, making me smile. "That and figuring out what you're going to do with the rest of your life."

"Deal," I said, lying. I was young, but I also knew there wasn't much he could do to fix my sad, sorry life.

18

Holly

"Oh come on, please? It'll be so much fun. And you owe me some friend time. You haven't hung out with me for weeks," Ivy whined, begging me to come to some masquerade ball in L.A. with her.

"It's too expensive. Where would I get the money for a dress?" I stated the obvious.

Ivy looked at me softly, placing her cool hand on my arm. "It's on me, you know that," she stated, giving me a smile. "I want you to come with me. You're always so busy and I miss you." She shot me her cutest pouty face that always made me laugh.

Pondering the trip again, I sighed, realizing everything —and everyone that would stand in the way of me leaving the city. "Three days? I can't leave my mom for that long."

"Get the neighbor to check in on her. It's not like you're there twenty-four seven anyway."

"Even if I could arrange it, there's no way I can miss out on three days of pay or finding someone to fill in for me."

"Hmm," she said, tapping her finger against her lips. "I bet I can. Are you working tonight? Mr. Turner loves me. It'll take me about ten seconds to convince him how much you need this break."

"You are listening but not hearing. I can't go without the money."

"Minor detail. Give me a second," she said, pulling out her phone, texting furiously. I tried to ignore her the best I could. Taking a bite of my sandwich, I stopped myself from even entertaining the thought of going to a huge, masquerade party with Ivy and how much fun it would actually be.

I refused to think about getting dressed up in a gorgeous dress, having my hair, nails, and makeup done and dancing the night away in a huge ballroom. Sighing, I took sip out of my water container.

"Done," Ivy squealed, throwing her hands up in the air, pumping them like a fool. "Who's your best friend in the world?"

"Alex?"

She hit me playfully in the shoulder. "Me, you big dork. I texted my aunt and you can help out in the kitchen before the ball for twice what you'd be making at the diner."

My tiny heart jumped at what she said. "Twice my wage?"

"Yep, so really, it would be fiscally irresponsible for you not to go." She raised an eyebrow as she crunched down on a baby carrot.

"It's still going to be impossible to get out of work."

"Leave that to me, young grasshopper." Ivy pointed her half-eaten carrot in my direction.

"WATCH AND LEARN," Ivy said to me as she swayed over to Mr. Turner, all full of smiles and over confidence. She'd said that she didn't want me around, so I watched from afar as she worked her magic. This was the final piece of the puzzle. I'd spoken with a few of our neighbors and they agreed to take turns checking in on Mom while I was gone.

If Ivy was able to swing this then I'd be home free to have my first real vacation—aside from a few hours of paid labor in the kitchen. Pretending to look busy, I kept a steady eye on my friend as she flipped her hair, giggled, and leaned in with a hand on my boss's arm.

She was actually a really good actress when she wasn't on the stage and was able to make up her own script. My boss nodded with a sad face then Ivy hugged him. The butterflies in my stomach were making me queasy. I hadn't allowed myself to actually hope everything would fall into place until now.

"Holly," my boss called to me, waving his hand. Walking up to them, my legs felt shaky as I tried my best not to let my nerves show.

"Your good friend here said you'd like to take some much deserved time off to visit her grandmother?" he asked, his face smiling down at me.

Visit her grandmother? Good one, Ivy. "It would be nice, but I totally understand if you can't find anyone to fill in my shifts," my hands clenched into fists as I answered.

"We can figure it out. You deserve a break," he said, standing up to leave. "Write everything down for me on the scheduling forms so I don't forget."

After the door closed behind him, Ivy grabbed my shoulders, jumping up and down as she squealed, "We did it."

"You did it. I can't believe I actually get to leave the city for the first time."

"Wait until you see the hotel we're staying at," she said to me, eyes wide with excitement.

A bit confused, I asked, "Aren't we staying with your family?" Ivy's parents had been insistent that she attend the private school in Santa Lena. They didn't want her influenced by the glitz and glam of L.A.

However, the amount of time they actually spent with her in this city was negligible. I often thought Ivy missed them, but I kept my nose out of their arrangement.

"My house is too far of a drive to the ball. Besides, it's harder to sneak around if I'm at home." She raised her eyebrows. "I told my parents you'd rather stay in a hotel. We'll still have to visit them," she said sighing. "Other than that, it's shopping, manicures, and hot guys galore."

"Thank you so much," I said to her, leaning in for a hug. "I owe you."

$\approx$

"WHERE ARE YOU GOING EXACTLY?" Evan asked me as I sat between his legs on the beach, watching the moonlight on the water.

"Ivy is taking me to some masquerade ball at a huge mansion in Los Angeles." I giggled at the sheer insanity of me being in such a place. "We're getting our hair done, manicures—the works," I said, twisting my head back to him.

"I assume there'll be handsome, masked men at this ball?" He squeezed his legs around me. I loved how safe and secure I felt when he held me like this—like nothing bad in the world could touch me.

"That would be a logical assumption. Although techni-cally, nobody will really be able to tell how handsome because we'll all be wearing masks." I teased him, knowing full well nobody would interest me except him.

"I see. And what will you do when one of these men—handsome or not—asks you to dance?"

"It's a ball. You dance."

"Do you know how to dance?"

Oh crap, I hadn't thought that far ahead. Panic shot through my stomach. Everything else seemed so unlikely I forgot about what I'd actually do if I got there. "Not exactly," I said, a small cloud now covering my formerly sunny antic-ipation.

"You're in luck, Miss Anderson. You'll find I'm quite a proficient dancer." He stood, swishing sand around in the process. He held his hand out to me with a formal little bow. "May I have this dance, m'lady?"

Laughing, I reached up, placing my tiny hand in his. "Why thank you, kind sir." I loved it when he was playful and fun.

"First, I'll teach you the waltz. It's the most popular at these types of things." He stepped into me, one hand on my waist as he held the other out to the side. "Hand on my shoulder," he said, nudging my arm up with his elbow.

"Pretend we're making a box. You're the bottom and I'm the top."

"What if I want to be on top?" I said in a naughty voice, glancing up at him as I fluttered my eyelashes.

He snickered as he kissed my lips—making my belly squeeze. "If you keep talking like that you'll never learn. I'm the man, I lead. That's just how it goes. Live with it." His eyebrow raised humorously as he gave me one last quick peck.

"Whatever," I said dryly, feigning annoyance as I shook out my hair.

"In your head, you need to count, one, two, three, one, two three. Okay?"

"Got it. One, two, three."

"I step forward, you step back. Like this." He showed me, making sure to avoid stepping on my much slower foot. "Good. Now a step to the side," he said, moving me with him. "Then you get to step forward."

After a few trips and missed steps, Evan somehow managed to get us in smooth rhythm as he hummed along. "Thanks for teaching me this," I said, feeling a blush begin.

"Anything for you," he said, kissing me while keeping up the slow, methodical beat.

19

Holly

"I've never been this relaxed in my whole life," I said, as firm, magical fingers dug into my back.

Ivy peeked up from her massage bed to look at me. "I go at least once a week. With the pressures of school, I need it to function." She laid back down.

Refusing to think about how our pressures differed in my eyes, I decided instead to be grateful. "Thanks for bringing me here. I've had so much fun already." And that was true. We'd had our nails done and were now getting massages.

"We need to look our best for tonight. I hope they didn't work you too hard in the kitchen?" she asked, sounding genuinely concerned for me.

The kitchen she referred to was the catering service. All I really did was wash dishes for about three hours straight. "It was okay. I don't think I worked hard enough to earn all the money they paid me, though."

"Ugh, trust me. Whatever they paid you wasn't nearly

enough. Yuck," she said as though I'd been emptying bedpans all morning or something.

"It was pretty easy work. I almost felt in the way." So much so, that I began wondering if Ivy had invented a job for me to do. My heart squeezed a bit as I thought about what a good friend she was to me.

"Holly, they were lucky they could find someone to do that grossness. Blah," she said, making herself fake shiver. "Let's talk about something else—like how many hot guys there'll be there tonight."

~

WE SAT READING GOSSIP RAGS, laughing, and joking as best as we could without cracking our facial masks. Sitting in this plush robe was so luxurious I could stay here forever—I'd never felt anything so decadent before.

"I'm still confused about why we had to take off all our clothes to get facials," I said, sipping on the champagne we were served, the tiny bubbles tickling my nose. Nobody had thought to card us, so we accepted.

"It's for after the facials," Ivy said, finishing her glass then signaling for more.

"What's next?"

"Waxing."

~

"I'M REALLY NOT sure about this. I'm more of a trimmer than a waxer," I said hesitantly while Olga's back was turned. My heart started to beat like drum. I'd never had anything waxed let alone down there.

"What if you meet, "the one" tonight? You don't want to

be all—unkempt down there," she said, whistling, waggling her eyebrows.

Evan had never complained about the state of "down there". I wondered if he'd prefer me waxed? "That's not likely." I snorted, rolling my eyes.

"Oh, you never know. Someday you'll get that cherry popped," she said, giggling as her hands wrapped around my arm. "I'll leave you to Olga. She's a pro." With a quick pat on the shoulder, she turned and left.

∾

"OHHH, this would look perfect under your dress," Ivy said, handing me a white bustier with pink roses sewn on it. It was breathtaking. I wondered how it would feel to wear something so lush.

Reality brought me back to Earth. There was no way I could afford it. Still, curiosity knocked and I flipped the price tag over, frowning. "I have a bra I can wear."

"You need to have something like this under your dress so you don't fall out, my dear. Trust me. I'll buy it for you." She stuffed it in my hands. "Look at the sexy matching undies," she squealed, waving them in my face.

Butterflies took up residence inside my stomach as I thought about owning such beautiful, expensive things. Pride took over. "It's okay, you've been too generous already. I can't ask you to buy this for me." My shoulders drooped when I attempted to put the items back.

"No way," Ivy said, halting my efforts. "You can't wear a regular bra under our gowns. It'll look awful. Trust me." Her eyes looked me over for a second before she whispered discreetly, "Stop worrying about how much everything costs, okay?" The sincerity in her eyes and voice made my eyes start to water. "My dad makes gobs of money, you know that. I wanted you to come—you're my guest—I pay."

I squeezed my eyes shut as I gave her a quick hug. My throat felt dry as I sniffed. "You're too nice."

Ivy hugged me back, then took a few steps to the side. "What do you think about this on me," she said, picking up a black lace bustier, holding it close to her body.

"That is hot," I said, feeling the intricate lace between my fingers. I didn't dare flip that tag over.

Posing in front of the mirrors, she said, "Not for tonight. For Mr. Marshall."

My stomach sunk as all the breath in my lungs fled. "What do you mean?"

"When I finally land him." She shimmied a bit, wiggling her hips in a seductive dance as she stared at herself in the mirror. "It's just a matter of time before he gives in," she said, tossing her curls around then suddenly doubling over, grabbing her belly. "Ouch," she said, her face contorting in discomfort.

"Are you okay?" I asked, holding onto her arms, scared she might fall.

Taking a few deep breaths, she shot back up. "I'm fine. Just a quick pain. Let's go try these on."

∾

Looking at myself in the mirror, I barely recognized the person staring back. I didn't even have my mask on yet. My fingers traced down my fitted bodice, feeling the intricately beaded appliques. The butterflies in my stomach had called their friends and were now having some kind of rave.

"Whoa, you clean up nicely, Anderson." Ivy walked out

of the bathroom in her bustier that needed to be commended for holding everything up. Without straps.

"How is that even staying up?" I asked, jaw dropping, sincerely amazed at the wonder before me.

Ivy laughed, giving me her signature shimmy. She stopped after a few shakes, holding her stomach again. "Are you all right?" I asked, rushing over to her, worried something was really wrong.

"Fine. Just a cramp or something. Help me get into my dress, will you?"

Fifteen minutes later, dressed, primped, waxed, exfoliated and entirely too excited for words, we left for the ball.

I'd never worn such a dress before. It was interesting navigating down the stairs and into the limo that Ivy ordered. When we were seated, she asked, "Champagne?" Holding up a green bottle?

"I'm a little lightheaded from the two glasses I had at the salon," I said, speaking the truth. Unlike Ivy, I had made a point of eating so I wouldn't feel sick.

"Come on, live a little. We're in L.A. now. Nobody here knows you," she said, passing me a half full flute. "To us finding hot, rich, trust fund babies tonight." She toasted, cracking me up me as we clinked our delicate glasses.

20

Holly

Afteer driving down the longest driveway in history, we finally arrived at the biggest house I'd ever seen. My imagination couldn't even fathom what kind of people lived here.

"Nice, right? It's Senator Stanton's house." Ivy fiddled with something in her purse. I was going to be inside of a senator's house? This was crazy. "Here, I almost forgot." Handing me a fancy mask with glitter, feathers, and ribbon that matched my dress. "Turn and I'll tie it for you."

Masks secured, she informed the driver we were ready. He got out, opening our door for us and helping us as we got out. The brightly lit water fountain held my attention as I waited to follow Ivy into the house.

Two doormen opened the oversized wooden doors for us. "Thank you," we both said to them as they nodded.

"Do people seriously live here? It looks more like a museum." Looking around, I was in complete and utter awe at the magnificence of the place. "Or a palace," I said, whispering to Ivy as I admired the huge chandelier hanging above us.

"Shhh, stop freaking out. Pretend like you've been here a thousand times," she said, turning her head to the side while she spoke.

"Margaret, is that you?" she said, spotting someone in the distance while I lagged behind. Ivy was clearly in her element—me, not so much. Wandering around the entryway, I paused to look at the artwork on the walls.

Pedestals held vases of elaborate floral displays that probably cost more than I made in an entire year. People walked up and down the wide, flowing staircase. Women in ballgowns of all design—men in tuxes.

Music echoed from the second level. When I finally caught Ivy's eye, I motioned that I was going upstairs. She nodded and waved. Holding my skirt so I didn't trip and fall, I took one step at a time feeling like a movie star or royalty as I went.

Entering what must be the ballroom, I stood there, stunned. An orchestra played at the front while people danced—waltzed—in the middle. The sides and back held tables and chairs where attendees sat, laughed, and drank.

Talk about a fish out of water. The song ended followed by the dancers on the floor clapping. Everything was so formal, like something out of a movie or a book.

Staying close to the wall, I headed toward the punch bowl. "Thirsty?" a gentleman asked beside me.

A bit shocked that someone spoke to me, I stopped and turned to him. "Not really, just trying to look busy," I said, giving him a brief smile. He had on a dark red and black mask and his hair was a well-combed sandy blond.

"I can do my best to keep you busy. Would you like to dance?" he asked, holding out his hand.

He seemed nice enough, so I agreed. We walked slowly, side by side to the dance floor. I mentally prayed that I didn't look as awkward as I felt. "Oooff," I said, the third time our bodies bumped into each other. "I'm sorry, I'm not a very good dancer." Apologizing for my ineptitude. Why was dancing so difficult with this man yet so easy with Evan?

"Completely my fault," he said, a kind smile on his face. I knew better, though. This was all me.

We started again, this time he stepped on my feet. "Ouch," I said, backing up hoping to end this disaster.

"May I?" A dark haired man appeared in front of me, asking my dance partner for permission to take his place. Boy, was he brave.

"Be my guest." My former partner slapped him on the arm, wishing him luck. He'd need it.

"Look, I'm not very good at this, I think I'll just sit this one out," I said as my new partner turned to me.

"M'lady," he said, bowing at the waist with his hand out.

I knew that voice. And that hair. "Evan?" I asked, touching my throat as I inhaled deeply, not believing that he of all people would be here.

He stepped into me, taking me hand with his. Pulling me closer, sliding his hand to my waist, we began to dance. "One, two, three, can you hear it?" he hummed into my ear, causing goose bumps to form.

Amazingly enough, I danced well with him. "Why are you here?"

"Because you're here," he said, leaning down to kiss my bare shoulder. Desire flickered to life as the heat from his lips traveled through my body.

"But how did you get in?" I asked, bewildered at how he managed to get an invite to a senator's ball.

He chuckled into my neck. "I know people who know

people. Are you not happy to see me? Shall I call that young man back here to finish your dance?"

Pushing back, I smiled at him. "He was more than eager to let you take over."

"The third time he stepped on your feet I knew I had to intervene."

Shaking my head, I said, "I don't understand why I can dance just fine with you but when I tried with him it was a huge fail."

"It's because I know your body, inside and out." His low, husky voice reminding me of how he spoke when he was deep inside me. "I know the sway of your hips—how you move underneath me when I'm making love to you. How you follow my lead—everywhere."

Looking up into his eyes, I slid my hand behind his neck, pulling him down to me for a kiss. He brought us to a halt, our bodies close, the fresh, manly scent of him surrounding me. "You look beautiful tonight, Holly. Simply irresistible, as always." One more kiss, then he smiled and said, "Follow me."

Not that I had a choice. My hand was in his firm grip as he tugged me to a set of ornate doors. Walking through, they led to a balcony where a few people stood chatting. He pulled me behind him until we arrived at a set of stairs.

One hand holding the railing, he kept possession of my other one. "Where are we going?"

"Shh," was all he said until we were at the bottom. "Over here." He led me to a tall gazebo, covered in mini fairy lights. Flowers sat in pots all around the perimeter.

"Are you sure it's okay for us to be here?" I asked, scared that a security guard was going to pop up and catch us.

Again, he chuckled. "It'll be fine, trust me." Spinning me

into the middle of the floor, he started dancing a slow waltz with me in his arms.

I laughed at his smooth moves. "I'm so happy you're here," I told him, running my hand over the back of his neck.

"Ready?" he asked.

I knew exactly what he was talking about. He spun me out then I circled back to him, his arms around me, my back to his front.

Turning my head, I giggled as he stole another kiss. His arms dropped mine, turning me around. We kissed for a moment before he said, "Follow me." He shot me a roguish grin before sweeping me off to who knows where.

21

Evan

Holly was always beautiful to me. But tonight, seeing her in that gown, dancing with her in the gazebo—she was stunning. Her golden hair fell in curls down the back of her pale, pink satin dress. If I hadn't known better, I'd think she was born to this life.

"Where are you taking me now?" she whispered, her chest rising and falling rapidly as we entered the staff doors.

"Just trust me," I whispered into her ear, lightly grazing the sensitive part of her ear with my lips.

Telltale goose bumps rose on her delicate skin as she shivered. "You always say that. Why can't you just tell me?"

"It'll ruin the surprise." I smirked then turned around, pulling her with me. What a surprise I had planned. My cock swelled just thinking about it. One more corner and we'd be—

"Why hello, Mr. Evan. I didn't expect you to be here," one of the maids said, shocking the shit out of me. My heart started beating faster.

"Laurette, nice to see you again. We're just passing through," I said, trying to dismiss us as quickly as possible before anyone else saw.

"What do you—"

"We'll talk later, we're in a rush." I gave her a fast wink before proceeding on at a quickened pace.

Zooming passed Laurette, Holly said, "We're in a rush?"

"Shh."

"These shoes weren't exactly made for stairs." She huffed, grappling at her long skirts as to avoid tripping. "How many more flights?" Holly said, likely feeling the burn of doing three flights of stairs in extremely high heels.

Relief ran through me as the door we needed finally appeared on the left-hand side. "Hold on, let me look first." I took a deep breath before carefully poking my head out, checking for anyone in the hallway, praying it would be empty. "All clear. Run if you can," I told her, taking off down the hall until we came to a familiar room. "Inside," I clipped nervously, shoving her in then closing the door behind us.

Leaning against the shut door, I let out a long, relieved sigh as I let my eyelids close for a moment.

"I don't think we're supposed to be here." Holly turned to me, frowning, her face filled with apprehension.

"It's okay, I know the guy who it belongs to." I smiled down at her.

She turned, walking further into the room. "It's someone's bedroom, Evan."

"Look at the pictures on the wall and the dresser," I said smirking, my back still against the door.

Unsure, she slowly wandered from picture to picture, gently grazing her fingertips on some before recognition finally hit. "This is you?" Confusion written all over her face as her eyes narrowed on me.

Locking the door behind me, I pushed away, nodding.

"I don't understand," she said, a framed photo of me in her hand. "This is Senator Stanton's house. Are you—"

"His son." Taking the picture from her, I set it back down on the dresser as I rolled my shoulders trying to rid the tension.

"But your last name is Marshall?" She looked up at me, perplexed.

Sweeping her hair behind her shoulder, I said, "It's my mother's maiden name. Stanton is too recognizable. If I use it then people treat me differently." My stomach knotting, hoping like hell she'd understand.

Turning away from me, she walked to the bed, sitting down. "I feel like you lied to me," she whispered in a breathy voice, her eyes wet.

I ripped off my mask, feeling an uncomfortable tightening in my chest. "I'm sorry. I couldn't tell you until I was certain you wouldn't say anything. The only person at school who knows is Principal McGreggor and I'd like to keep it that way." Sitting down beside her, I grabbed her hand.

She pulled it away. My heart sunk as my stomach churned with worry and disappointment. "You should have told me. Ugh," she said, putting her hands over her face. "You saw the trailer I live in and you grew up here? In a palace?" Her voice laced with pain—and perhaps embarrassment? Jesus, that was the last thing I wanted her to feel.

Laughing in a low voice, I said, "It's not a palace. Would you look at me, please?" I begged, reaching for her hands again, my heart hurt to see her act like this. "I can't help where I grew up any more than you can. And you know I don't think less of you for living in a trailer, right?"

"Why don't you?" Her eyes questioned me.

"Do you think less of me for having lived here?" I asked, scanning her face for the truth, worried she'd already changed her opinion of me.

"No, but it freaks me out a little. A lot, actually."

"It freaks everyone out, that's why I try to hide my family when I can."

"Same."

Unable to stop the chuckle that burst out, I rubbed her hands. "I don't mean to laugh, but you kill me sometimes." Gazing into her eyes, I asked, "I'm sorry I kept this from you. Can you forgive me?"

She didn't take any time at all to answer. "Are those trophies all yours?"

Squinting my eyes, I answered, "Yes, why?"

"Your parents didn't buy them for you?"

I threw my head back, laughing. "I'm very athletic and was rewarded accordingly. Now that you know my trophies are the real deal, can I kiss you?"

"Mmm hmm," she said, finally giving me a smile. I removed her mask then leaned down, taking her mouth gently, letting her know how sorry I was to keep a secret like this from her. As I began lowering her down on my bed, she protested. "No, my hair will get all messed up," she said, pushing me away.

Standing up with a groan, I took her hands, lifting her to her feet. Reaching behind her, I felt for her zipper, yanking it down slowly. Her eyes widened and her jaw dropped but she didn't say a word.

As her dress fell to the floor, my heart stopped beating. "You are stunning, my dear," I said, blood rushing to my cock in record time. The bustier she wore combined with matching panties drained my lungs of air. Helping her step out of the dress so she didn't trip, I held her to me. "I need you, Holly. So much." My kiss was not gentle this time. I crushed my lips to hers, feeling my erection hard against her stomach. Her hands wandered down to my button, carefully undoing it then the zipper. Easing her hand inside my underwear, the touch of her cool hand on my cock drove me wild.

"Turn around. Hands on the dresser," I ordered, my cock twitching and ready.

Doing exactly what I said, I kissed her shoulder, inhaling her flowery perfume before I began unhooking her bustier. Finally, at the last hook, I opened up my prize—a naked, gorgeous, Holly. Tossing the lingerie to the side I eagerly sidled up closer behind her as I got rid of my jacket.

My hands caressed her back then traveled around to her breasts, palming them as she closed her eyes. Squeezing her nipples between my fingers, she moaned. "Spread your legs," I growled, tapping my shoe beside hers. She opened for me. "More, honey. And bend over, like this." Moving my hand to her upper back, I pushed gently.

"Yes, that's good," I said, watching as desire transformed her beautiful face in the mirror as I moved her thong to the side and got my cock ready at her opening. Driving inside her, filling her, I inhaled sharply. "You are absolutely exquisite," I said, thrusting myself back and forth. Her tongue darted out, licking her lips as I went deeper.

Watching her breasts move in the mirror as I fucked her from behind nearly sent me to the brink. She needed to come first—she deserved to come first. My hand crept to her pussy. I gasped, feeling the soft skin.

"You're fuckin' bare, baby. I love it," I grunted, getting even harder the more I played with her. Touching her where I knew she liked it best, I felt her get even wetter. I could feel my orgasm coiling up in my balls, ready to shoot into her. "Open your eyes. I want to watch you come."

With those words her back arched even more as her eyelids opened. Staring into her eyes, I couldn't hold back any longer. "Ahh," I moaned with one last thrust. Seating myself to the hilt, my cock jerking a few more times as she, too, found her own release. I leaned over her, gasping for air as I placed my mouth against her neck for a gentle kiss before I reluctantly pulled out.

"I can't keep my hands off you," I said, turning her around, pulling her into my arms. God, she felt good as she let out a satisfied sigh, warming my heart to have her this close.

Her fingers dug into my shoulders. "Ditto." Kissing my chest, she clung onto me as we held each other in our afterglow.

"We should go back to the party before Ivy starts looking for you."

"I completely forgot about her," she said, leaning away from me, jaw slack. "I should check my phone." I couldn't help but watch the show in front of me—Holly in high heels and a pair of the sexiest panties I'd ever seen. Bending over to retrieve her phone out of her purse, she said, "Oh no, no, no, no, no."

22

Evan

Doing up my pants, I prowled up to her to see what was so upsetting. Snatching the phone from her hand, I read the texts.

Ivy: Where are you?

Ivy: Holly? Where did you go?

Ivy: I'm going to the hospital. The pain in my stomach is worse. Text me when you get this.

"She's sick?" I asked, unclear of what Ivy was talking about. From the look on Holly's face it seemed like she already had an idea of what was wrong.

Furiously typing into her phone, she spoke to me, "Her stomach was hurting her today, but she insisted she was fine. I bet something bad happened and I wasn't there to help. I'm such a horrible friend." Her voice hitched a bit at the end.

Rubbing her shoulders, I said, "You couldn't have known something was going to happen. This isn't your fault."

"I should have been there for her," she said, beginning to cry. "She says they are doing tests on her now."

Hugging her into my body, her back to my chest. "How is she feeling now?" I asked, snapping up her hand.

"Better, I guess. They gave her some painkillers and she's telling me about all the hot doctors." She giggled as she sniffed.

Putting my arm around her, I said, "That's a good sign." Kissing her cheek, she gazed over at me.

"I hope so."

"What do you want to do? Go back to your hotel or—go back to the party?" My thumb circled the top of her hand.

A sad look of indecision crossed her face. "I don't know what to do."

Pulling her in for a hug, I said, "It's okay, take your time. Why don't you ask Ivy what she thinks?"

Releasing me, she said, "That's a great idea." Texting madly on her phone again, she began to laugh herself silly.

"What?"

Unable to speak, she handed the phone to me.

Holly: What should I do? I can pack up and take the bus home.

Ivy: If you do that, I will personally come down there in my hospital gown and slap you! Enjoy yourself and pick up a hot male specimen. Tonight might be THE NIGHT.

Holly: I don't feel right about partying while you're in the hospital. I should go.

Ivy: DON'T YOU DARE LEAVE. After all the work we did to make this weekend special? You better enjoy it. Maybe I'll bust out of here tomorrow. Stay as long as you want at the party and I'll text you the limo driver's number. I paid him for the entire weekend so take the car wherever you want to go.

Holly: Are you sure?

Ivy: YES. Now stop bugging me. I just turned my hospital gown around "by mistake" so when the hot doc comes back in to check my heart, he'll get a nice surprise.

I passed the phone back to her. "She's very—"

"Aggressive?"

"Sure." I gazed down as Holly smiled at me. It was nice to see her a little less worried.

"So, Miss Anderson? The world is your oyster this evening. What's the verdict?"

"Stop in at the hospital for a bit? At least until Ivy's parents get there?" she said, uncertain of my reaction.

"Your wish is my command."

Holly

Stretching, I felt a strong, warm arm pull me closer. "Morning," Evan said, his voice a combination of sexy-sleepy deliciousness. My nipples immediately beaded up just hearing his voice.

His hardness up tight against my behind was a bit of a catalyst as well.

Turning in his arms, I said, "Morning." He smiled down at me, taking my lips for a quick kiss.

"You sleep?"

Nodding, I said, "Yeah, but not much. I was texting with Ivy until two or three." I yawned loudly. By the time Evan dropped me off at the hospital the doctors were already discussing sending Ivy home. She was not pleased to see me and gave me heck for leaving the ball.

I definitely got some looks stumbling into E.R., rolling

two huge suitcases behind me as I struggled with my long skirts.

Ivy had asked me to pack up her stuff and send it with the limo driver to the hospital. Instead, Evan drove me and her luggage then waited in the parking lot. Her mom had a fit with her on the phone, insisting Ivy had to go back home with them if/when she was released.

In the end, I was only there about an hour before her parents showed up and they all shooed me out. Relieved that my friend was going to be okay, Evan drove us back to the hotel.

"That's good. Is she home yet?"

"They released her but couldn't tell what the problem was. One doctor said maybe she had a cyst that broke or something. She was feeling no pain, though." I laughed, remembering some of the things Ivy had texted.

"I'm glad she's better. What do you want to do today?" he asked suggestively, tracing his finger along my cleavage.

"Whatever you want."

"Whatever I want?" he asked, his eyebrow raising as he smirked, causing my belly to do a delicious flip.

"Sure."

"Well, first," he said, kissing my neck as he rolled me over to my back, "there are a few things I'd like to do right here."

"Really?" I gasped as his hands roamed.

"Mmm hmm. And then I want to show you my favorite place in the world—other than this bed."

~

"THIS IS ALL YOURS?" I asked, looking out the windows of the Jeep, amazed at what I was seeing.

The smile that covered his face was contagious. "It's been in the family for generations." The massive ranch-style home was impressive. Even more amazing was the astounding grounds surrounding it.

"Is anyone else here?"

Shutting off the Jeep, he turned to me. "My parents are both back at the house in the city this week. They always stay there whenever they hold a big bash."

He'd pointed out his parents to me last night at the ball. There was a constant circle of partygoers surrounding them at any given time. Even still, Evan kept us far away from them, not wanting to catch their eyes. Which really wasn't difficult to do with the massive space and hundreds of people attending.

"Only the outdoor grounds staff. They'll be more than kind. It takes a lot of hands to run this kind of operation." Reaching over to click open my seat belt, he kissed me on the lips. "Let's go have some fun."

With a bit of hesitation, I opened my door, stepping out onto the brick driveway where he'd parked. Ahead of us was a sprawling bungalow that seemed to go on forever.

Evan sauntered around the Jeep then grabbed my hand. As we walked, I noticed an almost imperceptible shift in his mood. He seemed lighter—happier, like he was a kid walking into a toy store. We arrived at row upon row of grape vines as far as the eye could see.

"This is incredible," I said, reaching out to touch the rough vines. "There are so many, everywhere."

"Harvest is almost done for the year. It's an exciting time here," he said, tapping his finger to the fruit.

"How can you tell when the grapes are ready to be picked?"

He pulled a grape from a full bunch hanging down in front of us. "Open up," he asked.

Doing as he asked, Evan slowly popped it into my mouth. Biting down on it, the sweet, crisp flavor filled my mouth. "Mmm," I said, chewing. "So good."

"That's one way to know if they're ready." He grinned, wiping a drip from the side of my mouth. "We also have what's called a Brix that measures the amount of sugar in a grape."

"How much sugar does it need to have?"

Holding my hand, he led us further down the path. "It depends on what kind of wine we're using the grape for."

He continued to walk us down the row, telling me all the intricacies of growing successful vines. One thing bothered me but I didn't want to ask in case it came across as rude. Stopping us, he reached for my hand. "You okay? You're quiet." His finger lifted my chin as he scanned my face.

I smiled up at him, backing away as I kicked at the rocky soil. "This dirt is—"

"Complete crap?" he answered, booting a large stone down the pathway.

Raising my eyebrows, I answered back, "How can these vines survive?"

"They don't just survive—they prosper," he said, halt-ingly. Gazing down at me, he added, "The poor vitamins and nutrients in the soil cause the roots to shoot further down until they find what they need. Year after year the plants struggle against their surroundings to survive. Only the toughest make it through and what's left brings us the best quality, sweetest fruit possible."

"Too bad they have to fight so hard."

"You don't get it, do you?" he said in a near whisper. "It's the battle that makes them the best of the best, producing some of the highest quality stock in the world."

"I bet the plants feel differently."

Evan gave me a sweet smile then leaned down brushing a gentle kiss across my cheek. "I don't doubt that one bit. Their struggle is rewarded, though. Don't ever forget that. Sometimes a plant appears helpless and just when you think all is lost—boom—it starts growing like crazy because it's finally found what it's been searching for."

We both knew what he was alluding to. My eyes filled with unshed tears as I hugged him tight. "So, it's all worth it in the end?"

"I guarantee it," he said solemnly into my hair as he stroked my back.

Evan

"THIS HAS BEEN the best weekend of my life," Holly said to me, sipping her third, small glass of wine. I'd pulled out a few of my favorites for her to try.

"I would have to agree with you on that." My hand covered hers on the table. "I only hope I didn't bore you with my lengthy tour of the grounds and buildings." If there was one thing I could go on and on about besides literature, it was this vineyard.

Holly shook her head as she chewed one last forkful of salad. "It was fun. Seriously," she said, intertwining our fingers. "I had a great time."

Sitting out here on the terrace, eating supper that we'd cooked together, it was easy to forget what was waiting for us back home. Too easy. Being here with Holly felt so —right.

Not having to hide from anyone's prying eyes set us both at ease.

After swallowing a mouthful of Montoya Cabernet, she said, "Thanks for bringing me out here."

"It was my pleasure. Which of the three wines do you like the best?" I asked, curious what her answer would be.

"This one," she said, holding up her glass.

Smiling, I asked, "Can you tell what the subtle taste is?"

"I've been trying to figure it out," she responded, sitting back in her chair, looking a bit perplexed. "Take a guess."

Swishing the deep, red liquid around in her mouth, she pondered my question. A few moments later she said, "Plum?"

A huge grin erupted on my face. "Exactly. Well done."

We sat for another hour, watching the sun go down on the rows and rows of vines, chatting, enjoying our quiet time together. Eventually, we had to get up to clean the kitchen. Since my parents weren't here, neither were any inside house staff. Clean up was up to us.

I'd just finished putting the last plate in the cupboard when we heard the front door swing open. Holly's questioning eyes shot right to mine.

The entire open concept kitchen/living room was in full sight of the front door. It wasn't difficult to see who it was.

"Oh, Carl, stop." A woman's voice echoed from the entryway.

My dad's voice soon followed. "I'll go get your other ten suitcases after."

"After?" the woman questioned in a suggestive manner as they moved further into the entryway. My guts twisted, bile rising up once I realized who it was. My father was a real piece of work.

"Evan?" Dad called from across the wide expanse, his

voice loud and powerful. He stood stock still as though he were shocked to see me.

Clearing my throat, I answered back, "Hi."

He dropped the luggage in his hands, marching over to me. "What are you doing here?" he asked, coming to a stop in front of us, looking over Holly with his speculative eye. She actually took a step backward as though my father's gaze physically moved her.

Throwing the dishtowel down, I replied, "I was about to ask you the same thing." Hands on my hips, I stared him down. We both knew what and who he was doing here.

A crooked smile crossed his face as he ran a hand through his hair. "Samantha and I have planning to do. You know how crazy that house gets after your mother puts on a party. I couldn't hear myself think so we came out here instead." My stomach churned at his explanation. "Election year is nearly upon us. We need to discuss campaign strategies."

"I don't think we've met," he said, turning to Holly with his hand stuck out. "Carl Stanton, and you are?" his voice laced with condescension.

Holly's hesitation made me want to clock my dad in the head. "Holly Anderson."

"Nice to meet you, Holly." How he managed to say it in a way that made even me feel bad for Holly I'd never understand. I knew why he did it—Dad always had to be the biggest dog in the room and let everyone else know it.

"You didn't mention coming out here, Son," he said, glaring at me just as Samantha strutted up, swaying her ample hips.

"How nice to see you again, Evan. I didn't catch you at the party last night," she said, fluttering her eyelashes at me.

Giving her a fake smile, leaning my hip against the stove, I said, "The masks made socializing more challenging."

"True." She giggled back in her annoying tone.

Dad stepped forward a bit, almost in challenge. "You didn't say what you were doing here, Son," he asked as he crossed his arms.

Turning around to put a glass in the cupboard, I answered as nonchalantly as I could, "Just came out here to show the place to Holly. We'll be out of your way momentarily." Shutting the cupboard door, I snatched up Holly's hand, hoping to remove us from this situation without a confrontation.

Holly picked up her purse. Another thirty seconds and we'd be home free. "Evan, a moment of your time, please," Dad called from behind us. Damn.

Closing my eyes, I exhaled. "I'll be out in a minute," I said to Holly, nodding toward the still open door.

She looked at me with a worried expression on her face, nodding slightly.

Holly was barely out the door, and Dad started in on me. "You know how your mother worries about me working too hard," he said, slapping me on the back like we were old friends. "No need to upset her by mentioning I'm here to work with Sam. I told her I came up to relax and check on things."

It took everything in me not to hit him. "I won't say a word." Swinging my head towards him, I said, "Wouldn't want Mom to worry about you overextending yourself."

"With that out of the way," he said, patting me on the back again. "I picked up a few things for you. Meant to give them to you at breakfast but you were already gone." My eyes followed him while he walked to one of the bags. Shuffling through a pocket, he pulled out some papers. "I have more information on law school for you. I spoke with the dean and—"

"Dad, I don't want to go to law school." I raised both my palms toward him, taking a step back. Same old fucking fight. Anger spiraled through me.

Completely ignoring me, he continued on, shoving the stack of papers at me. "I got them to include forms for a business degree as well. It turns out you'll actually be able to transfer a lot of your classes—"

Hands on my hips, I barked back, "I don't want to go back to school."

His famous dead calm persona emerged. Dad was known in the media as The Piranha for the way he devoured his opponents during a debate. "You don't want to go back to school?" he said, eyes narrowing on me, preparing for attack.

Holding his gaze, unflinching, I said, "You know that." I ground my teeth so hard my jaw ached.

"How exactly do you propose to get into office if you don't get a real degree. Hmm?" He leaned in further. "Do you know how fucking embarrassing it is to tell people what you do?" he spat out the words in frustration. His face looked as though he'd tasted something bitter. "A son of mine—teaching?" he said as though it was one of the lowliest jobs around.

"There's nothing wrong with teaching for a living." Clenching my fists at my sides, I tried to keep myself under control. What made it worse was that I really didn't enjoy teaching, so my dad was partly correct. I didn't know what I wanted to do but law school was a definite no.

"No, Son, there's nothing right about it. It's a dead end. Where do you think you're going to end up in five or ten years?" He threw his hand with the forms up in the air. "You need to get your ass back to college." He leveled a glowering look at me. "And earn a useful diploma in something other than glorified babysitting." His words hit me like punch to the gut. He had no clue about the work involved in teaching teenagers.

I could feel the blood pulsing through my brain, ready to explode. "Have fun with your planning," I said, raising an eyebrow as I shot out the last word and stormed out.

23

Holly

"Get Nan in here to help. I need some pain pills, my back is killin'. Grab my smokes, too, will ya?"

Fear gripped my stomach so tight it was difficult to breathe. "Mom, Nanny passed away years ago. You know that." Holding my mom's hand, I squeezed it, hoping her mind would return.

"Don't talk such nonsense. She's in the kitchen. Now get her in here like I said," she attempted to yell but instead it came out as a wheeze. A knock on the door startled me.

"I'll be right back," I said, letting go of her cold hand.

Closing the bedroom door behind me, I hurried to the front door, the insistent noise echoing through the room. Turning the knob and shoving the door open with my hip, I saw Ivy standing on my steps. "I didn't know you were coming over? Were we supposed to go somewhere?" I asked her in confusion.

"We need to talk," she hissed, barging in, newspaper in

her hand. Now even more baffled at my friend's behavior, I shut the door then followed her.

Spinning around on her heel, her eyes flashed with such anger I was taken aback. What was Ivy so ticked off about?

Holding the paper to her chest, she said, "Anything you need to tell me?" Staring down at the black and white print, it said, "Senator's Son Smitten." I drew in a stuttered gasp as my stomach threatened to revolt. Below the bold words was a picture of Evan smiling down at me as we danced at the masquerade ball. My heart sunk as my brain raced for a reasonable explanation.

Ivy tossed the paper at me, displaying another. "Hearts Break across Cali as Vineyard Heir Finds Perfect Vintage." That had a photo of Evan kissing me in the gazebo at the ball. A heavy weight pressed on my chest, robbing me of breath.

Forgetting how to inhale and exhale, I somehow managed to squeak out a flustered, "I can explain." A cold shiver ran down my spine knowing there was no possible way to get out of this now.

The look on Ivy's face changed from angry to furious, her gaze slicing through me. "You knew I liked him, and you went after him anyway." I stood there, dumbfounded, unable to move. "After all I've done for you. I thought we were friends?"

"We are friends," I stammered, gazing downward, stunned into near silence for what this might mean not only for me but also for Evan's career. My heart clenched at the thought of him getting in trouble because of me.

"Really?" she shouted, stepping closer to me. "In my world, friends don't fuck their friend's boyfriends." Fear twisted in my gut as I registered exactly how angry she was.

"He's not your boyfriend, Ivy. It all just sort of happened.

We didn't mean—" I said, wringing my hands together, feeling trapped inside this aluminum cage.

"You didn't mean to sleep with the guy I was gunning for? I made it more than clear. You must've had a good laugh over me after you bagged him instead. Honestly, I never thought you had it in you to burn me like this."

"Ivy, I said—"

"It's a shame that Mr. Marshall's career is going to be over before it even starts," she snarled, an evil expression on her face.

My knees buckled as all the remaining air left my lungs. "You can't report him. Please, Ivy, you can't do that," I begged, placing my hand on the kitchen table to lean on it before I toppled over.

"I certainly can." Ivy positioned her hands on her hips, her foot jutting out.

Sitting down in the chair, I said, "No, please, this isn't his fault."

"You're trash, Holly. Everyone knows it. The only reason I was friends with you was because I felt sorry for you. Living in a dirty trailer park with a drunk for a mother."

If she'd physically punched me in the stomach, I couldn't have felt more pain. Tears flooded my eyes at her hurtful words. "Think what you want of me but don't take it out on Evan. You'll ruin his life. And his father's."

"Oh, I'm sure Senator Stanton would love to hear how his son has been slumming it."

Wiping my eyes, I continued to beg. "Please, there must be something I can do to make you change your mind."

"Stop seeing him."

I felt sick. The thought of ending things with Evan made me ill. My stomach churned at the thought of not having him in my life anymore. He was the only good thing I had. "Ivy, I—"

"It's simple. Dump him or I'll go straight to Principal McGreggor."

My voice caught in my throat. There was only one thing to do.

Evan

MARKING the English papers took twice as long as they should have with my mind continually wandering to the perfect weekend I'd had with Holly. Even my father's unexpected interruption didn't damper it.

Being away from the hustle and bustle of the city and spending two full days alone with Holly was incredible. No matter how hard I tried, I couldn't wipe the smile off my face.

Ding dong, ding dong, my doorbell went off. Some jerk kept pressing the button. "I'm coming, I'm coming," I yelled, shoving away from my desk.

Opening the door, I saw my very angry father there. "Move," he snapped, pushing past me forcefully. I stepped back to let him in.

"Where's the fire?" I asked sarcastically, not understanding what exactly could be the matter this late on a Monday evening.

"Where's the fire? On the front fucking page, that's where, you idiot," he shouted, marching into the living room.

Slamming the door, I said, "Excuse me?" Confused at what he could possibly be talking about, I followed him.

"Here, lover boy," he said, thwacking a newspaper into my stomach.

Bewildered, I peered at the front page. Holy shit. Me and Holly kissing in the gazebo at the masquerade ball splashed over the entirety of the front page. "So what? I kissed a girl at the ball. Who cares?"

"My constituents, that's who. And they will really care once they find out she's your damn student. How could you be so dumb?" he said, throwing his arms out, beginning to pace. "All these years I've spent building up my career, making the right friends, gathering support and you're going to throw it all out the window for a piece of trailer trash."

"Who told you she was my student?" I asked, my mind racing as I frowned.

"It doesn't matter. What matters is the field day the press is going to have when they find out you're sleeping with a minor."

"She's eighteen, Dad."

Veering straight for me, he stopped dead, nearly toe to toe. "That makes it better? I can't believe you did this to me. After everything I've worked so hard to get."

"She's wearing a mask and it's not even a very clear picture. Nobody's going to find out." Looking again at the grainy photo, it would be near impossible to tell.

"Somebody will find out, Evan. End this. Now."

～

SITTING ON MY DECK, feet on the railing, I stared out into my backyard. I didn't know what I was going to do. That's not true. The one thing I did know was that I wasn't about to end things with Holly. That was for certain.

We had a connection I'd never come close to feeling with anyone else. No way was I going to throw what we had away. Not even for my overbearing father.

I looked down after my phone rang. "Hey, beautiful. How was your night off?" I asked, knowing that Holly had a rare evening off. She felt guilty for being gone so she'd opted to spend time with her mom and her schoolbooks.

Instead of an answer, all I heard was crying. Standing up, I said, "Are you hurt?" Ready to go save Holly from whatever happened.

"Ivy saw the papers." She sniffed.

Sighing, I ran my hands through my hair. "She won't rat us out, will she?" After Dad left, I realized we could add Ivy to the small list of people who would now know about us. Ivy gave Holly the dress and mask to wear to the party. Of course, she would recognize her. I held out hope that she wouldn't see the pictures. It was naive of me to think a girl like Ivy wouldn't comb the society pages.

"Evan—she's had a crush on you ever since you came to the school. She's so angry."

Falling back into my chair, I rubbed the bridge of my nose. "Yeah, that was abundantly clear from day one."

"She said if I don't stop seeing you, she's going to the principal." Holly's crying got louder, breaking my heart even more.

"Let me speak to her. I bet I can change her mind."

"You don't get it. There's no changing her mind once she's made it. Ivy will get you dismissed and—" Her voice wobbled. "Who knows what she'll do to your father's career. We can't risk it."

"We've been careful, Holly. It's worked up until now. We can keep seeing each other—"

"Do you think I'll be in line for a scholarship if this

comes out? What college is going to want a student with that kind of a scandal following her?"

I sat back, feeling like the wind just got knocked out of me. "We'll figure it out. Don't worry."

"There's nothing to figure out," she whispered.

24

Holly

My wake-up alarm started beeping. There was no need for it since I hadn't so much as shut my eyes. A steady stream of tears trickled out all night long. Sitting up in bed, I turned on the light before standing.

The mirror was not kind.

Swollen eyes, red, puffy face. No amount of powder was going to cover this train wreck. It was a valid reflection of how I felt inside—like someone had socked me in the stomach repeatedly. With a hammer.

My head pounded as I stared at the unrecognizable person in the mirror. How had things gone so wrong so fast? Tears threatened again while I replayed my last conversation with Evan in my mind. "We'll figure it out," he'd said. No matter how much I wanted to believe that, I knew it would be a lie.

Our relationship would end up ruining two mens'

careers and possibly my hopes of getting a college scholarship—my only ticket out of this trailer park.

Several deep breaths later, I slogged into the bathroom to splash some cold water on my face. Nothing helped. Exhaustion seeped out of every pore.

Tip toeing past Mom's door, I heard the soft snores of sleep. Finally. She'd been up sick a few times in the night. Which meant I was also up to help. My level of worry for her was officially through the roof. No matter how many times I suggested going to the hospital she'd out and out refused.

The crushing weight of concern for her combined with the soul killing devastation of losing Evan was too much.

I had no one to lean on—nobody to help carry the burden.

My friendship with Ivy was over. She'd made that abundantly clear. I imagined her poisoning the minds of Paige and Alex as well. They'd side with her or whatever warped version she came up with to explain why she hated me. Unless she decided to tell them the truth.

Closing my eyes, taking another deep breath, I thought about what exactly I could control at this moment. Not much besides putting one foot in front of the other. Which is something I had gotten quite good at over the years.

～

"Aww, baby Hope, how are you?" I said, reaching immediately for my friend's baby. "Look how big you got." Extending my arms so she now looked down at me, Hope gave me the sweetest baby smile ever.

"She's good. So am I, thanks for asking," Jason replied,

nudging me. I hadn't seen Jason or his family in some time. Much too long.

"Grab a menu if you need one," I called back, carrying the baby with me to get a highchair. "Are you eating Auntie's hair?" I said, looking down as Hope mouthed a chunk of my ponytail. She answered me with a slobbery, toothless grin. Babies held some kind of special magic that could change your crappy mood on a dime—even when you'd just broken up with the love of your life.

"Here, let's wipe that," I said, dumping the silverware from the napkin to use on her wet face. Her Snow White skin was dripping with baby spit.

"It's pointless. You wipe off a bit and a bucket more comes in its place." Jason sighed, plopping down in the chair as only an exhausted, first time father can.

I sat opposite him, bouncing Hope on my knee as I quickly gave her a wipe down. She protested, putting her chubby arms in front of her. A quick tickle to her sweet, soft belly quickly brought back her grin.

"How was your trip?" he asked, eyes not leaving me.

"Good." I kissed Hope's hand, the delicious smell of baby powder wafting up my nose. "Thanks for checking in on Mom," I said, changing the subject.

"Holly," he said, commanding my attention.

Regretfully looking up at him, he said, "Your mom's even worse than the last time we saw her."

Nodding, I agreed, "She won't go to the doctor."

His eyebrows nearly hit his hairline. "Viv and I practically begged her to go. Offered to drive her and everything."

"I'll try talking to her again."

"How are you holding up?"

"I do my best."

"What about school? That okay?"

"Just because you lived beside me nearly my whole life doesn't mean you get to ask me what kind of grades I'm getting," I said, cracking a smile I never knew I had in me.

"How's school?" he asked, leaning in this time.

Rolling my eyes, I told him, "My grades are great."

Shaking his head as he sat back, he said, "I don't know how you do it. Work, school, work, your mom."

"How did you do it?" I asked, knowing full well he went through the same shit I am.

Blowing air out of his mouth, he confessed, "One fucking day at a time."

"Would you stop swearing in front of the baby?" Vivienne glided in, giving Jason a look from under her perfectly mascaraed eyelashes.

"She has no idea what I'm even saying," Jason argued.

"Even so—you need to stop or Heaven knows what her first word will be," Vivienne said as she sat down in her skirt, pulling at her matching jacket that didn't quite fit her properly. "Will I ever lose this baby weight?" she exclaimed discouragingly, yanking harder on the poor fabric.

Jason's eyes traveled down to her chest. "I hope not," he said in a low tone but still loud enough for me to hear. Vivienne rolled her eyes and narrowed her gaze at him as he winked back.

Giving baby Hope a kiss on her cheek. "Let Mommy wipe." Once again, the baby fought having her rosy complexion dried. "You are a regular drool machine."

"Why even bother? She's a constant fountain." Jason huffed, holding his hand out for the damp napkin. Vivienne handed it to him, but he held onto her fingers, pulling her down for a quick kiss. They really were sweet together. I had my doubts in the beginning because of their age difference, especially as Jason was so much younger. Seeing them together, you understand how well their personalities fit.

"Did you discuss, you know—" Vivienne asked, semi covertly as she cocked her head in my direction.

"Smooth, Viv." Jason shook his head. "We were just talking about Holly's mom, yes."

Vivienne's hand clasped over mine. "Sweetheart, you ever need anything—and I mean anything at all, you call us. Right? We have so many rooms in our house we don't know what to do with them all."

Jason smirked at her and said, "I thought we were going to fill them up with babies?"

She whacked him in the chest with her hand. "Hush. Aren't you supposed to be writing?"

He looked at me sheepishly. The fact that Jason had gotten out of our trailer park, worked hard to stay out, and found the love of his life made my heart unbelievably happy. "I thought you'd feed me first?"

"I suppose." Vivienne blinked at him then turned back to me. "I'm not kidding, girl. You need help, call."

≈

"THANKS, Mr. Turner. I had a great time," I told my boss as I prepared to rush out to catch the bus. He'd asked about my weekend, causing another stabbing pain to shoot through my already shattered heart. "See you tomorrow." Waving my goodbye, I ran past a few customers on my way out.

I stopped dead in my tracks at what awaited me. "Hey," Evan said, pushing away from the side of his Jeep. Slowly swaggering over to me, he carefully checked me out. "You look—" His hand moved out as if to touch my face.

Dodging him, I answered back, "Like shit, I know. You

need to leave. What were you thinking, coming here again?" I frowned at him then swung my head to watch for the bus.

"I was going to say, sad."

"Whatever. Just go before someone sees you."

"Get in the Jeep, Holly. We need to talk," he said, cocking his head toward the vehicle.

All I wanted to do was jump into his arms and kiss him while he assured me everything would be okay. The one part of my brain that still worked knew that was an awful idea. "Evan, leave. Please? Can't you see how much harder you're making this?" I pleaded, tears invading my eyes again as sorrow closed up my throat.

"Don't cry, we can fix this." He moved closer to me, the smell of his cologne wafting up my nose. I had to stop myself from doing something stupid.

"Please, I'm begging you," I sobbed, cursing the universe's cruel fate that kept us apart. A loud honk sounded drawing my attention down the street again.

"Get in the Jeep before the bus comes," Evan said more sternly now. I stepped further away from him, shaking my head. "Please," he said breathlessly as I shut my eyes, shaking my head. "You're fucking serious? You'd throw away what we have? Just like that?" His hands jerked to his hips.

Unable to move, I stared at him, tears in my eyes.

"I don't believe you." Turning on a dime, he hurried around the Jeep, hitting the hood with his fist as he went.

~

"SOMETHING UP WITH YOU TWO?" Alex asked me after Paige and Ivy left our lunch table.

Pretending to not understand, I said, "What do you mean?"

He rolled his eyes. "Girl, it was so frosty in here I could build a snowman," Alex said in his typical sing song tone.

Attempting to play it off, I countered back. "She's probably just upset about getting sick during the ball."

Alex narrowed his gaze. "Anything happen between you two at the big bash?"

I let out a big sigh. "Nothing at all. Would you just drop it already?" I asked, stabbing my salad with a bit more force than necessary.

"What did that romaine ever do to you?" he said, sliding my plate over a few inches.

Shoving it back, I glared at him.

"Ohhh, if looks could kill," he said, eyes wide, hand to his heart. "Fine, consider the subject—on hold for now. But if I may say, you're in need of my miracle eye serum today, missy." Digging through his backpack he pulled out a tiny pink tube. "This," he said, holding it up high with one hand while doing a game show model wave towards it with the other, "is the best thing since the invention of lip plumpers."

He screwed off the cap, squeezing a pea sized glob onto his finger. "If you won't tell me what's going on at least you can look fabulous as you scowl at everyone."

That made me giggle a bit. "You're crazy, you know that?" I said, closing my eyes as he lightly dabbed around them.

"Ain't tellin' me something I don't already know, sugar. Now open wide. We need to prevent those crow's feet at all cost." After he finished applying the cream to my face, he fanned me with the nearest book until everything dried.

Giving him a big hug, I said, "Thanks."

Alex pulled me in. "Anytime. You know I'm here for you, right?"

"I do, but it's still nice to hear."

"How's your mama been feeling?"

Shaking my head on his shoulder, my breath hitched. "Not good."

He squeezed me tighter. "I'm sorry. Now I feel bad for all the shit we talked about her. I didn't know she really wasn't well."

"It's fine, don't worry."

"Has she gone to the doctor yet?" Alex asked, pushing away from me a bit.

"My neighbors even tried to take her while I was away, but she refuses to go in." My eyes started to tear up.

"You ever need me to come over and help, just call, okay? Just because you've been ignoring our asses for weeks now doesn't mean I won't drive over in my silk pajamas to help my girl out."

Wrapping my hands around him again, I said, "Thanks, that means a lot."

25

Holly

"People, we have two weeks left to get this right. It's not fun and games anymore. You need to buckle down and memorize your lines." Evan slammed his dogeared script on the stage then removed his glasses, rubbing the bridge of his nose. We'd begun meeting during lunches as well, not that it was helping much.

From somewhere behind me, I heard a guy whisper, "Holy shit, Marshall is pissed right off." There was a low grumble as people reacted with whoever was nearest.

Ivy and her Romeo stood tight-lipped on the stage while the rest of the onlookers gawked. Their performance thus far had been dismal at best. Evan turned, storming out of a side door. After it slammed behind him, the volume in the theater got louder. "Do you think he's coming back?" one of the stagehands asked.

A war battled inside me. At this stage in the game I really didn't care if Ivy bombed. But something inside me took pride in my set and the work we'd all put into preparing for the big night. If they looked like a laughing-stock—so would we. Guilt by association.

Gathering up my courage, I used my big girl voice. "Take ten everyone. Mr. Marshall will be right back." The students looked at each other for a second before dispersing. Dropping my hammer on the stage, I headed toward the same door Evan had exited.

"Typical," Ivy said as I walked past. Twisting my head, I shot her back a nasty look to which she returned a condescending smile. Whatever. I had other more important things to deal with right now than her infantile attitude.

It took me a while to track him down. Closing the door to the costume room, I leaned my back against it as Evan looked up from where he sat on the floor. "You need to go back out there and get control of your group."

His dark brown eyes settled on me, looking me up and down. "You're talking to me now?"

"I never stopped speaking to you," I lied.

Tilting his head back against the brick wall, he scoffed. "You haven't said boo to me in a fucking month."

Keeping my distance, I straightened up a bit. "I'm in your class every day. That's not true."

His eyes shot to mine. "The only time you answer me in class is when I specifically call on you. Four weeks, Holly. Trust me, I've been keeping track."

"You lost your cool out there and everyone's wondering if you've quit," I asked, changing the subject.

"I'm still deciding."

Unable to help myself, a laugh bubbled out.

Evan's face fell. "I've missed that." The room filled with silence. "I go all day hoping to hear your voice. Thinking maybe today will be the day you pick up your phone when I call or text." He stood up, wiping his hands on his thighs.

"You have to stop calling," I said weakly, not meaning it at all. I, too, craved having him reach out—happy he hadn't forgotten me. Yet. It was a cruel kind of torture seeing his name pop up on my phone several times a day. Each time, I'd read the text or listen to his voice mail, wanting him so badly.

There was no sense to it, though. Being with him was impossible. We both needed to face that and move on.

Stalking toward me, my nipples hardened at the look of pure determination on his face. As he halted directly in front of me, I inhaled deeply smelling his fresh, spicy scent, not knowing what he was going to do. With everything inside of me, I fought against the invisible pull he still had on me.

Hands against the door, he leaned in, speaking directly into my ear. I shivered as his breath washed over my skin. "Tell me you don't want me. Tell me you don't miss me," he said, voice husky like he was trying to control it but failing miserably.

Feeling the heat radiate off him, my heart sped up to an impossible beat. His lips grazed my neck as I let out a sigh, my body remembering exactly what this man was capable of. He lightly kissed the edge of my jaw, creating a tingle that shot straight to my lower belly. Those soft lips traveled down my neck, his tongue gently licking as he went.

My brain fizzled as the heat from his touch made me clench my thighs together, seeking relief. I couldn't help it— I was weak. Turning my head, he captured my lips in an impossible kiss.

My arms shot around his neck, seeking to be as close to him as possible. Below, my belly tightened into a delicious ache already wanting more. Pulling me into his body, he moaned down my throat, searching almost angrily for my tongue. I responded immediately, opening up for him, matching his kiss.

Running my hands through his hair, he pushed me up further against the door while his hand found my breast. It wasn't a kiss—he devoured me, mind, body, and soul. "You taste so sweet," he said against my mouth before kissing me roughly down my neck.

Wetness pooled between my legs as I leaned my head to the side, giving him more room. I let out a squeak when his hands found my behind, lifting me up so my core was in line with his hardness. Forcing me further back into the door, I was willingly trapped.

Wrapping my legs around his waist, he continued kissing down my chest, letting go with one hand to use it on my top. Shoving aside my tank top, the strap slid down my arm. Once my nipple was free, his warm mouth found it, drawing it inside.

"Ohh," I almost whimpered, finally feeling what I'd wanted for so long. Waves of desire shot through my body as his tongue flicked at my nipple. My pelvis moved in time against his. The friction created by rubbing against his pants made me go faster, seeking my own release.

"Pull down the other side for me," Evan instructed, his breath coming in heavy pants, keeping his hands tight on my ass. I yanked the strap down, pulling my bra cup with it. He took my mouth in a deep kiss as his fingers did wonderful things to my breast.

A subtle tingling sensation began then quickly spread. My fingers dug into him, not believing what was about to happen. "Give in, honey. Let it take over," Evan groaned in between kisses.

There was no stopping it, so I gave in, just like he said. Sparks exploded behind my eyelids as my body finally found what it had been craving so desperately. Every muscle in my body contracted at precisely the same time overwhelming me with sensation.

Evan's mouth covered mine, absorbing my soft cries of relief. My legs tightened around him, jolts of ecstasy still shattering me from the inside out. As the roar of our passion faded and my extremities became limp, he turned then lowered us to the ground.

Sitting in his lap, his back leaning on the wall, I laid my head against his chest, listening as his heartbeat finally slowed like mine. His hands methodically rubbed my back as I unwillingly reentered the world—our screwed up, unfair world.

"I've missed you, Holly. You're all I think about," he repeated the same words he'd texted me over and over again during the last month. My only answer was to snuggle further into him. "Try with me."

Pushing back so I could see his face, I said, "Try what?"

"This," he said, pulling me toward him. "Us."

"We—" Was all I got out before there was a knock at the door. "Oh no," I whispered, jumping off his lap like it was on fire. Panic filled my brain as I rushed to fix my clothes before whomever was at the door barged in.

"Your hair," Evan motioned, one hand holding the door shut. As quick as I could, I undid my ponytail then redid it. "Go in the back," he said, barely audible. "Wait until I leave."

Doing as he said, I ran around the costumes to the back of the room. I heard some words that I couldn't make out then silence for about ten minutes. Figuring it was safe to leave, I carefully poked my head around the corner. Nobody else was in the room. My shoulders sagged with relief.

Double checking my top, I strolled out of the door

nearly bumping right into Ivy. She had her back against the wall, clearly waiting for me. Our eyes met then a snide little smirk formed on her flawlessly made up face. "Just what I thought," she said, looking me up and down before pushing off the wall and sauntering away.

26

Evan

"All right, are we all clear on inverted subjects? This will be on the test," I said, wanting to invert something other than subjects and stick it—

"Mr. Marshall?" a voice called from the corner.

"Yes, Leslie?"

"I still don't understand compound subjects." A sheepish smile crossed her freckled face. Honestly, if I had to explain this one more time, I was going to scream. Taking off my glasses, I turned around to sit on my desk.

"Um, I can help." Holly turned to talk to Leslie. "If your compound subjects are joined by "and" then they are always plural. Like, "The cat and dog are friends." Not, "The cat and dog is friends. Always use the plural form of the verb with compound subjects so they agree."

Holly should probably be teaching this instead of me. "Thank you, Holly. Leslie, does that clear things up?" She nodded her head, writing furiously in her notebook. "Good. Now on to Romeo and Juliet. Any questions or concerns?

Have you begun thinking about themes for possible essay questions?"

"Light and dark," one student said.

"Good, very good. There are a lot of possibilities with that. Anyone else?" I gazed around the classroom, glimpsing Holly with her hand up. It was increasingly more and more difficult seeing her in class—unable to really speak or touch her how I wanted. Constantly checking myself and my actions toward her was exhausting. However, the alternative was far worse.

Pointing to her, she answered, "Forbidden love," with a sexy, knowing smirk on her face.

My mouth opened slightly, suddenly unable to form a coherent sentence. Instead, wanting to grab her and kiss that smile right off. She stared back at me as we communicated something unspoken between us. Clearing my throat, I said, "Yes, that'll work."

Directing my gaze toward another student, he answered, "Conflict between children and parents."

"Good answer. The bell's about to ring but I think you all have a good grasp on what's expected. Go over your notes." Two seconds later, the bell rang. Everyone gathered their things while I wiped the boards.

When I turned around, Holly was there, books in her arms, staring at me. I tentatively gave her my most heartfelt smile. "Hi." My hands itched to reach out and pull her body into mine. The rose blush on her face, her lips still slightly swollen from our earlier rendezvous looked much too tempting to me.

Several times, she opened her mouth to speak but nothing came out. "You work tonight?" I asked, cocking my head to the side.

"Yeah, I have to leave right away so I can't make drama. The set is nearly finished though."

Sitting on the corner of my desk, I asked, "What time are you off?"

A cloud of hesitation passed behind her eyes before she said, "Early tonight, nine." My body clinched at the thought of being alone with her again.

∾

"LIFT YOUR LEG FOR ME. A bit more," I urged as I continued rocking inside the woman I'd missed so much. Her heel dug into my ass cheek, urging me to go faster.

"Ouch," Holly said as her head hit against the door of the backseat again.

"Damn, honey, I'm sorry." Sliding my hands underneath her, I pulled her down a bit. "Good?" She nodded, her hair splaying wildly around her. Leaning down, I slowly licked her nipple until I heard a gasp slip out of her panting mouth.

"Don't stop," she said, bucking up with her hips. I knew what that meant. Rising up, I pushed my hips forward, teasing her with an unhurried, languid pace. Watching her head move from side to side in sweet agony was almost too much for me.

She moaned as I bent down to nibble on her sweet neck. "Please, Evan," she begged, wrapping her arms around me, caging my body to hers. My mouth found hers while I reared back to give her what she wanted.

"Are you close?" I asked, my lips touching hers, my tongue teasing—licking her lower lip before I grasped it between my teeth. She sighed, her sweet breath washing over me.

"Yes," she said as I increased my rhythm. The throb of release grew insistent inside my balls, eager to finally climax. The second I felt her clench me tight—I let go, exploding as Holly writhed below me. I felt the searing, hot, wetness of our combined ecstasy dripping down around the most intimate parts of us.

Finally catching my breath, I kissed her and said, "I missed this so much. I missed us."

Her eyes sparkled up at me, reflecting the bright moon-light. "Me, too."

~

"Ivy was waiting for me after you left today," Holly said, taking a bite of her burger as I drove.

Glancing over at her, I said, "Outside the costume room?" She nodded, grabbing a few fries. "Shit. She needs to give up already."

"I don't think Ivy's the type to give up. What are we going to do if she goes to the principal?"

Signaling left, I said, "I really doubt she'll do that. And anyway, all she's got is a grainy picture of us. It's her word against ours."

Holly looked out the window. "I think her word has a lot more credibility than mine."

Putting my hand on her knee, I shook it. "Your word holds just as much weight as hers." It didn't sound the least bit convincing, even to my ears.

She spat out a bitter laugh. "Nice try. Who's going to trust trailer trash over a trust fund baby?"

"Hey, stop. You're no such thing. Besides." I looked over at her with a smirk. "I'm a trust fund baby, too."

Rolling her eyes at me, she said, "Whatever. Must be nice."

I shrugged, turning onto the gravel road near her place. "I haven't gotten it yet. Not until I turn twenty-three."

"Why do they make you wait?"

"Well, in my family, grandparents set it up for their grandkids. I guess their reasoning is not to put too much money in the hands of stupid kids."

Taking a swig of our shared drink, she said, "I doubt you were ever a stupid kid."

Laughing, I stole a few of her fries. "I did plenty of dumb things. Didn't you?'

She pondered my question for a second, frowning a bit. "Other than sleep with my teacher?" she said, raising her eyebrows at me as I shook my head. "Not really. Just sneaking into clubs and underage drinking."

"You never know who you'll meet in a bar," I said, grabbing her hand, remembering the night we danced at the bar and later, our first time together on the beach.

As we pulled into the trailer park, Holly sighed, squeezing my hand. Pulling over to the side, I parked the Jeep and turned to her. "You're thinking too much. Stop."

The look of concern on her face broke my heart. "I'm worried that Ivy won't keep quiet."

Placing my fingers on her chin, I moved her face so I could look into her eyes. "There's nothing we can do about that right now. She's either going to tell or not. That ball is in her court now. The only thing for us to do is be as careful as possible."

"But we weren't careful—"

"Holly, I didn't think for a minute that the stupid newspapers would give a shit about who I danced with at the masquerade ball. If I had, I would have been more cautious. I'm sorry, that was my fault."

Her hand snaked behind my neck, pulling me closer until our foreheads touched. "No, it was a fluke, you're right. Seeing you there—being able to dance with you—"

"Other than our first night at the beach, it was the best night I've ever had." My lips entwined with hers, forcing her mouth open under mine—leaving her no choice but to take what I was giving.

27

Evan

"Juliet," I said to Ivy. "With more feeling. The love of your life just killed himself for you. We need more emotion." I don't know why I bothered. All Ivy did was scowl at me now. At least her annoying flirting days seemed to be over.

"Mr. Marshall, please come down to the office," a voice said through the intercom in the theater.

"I'm busy with students. Can I come in an hour?"

A minute of silence before it clicked on again. "No, I'm sorry. You are needed urgently."

What the hell could be so important at four o'clock? "All right, everyone take fifteen minutes." The students scattered as I gathered my notes together. A sick feeling overcame me when my eyes met Ivy's. She sent me a half-smirk but not the usual kind. This smile had more of a "fuck you" written all over it.

Holly peered up at me with a worried glance where she

knelt, pinning an actor's costume. "I'll be right back," I said, trying to be comforting.

By the time I entered the office, my blood pressure was through the roof. "Go right in," our admin assistant said, not looking me in the eyes.

Principal McGreggor's door was open. Knocking lightly anyway, I hesitated to go in. "Have a seat, Mr. Marshall. Close the door first, please."

Holly

MY KNEE WOULDN'T QUIT BOUNCING no matter how hard I tried to stop it. The palms of my hands left sweaty patches on the skirt I wore. I wiped them on my calves while I sat patiently as possible on a chair.

Evan hadn't come back after the office called for him. Twenty minutes later, they called my name. The kids had all hollered like they always did whenever someone got paged to the office. As I walked past Ivy, she stared right at me with a grin on her face.

I nearly fainted. Had she reported us?

That was the only thought going through my mind right now—other than where I'd have to transfer to if Ivy had ratted us out.

Finally, the principal's door opened. Evan walked out, looking pissed. His eyes darted to me as he tilted an empty box my way.

They knew.

I simultaneously wanted to throw up, run away, and scream. Fortunately—or unfortunately, depending how you looked at it—I was so frozen with fear I couldn't even breathe.

"Miss Anderson," Principal McGreggor said in her doorway.

My poor brain just about exploded. What was I going to say?

As calmly as possible, I stood then walked into her office.

Closing the door behind me, she said, "Have a seat, Holly." Not once in my life had I been called to the principal's office. Sitting down, I wiped my hands on my skirt again.

Giving me a short smile, she finally sat behind her desk. "Look, this is a difficult thing to ask." Her dark brown eyes looked at me almost sympathetically. "First of all, because of the subject matter and secondly because you've been over to my house for supper more times than I can count. You and Alex have been friends for years." She gazed down for a second, as though collecting her thoughts.

"Someone has come forward with a very serious accusation against one of the teachers," she said, cutting her eyes back to me. My blood ran cold. Ivy did it. She actually went ahead and did it. "They said Mr. Marshall and you are having an—affair. Is there any truth to this?"

I thought I had prepared myself to hear this—apparently, I was wrong. The air in my lungs was sucked out and I was sure I'd fall forward onto my face. That would be no help to Evan, though. Instead of bursting into tears, I allowed myself to process the shock then gave the most convincing performance I could muster.

"What? That's crazy? Who would even say such a thing?" I shook my head, curling one hand on my leg.

"I can't betray that confidentiality, Holly. Now, I need you to think hard on this. If Mr. Marshall has in some way stepped over the line, I need to know." Principal McGreggor leaned forward onto her elbows.

"Mr. Marshall is my teacher and nothing more. I don't know why anyone would think differently."

28

Holly

The waves lapped methodically onto the beach. I loved hearing and watching the guaranteed predictability of it all.

Such enormous strength harnessed against its will. Just waiting for the time when it was unleashed and exposed the true power held secretly beneath the calm.

"What are you thinking?" Evan bent his head down, whispering in my ear as I leaned my back against his body. His legs and arms held me in a false cocoon of safety.

"I wondered if the ocean was happiest now in its serenity or when it lets loose, surprising everyone with its strength."

He hugged me tight. "I think it's happiest when it finally gets to do and be what it was always meant to."

I sniffed as a few tears finally escaped my tired eyes. "I bet you're right."

We stayed like that under the light of the moon and stars as the minutes inevitably turned into hours. "When do you have to go?" I asked, not wanting to know the answer.

"Not sure. I'm on suspension right now but there's no way they'll let me back in after today."

My heart physically hurt. Nodding, only slightly relieved he wasn't actually fired, I said, "I'm so sorry. I never thought Ivy would tell." More tears streamed down my face as I sobbed.

"No crying. This is not your fault."

"Then whose fault is it?"

He had no answer because sometimes shit just happened.

If you were me—it was pretty much guaranteed.

∾

"I HEARD he was banging a student, so they canned him," Ivy said, looking straight at me as she pinned up her hair.

"What? For real?" the girl who played Juliet's nurse asked while she fiddled with her wig.

"That's what I heard, too. Lucky, whoever she—or he is," Alex cackled as he worked on Ivy's makeup.

Ivy dabbed her lipstick. "I'm sure we'll find out soon enough. That kind of thing never stays a secret long." She stared at me in the makeup mirror giving me a look that could kill.

"For realzies, I'd like to shake the hand of whoever got into the panties of that fine, fine man. It takes skill and superior trapping abilities to snag that kind of quality tail," Alex said, shaking his makeup brush around like he was conducting an orchestra.

"Holly, you were in the office around the same time. Did you see anything? And why did they call you up there during drama practice?" Ivy asked, lifting her chin so Alex could continue applying powder.

Playing it off as no big deal, I kept sewing the loose button on our Mercutio's shirt, refusing to look at Ivy anymore. "I had some scholarship papers to deal with. Yeah, I saw him walking out of Principal McGreggor's with an empty cardboard box."

"That is one huge shame to no longer have his gorgeous self gracing our hallowed halls. I'd like to bitch slap the idiot who reported him," Alex said, hands on his hips looking ready to do just that.

So would I, Alex. So would I.

Evan

"WHAT DID I tell you to do, man? Jesus, is your head made of stone?" Jake asked, chucking a couch pillow at my head.

Catching it with one hand, I scowled at my friend. "We were careful," I said, frowning as I put my feet on the coffee table.

Jake stood, raising his arms. "Careful? You call it being careful to be in the social pages of at least two large newspapers?"

"Settle down, we were wearing masks."

"You think the press won't be able to track down your teenage lover?" he said, storming over towards me.

Leaning my head back against the couch, I sighed. "I told you, she's of age. Besides, I'm using mom's last name now. They won't find me here."

He laughed, flopping down onto the couch opposite me. "You stupid, stupid bastard. I know I'm older than you but how can I be this much wiser?"

"Five years makes such a difference," I mumbled sarcastically, shaking my head.

"It does, you moron. For one thing, I know how to choose my lays a hell of a lot better than you. Keep it casual. That's the only way. You need to be like me and use the right head when you pick up pussy from now on."

"Yeah, you're a real pro."

"My rules have never failed me."

Shaking my head, I barely stopped myself from rolling my eyes. "Yes, your famous rules."

He took this as a personal challenge. "Mr. Richter's fail-proof, ironclad rules," he said, sitting back up. Holding out one hand he began to count off on his fingers.

"More like, Mr. Richter's Ridiculous Rules," I mumbled under my breath.

If he heard me, he ignored my comment completely. "Number one, never date a student." His eyebrows raised at me as his mouth slightly opened. "Number two, use a different name. But make sure you remember which name you used—"

Jake really was crazy. I huffed knowing there were still more stupid rules to come.

"Number three, only one night. Number four—or technically it could be just an addendum to number three—never stay overnight."

Holly and I had broken that rule. The thought of having her in my arms all night long made me grin to myself.

"Get that stupid smile off your face, man," Jake scoffed, briefly halting his information session before carrying on. "Number five, do not—and I repeat for those in the back," he said in his very best professor voice, "do not get attached."

"Sometimes things just—happen. You don't plan it. The same thing could just as easily happen to you." And man, if that wasn't the honest to God truth. There was no way I saw this thing with Holly coming.

Jake laughed, shaking his head. "I'm smart about it. Way too smart to sleep with a barely legal student."

Looking over at him, I said, "This isn't casual."

"What?" He leaned forward, elbows resting on his knees. "You in love with her?" I didn't answer, instead letting my silence speak for itself. Jake groaned, falling back onto the cushions, "You're so screwed."

29

Holly

"You have a good day. Text me when you're off," Evan said, kissing me once more inside his Jeep. I undid my seat belt, hopping out. Waiting on the side of the road, I waved to him, still basking in the glow of spending the day with him.

Looking both ways, something caught my eye off to the side. Paige.

My heart came to a screeching stop when I saw her shocked, pale face staring at me, her arms stiff against the side of her body. She didn't blink, she didn't move—she didn't take her unbelieving eyes off me.

Closing my eyes, I restarted my heart as I gulped in air, hoping my legs wouldn't give out. I swung my bag onto my shoulder and crossed the street to talk to my motionless, stunned friend.

"You—"

"Yeah," I replied, gazing down at the sidewalk for a second.

"And—"

"Yeah."

Her entire upper body nearly collapsed in on itself as she heaved out a breath so hard, I wondered if she was going to topple over. "What are you doing? Are you crazy?" she asked, her voice choppy and breathless like she'd just finished a marathon.

Shifting on my feet, I silently thanked my knees for holding me up. Fear clenched my heart, afraid I'd lose another friend now that she knew the truth about me and Evan. "Probably."

"What—"

Letting out a breath, I asked, "Can we talk in your car?" I looked around the abandoned sidewalks. We were alone out here, true. Except I felt so open—so exposed here. More than likely I'd be late for my shift, but I had to explain things to Paige.

Paige nodded faintly, crossing her arms in front of her as though she was trying to hold herself together. Her car was right beside us, so we climbed into it. Doors closed, I turned to her as my heart thudded harder inside my chest.

"It just happened. We didn't mean for it to—"

"You're sleeping with Mr. Marshall?" she asked, her hand gripping the handle on her door.

"Uh, yes."

Her head thunked against the seat. "You're insane. Do you know how much trouble you could get in?" Paige's bright blue eyes shot back with disbelief. "A teacher, Holly? Really? You could have any guy at school, and you choose the English teacher?" She gasped, drawing in a sharp breath.

Tears threatened as I searched for air, my lungs screaming for oxygen. "It just happened," I said, my hand covering hers. Immediately, she snatched it away as though I'd burnt her. She shook her head back and forth. "I—I really like him," I whispered to her, my voice barely audible over the sound of my own heart.

"Ivy knows, doesn't she? That's why you two are acting all weird." Her shoulders sagged as her eyes filled up.

Nodding, my voice tripped over itself. "She knows." A single tear fell down my cheek, the ache in my chest almost too much to take. Paige needed to understand. "I can't lose another friend. Please don't hate me, too." That was it—all my emotions could take before bursting into loud sobs.

My hands covered my face as my body shook, not able to handle the possibility of Paige hating me. Arms wrapped around me, then a hand pulled my head to her shoulder. "Don't be stupid, I don't hate you." She sighed into my hair. My face was buried in her soft, silky, black hair—a hint of coconut traveling up my nose. "I think you've lost your freaking mind—a teacher?" She let out another breath.

"Not just a teacher," I said, moving back so I could see her face. "We really—connect."

Her loud snort broke some of the tension. "I bet." Her perfectly shaped eyebrows raised as she gazed at me knowingly.

Rolling my eyes, I said, "Not exactly what I meant." We broke out into nervous giggles, her hand gently rubbing my shoulder.

"You know what you're doing?" Her eyes narrowed on me as she looked me over.

A warmness flowed through me almost like I could feel her concern and worry so acutely it made my heart swell. "Not really," I said, a few more tears sneaking out before I could wipe them away. "But it feels so right. You know?"

"Not personally, but according to every love song ever

written there are billions of people who do." Her lips parted in a whisp of a smile.

"You're gorgeous, my friend," I said, reaching out to take a lock of her hair between my fingers. "If you left your living room once in a while you'd find someone in a minute." It was the truth, too. I'd never met anyone as naturally pretty as Paige.

Her long, dark eyelashes flawlessly framed her almond shaped eyes. The girl really didn't need a lick of makeup but the way she added her smoky eyeliner added to her allure.

Her head shook vehemently side to side. "No time for that nonsense. Besides, who wants to risk ending up like my mom?" she stated, eyebrows raised. "That's all I'd need. Some jerk to walk into my life, leave me with a bundle of joy then run off. No thanks." Paige's greatest fear in life was to be knocked up and alone. It wasn't difficult to see the emotional damage her father's abandonment had caused.

"Paige—" I started but she cut me off, never wanting to talk in detail about her family life.

"Ivy must be freaking jealous," she said, her eyes wide as she beamed an even bigger smile at me.

I sat back in the seat, fixing my uniform as my stomach sank at the mention of Ivy. "You could say that."

A loud gasp came from her mouth as she covered it with one hand. "Did she rat you out?" Her eyebrows nearly at her hairline.

There was no sense in denying it. I mean, she could easily just ask Ivy what happened. "She told on us."

"That little—"

"Like you said, she's jealous," I said, cutting her off as I grabbed my bag. "Promise me something?" I pleaded, tilting my head to the side. "Pretend you don't know? I would rather not give her more fuel to add to the fire. Right now,

I'm just grateful she hasn't actually told the whole school I was the reason Evan got suspended."

"Evan. Oh man, you're on a first name basis with our English teacher." Her beautiful face stared back at me, still dazed.

"Former English teacher," I corrected with a small sigh.

"You be careful, okay? If you need anything, you call me." The look of sincerity in her eyes squeezed at my heart as relief flowed through me, grateful she still liked me.

"Thanks," I said, sniffing one last time as I hugged her so hard I worried I might have broken a rib. Then I ran out to my shift, thankful to still have one friend at my back.

30

Holly

"We don't actually have to do this," Ivy said, giving me a snooty look.

Shooting her my nastiest glance, I said, "Trust me, I'd rather be anywhere than here. Mrs. White is right, though. You need to work on your lines. Opening night is in a week."

"I'll be—" she said, doubling over, holding her side.

"Are you okay?"

"Fine," she said out of breath, both hands on her side now.

Gathering my patience in case this was some kind of stunt, I walked over to her. "Is it that same kind of pain you had at the masquerade ball?"

"You mean the one you spent fucking our English teacher the whole night?" she grunted out.

"That would be the one," I said dryly, arms crossed in front of me.

"It's worse. Go get my keys," she said, flapping her hand at me. "I need to go home."

Assessing the situation, I decided to take her at her word. "You need a hospital. I'll go get Mrs. White."

Attempting to stand up unsuccessfully, she yelled out in pain before bending back over, "Ouch, no. Get me my keys and I'll drive myself. My backpack is in the theater."

Exhaling loudly, I ran to get her bag.

~

"Do you have any disorders? Other than your desire to ruin lives?" I asked sarcastically as I filled out the form on the clipboard.

Ivy looked up. "Nice. I'm dying here in pain and you're making stupid jokes."

"Wasn't joking," I said, cutting her a serious look.

Putting her hands on the wheels, she tried to move away from me in her wheelchair. "Nope, you're not going anywhere, slick," I said as I locked the brake handle down.

"Ms. Davenport, the doctor can see you now," a nurse in dark pink scrubs said.

I stood up, handed the papers to Ivy, unlocked the brake, and wheeled the patient down the hall.

~

"Your mom wants to talk to you," I said, holding Ivy's phone up to her ear.

"Hi, Mom. No, it's way worse than last time." I could hear her mom's raised, worried voice reply. "They think it's my appendix. Nothing showed on the ultrasound but they're going to go in and take it out. The doctor said it's probably what's been causing my issues."

Ivy's mom must've yapped non-stop for five minutes without taking a breath or letting Ivy get a word in edge-wise. "I'm really scared. What if it's not my appendix? What if it's something even worse?" Ivy sniffed, starting to cry. "No, he seems capable. But they also don't know for sure." Now her tears were really falling as her face contorted in fear.

Removing the phone from her ear, I took over. "Hi, Mrs. Davenport, it's Holly again. I'll wait here until you guys arrive. The nurse said they're taking her into the O.R. any minute now."

"Thanks, Holly. I'm so glad you're there with her. I can't believe this has flared up again," her voice hitched as she spoke, unable to continue.

"She's going to be just fine. The doctor and surgeon were confident it's her appendix. They said sometimes it hides and they can't get a good look at it until they're inside."

"Hug her for us, will you? She sounds so scared."

I swallowed the lump in my throat. "Of course. I'll keep the phone with me until you get here." She hung up and I stood, grabbing onto Ivy's hand.

"What are you doing?" she asked, peering up at me with suspicion in her eyes.

Leaning over her, I lightly wrapped my arms around her shoulders. "Your mom wanted me to give you a hug from them."

Her arms wrapped around me, her fingers clinging to me in a death grip. "You're hugging me after everything I've done?"

"It's not from me, it's from your parents," I said, not letting go.

She let out a loud, mournful sob. "I'm a shitty friend."

"The shittiest."

She did a painful sounding laugh-cry that echoed in the otherwise quiet room. "I might die and the last thing I did was hurt my best friend because I was jealous. I'm going straight to Hell."

"You're not going to die. They do tons of appendectomies every day."

Ivy hugged me tighter. "I love you and I'm sorry for being the worst friend in the history of friends. Can you ever forgive me?"

Her pain, fear, and pure patheticness tugged at my heart. Don't get me wrong, I was still mad at what she'd done to ruin Evan's job and end our friendship over a guy. But there was really nothing else to do right now. "Yeah, I forgive you. We didn't plan for it to happen and when it did—I just— couldn't tell you. I couldn't tell anyone."

She cried some more until I felt a wet spot on my shoulder. "But I should have been there for you and I wasn't."

"It's okay."

"All right, ladies. It's showtime," the nurse said, startling us.

As I stepped out of Ivy's embrace, she whispered to me, "I'll make this right again. After my surgery, I'll fix everything."

Nodding, I gave my friend a small smile, knowing in my heart there was nothing anyone could do to fix what she'd done.

31

Holly

"Regrettably, with no lead heroine, we will have to shut down this production." Mrs. White announced on the stage to everyone.

Loud protests of, "That's not fair", and "But we've been working so hard every day" rang out from the actors, stage-hands, and other various helpers.

"Why can't Tara take over? She's the Juliet understudy, after all," another angry student shouted.

Mrs. White cleared her throat. "Tara has stepped down as understudy. There really is no other option than to call it a day. We can't go forward without a Juliet."

"Holly can do it," Alex practically screamed as he jumped up and down. "She knows every boring—she knows every Shakespeare play by heart." He clapped his hands, proud of his suggestion.

I stood there, unable to blink, breathe, or think. What was he doing?

Turning to me, Mrs. White said, "Is this true?"

Taking a deep breath, I said, "I've never acted before, Mrs. White. I'm afraid I wouldn't know what to do, I'm sorry."

"We have six days to prepare you."

Shaking my head, I blurted out, "Honestly, I wouldn't know the first thing."

"Baloney," Alex said, running up behind me, shoving me onto the stage with his hand on my lower back. "You know the words. Which is more than anyone else can say at this point." Pulling me over to Noah, he said, "Romeo, meet your new Juliet. Start at the part where you hold hands, talking about pilgrims and lips. I have no idea what it means but it sounds dirty." Alex giggled hysterically, placing our hands together.

"It'll be okay. Being up here is actually kind of fun," my Romeo whispered with a comforting grin on his face. He looked the picture of calm, cool, and collected while I was relatively sure fainting would be in my near future. "Ready?" I shrugged, looking around at all the hopeful faces looking up at us with excitement.

"If I profane with my unworthiest hand, This holy shrine, the gentle sin is this, My lips, two blushing pilgrims, ready stand, To smooth the rough touch with a tender kiss," he said, holding my hand tightly in his hand.

"Good pilgrim—" I started before he cut me off.

"Louder. Almost like you're shouting. It feels weird at first. Try it again." He let go of my hand.

Filling my lungs like he demonstrated, I made a second attempt. "Good pilgrim, you do wrong your hand too much, Which mannerly devotion shows in this: For saints have hands that pilgrims' hands do touch, And palm to palm is holy palmer's kiss." We held our hands out, touching the palms of our hands together.

Smiling down at me, he said, "Have saints lips, and holy palmers too?"

"Ay, pilgrim, lips that must use in pray'r."

"O then, dear saint, let lips do what hands do, They pray —grant thou, lest faith turn to despair.

"Saints do not move, though grant for prayers' sake.

"Then move not while my prayer's effect I take," he said, lifting my chin up with his fingers. "Thus from my lips, by thine, my sin is purg'd," he said as he put his arms around me, dipping me back slightly, away from the audience— making it look as though we were kissing.

Everyone in the theater exploded with cheers and whistles.

~

"You're joking."

"I'm not," I said, cutting into the chicken and pasta Evan had made for us. "It's completely crazy."

Evan sat there, fork suspended in the air, staring at me. "You'd make a perfect Juliet."

"Correction. I make a Juliet. Desperate times call for desperate measures," I said, stuffing a forkful into my mouth.

"No, I bet you're a natural. It never really occurred to me before now. Good for Alex for pointing it out."

"Yeah, I'm thrilled," I said sarcastically, lifting an eyebrow.

Evan laughed, picking up his water. "When are you going to have time to practice with them?" he asked, his eyebrows furrowing together.

Wiping my mouth with the napkin, I said, "Get this. The powers that be called my boss, begging to steal me away until after the performance. They worked something out and I'll be financially compensated through some kind of Angel Fund at the school. I won't technically miss a paycheck."

He dropped his fork on the plate. "You're kidding me."

Shaking my head, I reached for my drink. "Nope. This is out of control."

Evan sat back in his chair. "How's Ivy doing?"

"She called me right after practice. I guess she spoke to Principal McGreggor and told her she lied."

"Too little, too late."

Regretfully, I nodded in understanding. "I thought so."

"Once the rumor mill starts there's no taking it back. They'd have parents protesting, calling the office. There's no way they'd ever take me back now. Not at a private school." His hand covered mine, squeezing it. "I can help you with your lines, though."

Smiling over at him, I said, "I need to run lines. No funny business." I shook my fork at him.

"Forget it then," he said jokingly, kissing my forehead.

Evan

HOLDING HER IN MY ARMS, I stroked down her ribs, past the dip in her waist and over her hips. Memorizing every curve.

Time was like a guillotine above us—uncertain of when or how it would drop. The only thing we both knew for certain was that it would. Soon.

"You promised no monkey business," she said lazily, kissing my chest.

Hugging her closer, I bent forward to kiss the top of her head. "I could never do that."

We stayed like that, wrapped in each other's arms, refusing to let the real world and all its problems in.

"When do you have to leave?" she asked the question neither of us wanted to think about.

"Soon."

32

Holly

"You look perfect," Alex said, adding more blush to my face as I stared blankly into the long, rectangular mirror. The round lights along its perimeter shining almost too brightly into my eyes.

"I can't believe I'm doing this," I muttered, unblinking, barely able to move my lips. Anxiety settled inside of me, more unsure of myself than ever.

Alex bent down, his face right next to mine. "I can't believe you've never done this before. You're a real pro out there, my dear. Everyone says you're the next big thing."

I shook my head. "That's not true."

"It is. When you get up on that stage, you become—someone else. We're all sitting here like, where did Holly go?" he said, moving his head comically from side to side.

That made me giggle a bit. "I feel different up there, you know?" I tried but failed to find the words to explain the sheer joy I felt on the stage. Everyone had been extremely kind and helpful, working with me until all hours to make sure I was prepared.

The bulk of the training I'd received was from Evan. He went over scene after scene with me, making sure I had a good feel for my lines, movement, and placement.

They'd all made it fun. Even when I was ready to throw in the towel. They had my back.

"You are different out there. Now go break a leg, kid."

~

"Nervous?" Romeo asked with a cute grin on his face. His costume and makeup made him seem almost unrecognizable to me.

"Very," I responded, allowing my shivers to show for a second.

"You have fun out there, right?" he asked, staring down at me, giving me a serious look. I nodded, not understanding what he was getting at. "It's like the world disappears and you get to be whatever you want—whoever you want."

Taking a deep breath, I smiled. "It's like a totally new world out there."

His dimples showed as he chuckled. "You've got the acting bug, congratulations. I can see it in your eyes—you come alive when the curtain opens."

"I've been doing this a week," I said, shaking my head as I poked him in the arm.

"Doesn't matter. You're either born for this or you're not. You feel it—or you don't."

His words struck a chord inside of me. Everything he'd said was true. "It's weird but when I'm out there, I feel like I

—belong," I said, shifting nervously from one foot to the other, hoping what I said wasn't too out there.

"That's because you do." The curtains began to open. "See you out there," he said with a wink.

∽

"Yea, noise? Then I'll be brief. O happy dagger," I said, picking up Romeo's dagger, holding it out for everyone to see. "This is thy sheath;" I said, pretending to stab myself. "there, rust, and let me die." In dramatic fashion, I collapsed on top of Romeo's already perished form.

There was silence for a few seconds before the others entered and finished up the final minutes of the play. After our Prince Escalus exclaimed, "For never was a story of more woe, Than this of Juliet and her Romeo." My breath hitched as tears came to my eyes.

"You did it," Romeo said beneath me as the gentle breeze from the closing curtains blew on my face. The audience exploded in applause.

"All right everyone, up, up, up," Mrs. White said, rushing around with the stage crew to move props and actors around in one giant flurry of excitement.

"You were awesome," Anna, the actress who played the nurse said, hugging me fiercely. "We knew you'd save this shitty play."

"Hey, it wasn't that bad," our Mercutio said, dusting off his pants.

Anna said, "Before Holly showed up, we sucked." Others chimed in with their agreement. Before I could disagree, the curtains opened again, and we all bowed. One by one the actors took their turns stepping up to the edge of the stage while the audience clapped.

When it was our turn, Romeo turned to me and said, "Stay here, let me go first, okay?" I frowned a bit, not understanding. This wasn't what we'd rehearsed. "Just trust me." Then he strode up to the front by himself, giving a few hardy bows and waves.

Striding back to me, he took my hand, leading me up to the front then he bowed grandly toward me, his knee on the floor. "You saved our asses, Juliette." He hurried back to the line of actors behind me. In one fluid, wave like motion everyone stood, clapping, and whistling even louder.

I smiled, absorbing their applause and acceptance into the depths of my soul. After a few curtseys, the curtains began closing. Turning back toward the cast members, they rushed at me all at once. "You were the best," our nurse said, squeezing me tight. "That was incredible," Romeo said, forcing me to turn and face him. He gave me a quick hug before letting the rest of them at me.

Once my fellow actors took turns thanking and congratulating me, I noticed someone in a wheelchair off to the side. She smiled as she motioned for me to come to her.

Unsure of what she wanted, I walked over. "Hey."

"You were fantastic," she said, smiling up at me with glossy eyes.

Shrugging, I said, "Nah, you'd have been better."

Ivy let out a loud laugh, holding her side, clearly still in discomfort from the operation. "Not even close. Everyone knows I sucked. Luckily my appendix saved me from public humiliation."

I shook my head. "You would have been great."

She looked down for a second before gazing back at me. "I'm really sorry for the shitstorm I caused."

Pursing my lips together, I grabbed onto my skirts. "It's—"

"It was a terrible thing to do all because I was jealous." We stared at each other for a minute, feeling awkward, not knowing what to say or do. "If it's any consolation I wish I could take it all back."

Taking a deep breath, I said, "Thanks, that means a lot."

"There's someone waiting for you in the park behind the school," she said, quirking her head to the side.

Frowning, I said, "An axe murderer?"

Laughing, she replied, "Someone better."

∽

TAKING my chances on it not being an axe murderer I managed to sneak away from the hubbub of the crowd. The night was dark and quiet except for the scraping of my shoes on the asphalt in the parking lot.

The grass was getting dewy so I picked up my long skirts with my hands as I walked. "Hello?" I said, feeling some trepidation as I walked further into the park.

I heard a rustling of leaves to the right and then, "She speaks. O, speak again, bright angel, for thou art As glorious to this night, being o'er my head, As is a winged messenger of heaven Unto the white-upturned wondering eyes Of mortal that fall back to gaze on him When he bestrides the lazy-puffing clouds And sails upon the bosom of the air."

Smiling into the darkness, I said, "O Romeo, Romeo! Wherefore art thou Romeo?"

I let out a gasp as I was suddenly lifted high into the air and spun around. "You were the most perfect Juliet in the history of Juliets," Evan said as I slid down the front of his warm, hard body.

Giggling in shock, I wrapped my arms around his neck.

"There've been a lot of Juliets in the last four hundred years."

"And you were by far the best," he said against my mouth, his breath minty as it wafted over me.

Kissing his cool lips, he pulled me closer. "Did you watch?" I asked, hoping he'd say, yes. I was no great judge, but I felt pretty proud of my performance.

"Of course."

"Did anyone see you?"

His head shook. "I stayed in the storage room off to the side until the curtains went up. Ivy spotted me because she was at the back in her chair."

Tilting my head to the side, I asked, "You guys talked?"

"Mmm, hmm. We had a nice little chat," was all he said, not offering more.

"What did she say?"

He touched his lips to my cheek. "She apologized. Explained why she did what she did."

Nodding, I squeezed him tighter. "When do you have to go?"

Our cheeks pressed together as he spoke gently into my ear, "Now."

My stomach dropped as a heaviness settled over top of me. Grateful for his big arms holding me up, my legs felt weak. "Okay," I said as stoically as possible—which in reality wasn't at all.

"I got offered a position in Boston."

"For the rest of the school year?"

"Yeah."

I promised myself that when the time came, I wouldn't cry. "Boston's far away." My voice shook slightly anyway despite my efforts.

He looked me in the eyes, lifting my chin with his finger.

"You need to be with your friends—live your senior year like a regular eighteen year old," he said, his fingers digging into my skin. "Take the leading role in the next drama production. Show everyone what you can do on the stage—not just behind it." His voice was gruff, filled with emotion.

This was his version of letting me down gently. Only problem was that it killed me just as much. Relaxing my body while my mind remained a virtual landmine of questions and oppositions was one of the most difficult things I'd ever had to do.

If there was one thing I was, it was proud. The petty, mad, selfish part of me wanted to yell and scream and beg him to stay with me. The realistic part of me knew he wouldn't change his mind. Instead I'd just end up embarrassing myself. "I'll miss you," I whispered as I felt my tiny heart officially crack in two. Holding back my tears, I kissed him one last time.

33

Holly

"Thanks, Dave. See you tomorrow," I yelled to my boss as I shoved my shoulder against the door of the diner. My hands were busy attempting to find that elusive bus pass. "Where the heck did I put it this time?" I mumbled to myself as I rummaged through my backpack.

"Holly?" I heard my voice being called a few yards away. My heart stopped in my throat as I gazed up into a pair of handsome eyes.

Recognition only took a moment before realization kicked in. Evan's rude friend. Great. We'd never been formally introduced—Evan had made sure of that. "Yeah. What are you doing here?" Suspicious, I took a few steps back, placing my hand back on the door.

He immediately put his hands up—palms toward me. Shuffling away a bit, he shook his head. "Just wanted to talk."

Defenses still up while my stomach twisted, I said, "I

doubt we have anything to talk about." From what I'd over-heard him say to Evan, he wasn't exactly my biggest fan.

Eyes closing briefly, he cleared his throat. "Look, I—I'm a dick sometimes. No, not sometimes," he said, shrugging his shoulders. "A lot of the time. With Evan being gone now, I just wanted to say that you can call me if you ever need—help. Or anything. He told me about your, um, situation."

When he said Evan's name it felt like a knife through my gut. The last thing I wanted was to give him the satisfaction of knowing how much I still hurt.

My laugh came out as more of a cackle as I threw my head back. "I've been dealing with my situation for years now. But thanks for the offer." I glared up at him for a second before squinting back into my bag. Ah, success. Closing my hand around the bus pass, I zipped up my back-pack, slinging it on my shoulder. "I'm going to be late."

Attempting to rush past him to the bus stop, his hand darted out, seizing my elbow. "I just want you know that I'm here if you need me." The shock of his warm hand on my skin almost made me panic. His eyes darted down to where he was grabbing me then let go instantly. "You don't need to be afraid of me. I only—look, if you need any kind of help call."

Jamming his hand into the back pocket of his jeans he yanked out a shiny, white card. Stuffing it into my hand, he held my eyes with his. "Any time of the day or night." Jake's eyes shone with such sincerity I almost believed him. "I swear I'm not a bad guy."

"Isn't that what all bad guys say?"

A huge smile crossed his face. "Good point, Miss Ander-son. Good point." He did a quick scan of me and said, "I like you. You're—spunky."

"Let me guess," I said, tilting my head. "Under different

circumstances we'd be friends?" I snarked at him with a fair bit of sarcasm.

His grin grew. "I bet we would. Take care, Miss Anderson." He gave me a quick wink before he turned to walk away. After a few steps, Jake pivoted then continued walking backward as he spoke one last thing, "Anything you need. Call." His finger shot out at me to further punctuate his statement.

Peering down at his card, it read: Professor Jake Richter.

34

Holly

"Really, Ms. Anderson. After your performance three months ago as Juliet, I'd have expected you to jump at this next challenge," Principal McGreggor said as she sat across from me with a stern look on her face.

"I appreciate that you thought of me but—"

She shook her head sharply, deep frown on her face. "How many interviews did you do after the play?"

Closing my mouth, I looked off to the side. "A few."

"How many?"

"A dozen." Give or take.

"Right. And how are your acting classes going?" she asked, drumming her fingers on the desk.

I had to smile at her question. "Really well." There was no way I could lie about that. Somehow, one of the most prominent acting schools got wind of me after my debut performance and invited me—free of charge—to join them twice a week.

It was seriously some of the most fun I'd ever had. Evan had left a huge hole in my heart that was impossible to fill. But being on stage and acting in Romeo and Juliet had ignited something inside of me that I didn't know existed.

The acting classes fanned that flame into a new passion and a new world opened up before me that I'd never even dreamed of.

"With my job and school, I'm not sure I'll have the time," I said, grasping the arms of the chair.

Her lips came together before she sighed. "You're down to much fewer hours at work now since your scholarship funds were increased, correct?" A stern eyebrow raised.

"Well, yes. My mother needs me at home quite often to help her as well, though."

"Is she still refusing to see a doctor?" she asked gently. I nodded, resigned to the fact that my mother would never receive the help she needed. "I see. Well, it's completely up to you. If there's anything the school can do to help make your life easier, you know we're here for you, right?"

They had already done so much to help, I was reluctant to ask for anything more. "Thank you, that means a lot."

She nodded before rising from her chair. "Think about it. The leading role is yours if you want it."

～

"DID YOU SEE THIS?" Ivy asked me as she bit into an apple. Shielding her phone from any snoopers, she shoved it in my face.

The title of the article read, "The Pirhana's New Prey". Below it was a picture of Evan's dad and his assistant, Samantha, in a heated clinch.

Eyes wide, I read the article, not taking the time to even

blink. "Holy crap," I whispered to her, clicking off the screen.

"I know. My dad said he'll have to step down from his campaign."

"Really?" I asked, my voice almost squeaking.

Nodding, she said, "This isn't something he can just sweep under the rug."

"I wonder if they'll get a divorce?" I asked in a low voice.

"You ever hear from him?"

I stared at her as my stomach twisted. It felt like so long since I'd said his name out loud. "Evan? No."

"Not at all?" she asked, eyes squinting in disbelief.

"Nope." I gazed down at the beige tile flooring, hoping Ivy would change the subject. My shoulders slumped as I slid my arm onto the table and rested my head in my hand. The pain from losing Evan was a palpable force I tried extremely hard to keep at bay. If I allowed myself to wallow, I'd never leave my bed.

"Let's go out tonight," she said, tossing her hair over her shoulder. "Find us some men. I haven't been able to show off my appendectomy scar to anyone yet," she said, a hint of mischief in her eyes.

I laughed. "Mom's been even more sick lately. I should just go home."

"Can I help with anything?" she asked, placing her hand on my arm. "How about I bring over pizza?"

My eyes got a bit misty. "That would be nice."

～

"OH MAN, if she picks that loser I'm going to scream," Ivy said, scooping up another piece of pepperoni pizza, pointing at the TV.

I had to agree. "He's hot but stupid," I said, taking a bite of my breadstick.

"Who would even go on these shows? It's so humiliating." I shrugged.

"Holly," we heard my mom call from her room before a loud thump rocked the floor of the trailer.

Dropping our food, we both rushed into the dark room to find her on the floor, unresponsive. "Mom, Mom," I said over and over, turning her onto her back. This was far from the first time I'd found her on the floor, but this time was different.

In the past, she would have reeked of alcohol. For the last week or two, she hadn't touched any booze at all. I could feel my heart beating in my throat. "Should I call 911?"

Looking up at my friend, I nodded.

35

Holly

"You'll be fine," I lied to my mother, holding her cool, frail hand in mine. Her skin was mottled with a yellowish tinge. She looked so tiny and frail in the hospital bed.

The whites of her eyes were even tinted a sickly mustard gray. Shaking her head, she said, "We both know I'm not going to be fine." Her cough shook deep from within her tiny body.

"Of course—"

"It's my liver. They told me last year it was incurable."

My hands instinctively clasped hers even harder as my stomach fell. "What do you mean? You went to the doctor and didn't tell me?"

The thin, wispy hair on her head moved slightly as she admitted her secret. "They said there was nothing they could do, I was too far gone. One doc offered me a line of treatments that sounded worse than the actual disease," she said, starting into another coughing fit.

I put my arm behind her back, feeling the sharp bones poke into my skin. Lifting her slightly forward until she finished and could lay back down. "Why didn't you tell me." I gasped, finding it difficult to breathe.

"What would it change?"

"We could have gotten you some help?"

"Nothing anyone could do. I chose to drink myself to death. Figured I'd finish the job and save the taxpayers some money."

The bright florescent light above us flickered. "What about me?" I asked, realizing that soon I'd be left all alone. No mother, no grandmother, no father.

"You'll be better off. The trailer is paid for and Nanny set aside some money for you. There's papers in my bottom drawer."

The room around me spun while I closed my eyes, trying to absorb my mother's words. Months of refusals to see a doctor when she'd already gone but not told me about. I felt like I was going to slide right onto the hard, tiled floor.

"Good afternoon," a deep voice sounded from the door. Gazing over, my eyes focused on a tall, white haired man in a white coat. "I'm Dr. Perry," he said, walking over to us, hand stretched out to shake mine and then my mom's.

He cleared his throat. "Holly, do you mind if I take a minute to examine your mother alone, please?"

"I'll wait outside," I said, quickly finding my feet then walking out the door. The hallway was bustling with nurses, doctors, patients, and worried family members. Everything around me began spinning again.

"Whoa, there sunshine," a female voice said before wrapping an arm around my waist. "What'dya say we go find a seat?" I looked up into the kindest eyes I'd ever seen as I burst into tears. It was all too much. "No, no, hang onto me. Let's go into the greeting room for a minute," the nurse said, guiding me past the craziness into a quiet room. My fingers grabbed tightly into her pink scrubs, afraid of letting go.

I sat down and a moment later she handed me a cold, Styrofoam cup of water and ice. "Here, have a sip." I didn't know where it came from but I was grateful all the same.

"Thanks," I said, my hands and voice shaky as I drank the cool liquid.

The nurse sat down beside me, arm around my body for a side hug. "I'm Laura. Is Julia your mother?"

"Yeah."

"Did the doctor speak with you yet?"

I shook my head, taking another sip.

She rubbed my back. "She's real sick. You understand that, right?" she asked as I looked up at her with teary eyes and nodded. I understood now. "Can I go and grab the doctor to explain things more clearly to you? I bet this is all very confusing for you. Is there anyone we can call to be with you? Any family?"

"No, it's just us." Tears fell as I realized it would be just me now.

"Stay here, I'll be right back with the doctor, okay?" I nodded, shrugging my shoulders as my mind raced. What was I going to do now?

A silent TV on the wall played a well-known talk show. I swirled the ice around in my cup, thinking how much my life had changed in the last six months.

"Holly, I'm sorry to make you wait." Dr. Perry stepped in the room, Nurse Laura close by his side.

Gazing up at his stoic face, my stomach churned, acid rising further. Barely able to swallow, I did my best to not get sick. "It's fine."

His white lab coat flapped when he sat down in a hurry. Hands threaded together, he sighed. "This is difficult to discuss. Is there another family member we can call to be here with you?" His bright blue eyes searched mine. Deep frown lines on his forehead spoke of how stressful his job must be.

"It's just me. Nobody else is left," I said, stopping my chin from quivering.

He looked down, taking another breath. "Your mother is in the final stages of liver failure. I'm afraid the only thing we can do now is make her as comfortable as possible."

Again, my world spun as Nurse Laura sat beside me. The doctor continued. "We have a call into hospice."

"Hospice?" I asked, the word vaguely familiar.

Dr. Perry reached out for my hand. "It's where patients who are at the final stage of their illness go."

Final stage. Those words smacked me hard in the face.

Nurse Laura spoke up, "They'll make sure to manage your mom's pain and keep her as comfortable as they possibly can."

Wiping my eyes, I sniffed. "That would be good." She handed me a tissue. "How long do you think she's got?" I asked the question I didn't really want an answer to.

His answer shot right through my gut. "Not long."

⌒

"DO YOU WANT ANYTHING?" I asked, watching my mother struggling to breathe.

Her boney hand found mine. "No sense. It won't be long now." Closing my eyes, I tried to keep myself composed, tears leaking out despite my efforts. "I should have been a better mother." She gasped, turning her head slowly to look at me.

"You were fine," I lied, placing my other hand on her arm.

That started another coughing episode. "I was a shitty mom. I'm sorry you got stuck with me, kid. Thems the breaks, though. Ya get what ya get. At least when Nanny was around, she looked after you."

Then she closed her eyes, drifting halfway between here and somewhere else.

∿

THE STALE SMELL of cigarette smoke and sickness filled the air as I walked into the trailer for the first time in three days —or had it been longer? One day had dragged into the next making it impossible to tell how long I'd been there.

Slamming the door shut behind me, everything looked so foreign but the same. My mind pulled me to Mom's room, clumsily finding the switch, illuminating the mess. This was the one place she refused to allow me to clean.

Shoving boxes and clothes away from the solitary dresser, I pulled the handles on the bottom drawer. It was stuffed full of papers, manila folders, envelopes, and pictures. Things I never knew she'd kept, like my school photos and report cards.

One by one, I sorted everything into pictures, papers, and important documents until halfway through, I found a pink envelope that didn't seem to fit in with the rest—the edges faded lighter from the passage of time. Turning it around, it read, "To Holly", on the front.

Opening it up, I immediately recognized the hand-writing as my Nanny's.

Dearest Holly,

You'll never know how sad I am to be leaving you. Ever since you were born, you brought such light into my life.

I had full intentions of being here to watch you graduate, venture out into the world, get married, and one day have little ones of your own. But this damn disease had other plans.

I'm not sure if your mother will ever tell you about your father. If not, I've included that information for you. One day, you may be curious about what happened and who he is—which is your right.

All I'll say is that your mother changed the day he left. She stopped caring about anything or anyone. Instead of being thankful for you, I think she saw you as the reminder of what would never be.

Promise me one thing? No matter what happens in your life, don't do what your mother did. Being bitter and blaming others for your lot in life only hurts you in the long run. You've been given many gifts and talents—I could tell that almost instantly. Use what you have to live a happy life.

No doubt your road may be bumpier with more twists and turns than most. That just makes life more interesting.

Hearing the ticking of time is difficult, especially now. When I'm with you, it's nearly deafening. It's hard to believe I'll be gone, leaving you here.

Hopefully you remember our many happy times—how we listened to Shakespeare's plays, acting them out while we baked, cooked, cleaned. I'd read them to you, too, in hopes that one day you'd find a love in literature like I did.

Right now, a quote that sticks in my mind is from As You Like it:

"All the world's a stage,

And all the men and women merely players:

They have their exits and their entrances;
And one man in his time plays many parts."

It's my time to exit the stage, Holly. For you? It's time to make your grand entrance.

You're a reasonable child, so I expect you'll always have a good head on your shoulders. What I'm about to say will seem strange and at first, you'll think I've already gone crazy.

I'm leaving you money to do what you want with. No strings attached. You do well in school, I'm sure college is in your sights. But if something else calls to you, my dear, I want you to follow your dreams. No matter how silly or impulsive they may seem.

Life is short. Trust me.

Don't be so overly sensible that you forget to enjoy it.

I'm not gone yet so I intend to listen to you laugh and watch you play as much as I possibly can until it's my time to go.

I love you, my sweet, Holly.

Nanny.

TEARS FELL SO QUICKLY onto the letter, I was scared it would get ruined. Pulling it away, I wiped my eyes with my hand as I sniffled loudly into the silent room.

I truly was all alone.

36

Holly

Out of pure exhaustion I finally dropped into my bed some time the early hours of the morning, eventually finding sleep. I didn't know what time it was but I could feel the steady knocking on the front door all the way through the trailer. Blinking against the light shining through my window, I groaned as I moved my tired legs over the side of the bed.

The weight of what had happened fell down me like an anvil in a children's cartoon show. Only I had no desire to pop back up like an adorable character. Instead, I shuffled to the front door. Jason's anxious face pressed up close to the window.

His shoulders sagged when he caught sight of me and stepped back as I opened the door for him. "Hey kid. How are you doing?" His voice was low and wrought with concern for me as he stepped inside, looking around.

"Did you use your key? She's still not answering her phone," Vivienne said, rushing inside holding baby Hope on her hip with one hand and her phone plastered to her head with her other. "Oh, child." She gasped, clutching the phone to her chest as she stopped short. "You scared the living daylights out of us."

Viv's eyes got watery then she handed off the baby to Jason. "Come here," she said, her voice hitching, full of pity. I took a few steps toward her as she met me halfway. Her arms surrounded me like vices, gripping on like she was singlehandedly going to hold me together.

My vision blurred as pain gripped my heart so acutely, I figured for sure I was going to fall. If it weren't for Vivienne's strong arms, I would have. "We are so, so sorry, my dear. I wish you would have called us so we could have been with you and—" She ceased for a second, taking a deep breath. "And you wouldn't have been all alone."

We stayed like that for a while, her just holding me, gently rocking from side to side as we both cried in each other's arms. My already broken heart was shattered beyond repair.

"Come here, kid," Jason said, lifting one of Viv's arms up to move her away. She took the baby from him, wiping her eyes with the back of her hand. Jason's arms engulfed me in a huge bear hug. "Should've called us, Viv's right. When your boss told us just now, we ran right over." More tears burst out, knowing that I'd caused my friends to worry about me.

"Pack some stuff, missy. You're coming home with us." Vivienne rubbed my back then I felt a sudden patting from a tiny hand. Hope started making baby noises as she hit my shoulder. It was enough to bring me back to Earth.

Turning around, I let go of Jason, capturing her little hand in mine. "Hi, baby," I said, blinking away the tears that refused to stop. She pulled my hair, letting out a big, belly laugh as she did it.

"You need to stop laughing when she pulls your hair, Viv. Now she thinks it's a big joke." Jason scolded her as he untangled Hope's relentless hand from my hair.

"It is a big joke," Vivienne said, her eyes already swollen from crying. "Look at her laugh." She pointed at Hope's smiley face.

"Her hand's going to grow. You know that right? It'll be a whole lot less funny then."

Vivienne rolled her eyes, reaching for my hand. "Yeah, she's a regular monster." She gazed up at me and said, "Go pack some things. You're staying with us."

"I couldn't impose, really, I'm fine—"

"You need to be around family now," she said softly. "And we need to be around you."

Her words filled my heart with a warm, fuzzy feeling. In no way, shape, or form was I related to any of these people in my living room. "She's right, kid. Go pack."

37

Holly

"You're really leaving us?" Paige asked, her face pouty and sad. I answered her with a nod. She launched forward, pulling me in for a hug.

"What a waste of a great prom dress." Alex frowned, crossing his arms in front of him as he fake glowered. I knew how happy he was for me.

Pushing away from Paige, I poked Alex's shoulder. "You said you'd do my hair and makeup for pictures before I go."

He sighed, placing one hand on his hip. "It won't be the same as if you were actually here, though, instead of abandoning us for greener pastures."

I couldn't help the smile that completely overtook my face. I was leaving for greener pastures. Way greener. "But we'll have pictures and Ivy said we'd have a mini-prom at her house before I leave."

"Repeat after me: Not. The. Same." His stare refused to let me off the hook.

"Alex, chill. We'll have a fabulous sendoff party for

Holly," Ivy's head twisted in his direction, shooting him a look that could kill. "Who we are so incredibly happy for."

"Yeah, yeah." He sighed dramatically then wrapped his arms around my shoulders, pulling me close. "I'm going to miss you so much. Who's going to make sure you're using the right mascara with the correct liner? Or who'll remind you to use the under-eye cream so you don't get horrible bags and premature aging?"

My shoulders shook even though I tried my hardest to hold in my laugh. "Uh huh, it's all fun and games until you wake up one morning resembling a Shar-Pei instead of a hot, young actress." He scolded, not at all kidding.

That was it. All I could handle. I burst out laughing as did the other two girls. Alex just continued to glare. "I'll video message you all the time so you can still control my moisturizing regime," I said, trying to placate him.

"Uhhhggg, those cameras are awful. I'll need you to send me daily snaps on top of that," he replied all matter of fact.

"Deal."

"Can I text you? Gosh, our time zones are going to be murder to line up," Paige worried, looking off to the side like she was calculating in her head. She was correct—our time difference was going to suck.

"You better text me." Pointing at the rest of my friends, I said, "You all better text me. Often." My eyes began to water thinking about not seeing them for a while.

"Paige will still be up at all hours studying her brains out so that won't be an issue," Ivy said dryly, tossing her hair over her shoulder.

Alex cleared his throat. "Paige needs to stop studying her brains out and instead get her brains—"

"Alex," I yelled before he was able to finish. "Baby steps. But I agree you need to go out more, Paige."

"More?" Ivy scoffed. "That would imply the girl ever left her desk."

Paige rolled her eyes. "I leave my desk."

"Yeah, to pick up another book," Alex shouted, laying down on the couch.

"They're right, honey. You need to cut loose sometimes. It's not healthy to stay cooped up studying all the time." I squeezed her hand lightly.

"Look who's talking. When was the last time you went out with us?" Ivy questioned me and rightly so. Between work, school classes, acting classes and getting ready to move, there had been not a lot of free time. Whenever I did have a spare moment I liked just hanging with Viv, Jason, and the baby.

Over the last six months we'd gotten even closer. Whenever I'd suggested getting my own place and moving out they'd both out and out refused to hear of it. But when this opportunity came up for me even they couldn't deny how wonderful it was.

I was really going to miss them. They'd stepped in and become the family I never had. Just like this group in front of me. I guess when you aren't given family—you find it.

"You guys pick a date for mini-prom and let's start planning. Oh, and don't forget Viv is having a big supper for me before I go, too. You're all invited."

"That woman can cook," Alex announced, jumping up from the couch, wiggling to a beat only he could hear. "Count me in."

Paige hesitantly said, "Finals are only two months away, I should probably stay home and study."

Ivy's jaw dropped open. "After finals, you, and I, are going out and we're finding you a man."

The look of shock on Paige's face was too funny. "I don't need a man."

"Girlfriend, we all need a man. But you especially. Keeping all this," Alex said, gliding up beside us again, pointing to her face and body with his finger, "locked up in a tower is a crying shame. You need to let it all hang out sometimes."

She looked to me for support. "They're right, you know. You've gotta put the books down more often. Promise me you'll try?"

Sighing, she slumped her shoulders. "I suppose. But not until after finals."

38

Holly

"Absolutely marvelous, darling," the stage director said to me in her strong English accent as she put her arm around my shoulders. Her perfume almost as overbearing as her personality. "Just remember to keep in mind that your voice carries differently in the outdoors. You'll be a roaring success. I just know it. Oh, and your Romeo finally arrived. He's three days late but he makes up for it with his looks and charm. Trust me." She squeezed me closer to her side.

"He wanted to meet you in person. Just stop by his dressing room before you leave." One last hug and she pushed me toward the stairs that led to our tiny dressing rooms.

Lifting my skirt as I ascended the steps, I gazed thoughtfully at the many empty seats surrounding me. Without a doubt they would all be filled on opening night. A tiny smile came to my mouth as I thought about what performing on this kind of a stage would be like at night, under the stars— just how it was meant to be.

The well-placed lanterns swung in the breeze, just as happy to be here as I was. "Holy crap, did you see him? He's hot," the actress who played Juliet's mother said to a costume designer before she caught my eye and my sleeve. "Wait until you see Romeo," she said, pulling hard on the fabric. Her eyebrows waggled, making me laugh.

"I'm headed to his dressing room right now. Thanks for the heads up." I smirked as I kept on walking past her into the building.

My fingers grazed the makeshift sign on my dressing room door while I strolled on by. I'd been so happy to see my name on it. The room beside mine now had a hand-written nameplate as well. But all it said on it was, "Romeo". No real name on it.

My knuckles lightly rapped the old, wooden door. A minute or so passed before I knocked again, harder this time. The door opened only slightly then stilled. Frowning, I pushed it the rest of the way.

My heart stopped.

"Hi," Evan said with that sexy smile on his face that I'd missed so much.

Unable to move, I stood there, frozen. My brain couldn't make sense of what was going on. "I was hoping for a more enthusiastic reaction than that."

"What—"

He stepped forward, reaching around me to slam the door shut. "Let's try this again," he said in his low voice, those brown eyes piercing mine. "Hi." His hands touched my arms, pulling me closer.

My lungs still not fully working, I replied with a breathy, "Hi."

"I missed you," he said as his fingertips gently pushed my hair behind my ears.

"You did?" I asked, still muddled and confused.

He cracked a smile. "Mmm hmm. Did you miss me?"

Nodding ever so slightly, I said, "You're here."

He chuckled, tilting my head back as his lips came down on mine. "I'm here." Evan stole whatever breath was left in me as his mouth moved over mine. My heart fluttered while his arms folded around me. When my mind finally caught up with what was happening, I kissed him back, hands on his shoulders, pulling him closer.

"But why? I don't understand why you came?" I pushed back a bit, needing answers.

"For you," he said, the back of his hand grazing my cheek. "I nearly counted the days until your graduation."

"I didn't go."

Evan laughed, throwing his head back. "I noticed."

My face dropped at his words. "You came back for me?"

"Yep. Flew all the way there, stayed incognito and couldn't find out where the hell you'd gone."

Looking to the side, I explained. "Somehow, I got on with this drama company over here. They offered me a position, but wanted me early."

"So, you took finals a month early and ran off to England. I know, Ivy told me."

"She did?"

"I'm so sorry about your mom," he said, his eyes getting serious. "I wish—"

"I know," I said, placing my index finger on his lips to quiet him.

Reaching up, his hand grasped mine, kissing it before

pulling it down. "I wish I could have been there for you." His words traveled through me, creating warmth and a—calmness in their wake. My vision blurred as my emotions caught up. "It must've been so hard to do that all by yourself. You're so brave."

Immediately, my arms circled his body as my head crashed into his chest. Since I'd read Nanny's letter, I hadn't cried at all. Now it felt like months of tears and heartache burst out all at once. "I stayed with friends for a while. They looked after me." Memories of Vivienne and Jason coming to my aid during that horrible time choked me up even more.

Evan held me, my body wracked with grief and unshed emotions I'd somehow managed to bottle up for so long. Until now. "I'm so sorry. You have no idea how much." Our bodies swayed as he absorbed the hefty weight of my burdens.

"I haven't seen you in so long and now I'm bawling all over the place," I said, shaking my head as I gazed up at him.

"You're beautiful," he said, wiping the tears under my eyes with his thumbs.

"Liar," I said, rolling my eyes, a hint of a smile emerging.

"Where are you staying?" he asked, changing the subject.

"With the director and her husband for now. Everything's so expensive over here."

A huge grin spread on his face. "I know a good place."

"Really? Any strings attached?"

He leaned down, whispering right against my lips, "Lots."

CHAPTER 39—A FEW MONTHS LATER OR AN EPILOGUE OF SORTS...

Holly

"You ever miss home?" Evan asked me as we walked barefoot along the beach. This was still one of our favorite things to do when I was wasn't busy rehearsing or he wasn't dealing with business.

"Almost never," I replied truthfully. "I mean, I miss Viv and Jason and baby Hope. And my friends of course." However, I didn't miss the restlessness I felt there—like I was wearing an ill-fitting outfit.

"Seeing as they call you all the time you haven't had much opportunity to miss them," Evan stated, giving me the side eye.

I giggled, pushing my shoulder into the side of his body. He reached around, pulling my body closer. "That's mostly Alex. He's very concerned with my skin care regime and what the English countryside is doing to it."

"Well that makes sense," he said with sigh, shaking his head. Just then, his phone started ringing and he pulled it out of his pocket to take a look. "Just Jared. He's probably wondering about the vineyard in Italy."

"How many vineyards does one man need?" I teased him.

"Two, apparently. Maybe three if they accept my offer." We waded into the ocean a little further, our pants rolled up a bit. "Did you like it there?"

I turned my head to him. "In Italy? Who wouldn't? All that pasta and bread went straight to my hips and ass though. I have to be more careful in carb country." All that was true—just ask my pants.

He laughed, squeezing me tighter. "You look just as gorgeous as you did before we left."

"Uh, huh."

"You're beautiful."

"My agent said I need to stop with the carb comas if I'm going to audition for that new Blade Bodwin series." My stomach tightened at the thought. I tried not to think about it but Blade Bodwin was huge. As in big, huge.

"*When* you audition."

"I don't know. I can't see any reason for them to pick me out of all the other options they have." I dug my fingernails into my hands as I squeezed them into fists.

"Number one, you're a fantastic actress. Number two, they specifically contacted your agent and gave you a personal invitation to the audition. They want you. Don't you want to try?"

I wanted it more than anything. Whoever got in with Blade Bodwin would get more exposure than you could ever dream of. "Of course I do. I'd have to be crazy to turn that down. Besides, you're right—It would be nice to stop in and visit everyone while we're there. Show off my new English accent."

"I thought we could show them something else, too."

"My superior English toffee recipes?" I joked with him. In fact, I had yet to not burn a toffee concoction.

"Yeah—and this," he said, stopping us in the water as he pulled out a blue velvet box.

Any and all breath left my lungs. My heart pounded so loudly I was sure he could hear it. Evan opened the box slowly, holding it out for me to see. I'd never in all my life seen a ring with a diamond that big before. It was a huge, square rock with smaller ones traveling down the band. The way it sparkled in the light made me dizzy. "What—"

"Will you marry me?"

I slapped my hand to my heart as my skin tingled all over. "You're serious?" I breathed out, barely having enough air to say those two words.

"We spent months together and months apart. I can't be away from you again."

Fear clutched at my stomach. "But if I get this part—filming is in Los Angeles. I'll have to—"

"We'll have to—" he cut me off.

"We?"

"Yep. We'll go wherever your career takes us."

"What about your businesses? You've got vineyards to run."

"I'll run them *and* be with you. We'll make it work."

"My *career*?" It sounded funny to say that word about something that was so much fun for me, most of the time it didn't even feel like work. Evan nodded. "You make it all sound so simple."

"It is. Wherever you are—so am I. Simple." He shrugged as if it was no big deal to follow me around at a moment's notice.

"What if I fail?"

"What if you succeed?" he asked, his eyes holding mine until a big, goofy grin emerged on my face. Evan had always been my biggest supporter.

"I'm only nineteen. Who gets married at nineteen?"

"You're the oldest nineteen year old in the world. And my mother is going to want us to have a huge wedding. That'll mean months of planning."

"Months? I haven't even met your mother," I said, eyes wide and unblinking as my heart caught in my throat.

"You will when we go home and tell her we're engaged."

"It's kind of bad timing—with their divorce and everything." And what a divorce that was. Public, humiliating, and messy were the nicest words I could use to describe it.

"With those two it'll always be bad timing. I'm not waiting to marry the woman I love because my father couldn't keep it in his pants." There was a weighted silence between us as he continued to hold out the ring. "You haven't answered me yet."

"Answered what?"

His large, warm hand reached out for mine. "Holly Elizabeth Anderson, I love you more than I ever thought I could love anyone. Will you do me the honor of becoming my wife?"

"Are you sure?" I squinted at him and then one more time at the ring to make sure it was really as monstrous as I'd thought.

It was.

"You're giving me a complex here," he said, raising an eyebrow as he tilted his head.

He looked so cute I dove forward to hug him, my heart ready to explode. Mumbling into his chest, I answered,

"Evan Alistair Marshall-Stanton, I love you more than I ever thought I could ever love anyone." Tipping my head back, gazing into his handsome face, I said, "I would love to be your wife."

CHAPTER 40—OR—WHAT'S NEXT?

Paige

"This is seriously the lamest," Alex said, rolling his eyes as he sipped on a martini. He bumped my arm with his elbow and said, "Let's give it five more minutes then we can take off."

Giving him my best smile, I made a different suggestion. "Or we could leave now and go home to watch a movie?"

His head tipped to the side, eyes narrowing. "You're not getting out of this. You promised Holly you'd come out with us and that," he said, pointing his finger into my bare shoulder, "is exactly what you're doing. We'll find you a man even if I have to go to extreme measures."

My eyes widened. Alex's extreme measures were to be avoided at all costs. They were sometimes loud and always —guaranteed—embarrassing. "No, no, no, that's not necessary at all," I said, shaking my head, grabbing onto his hands. "Five minutes it is." I prayed that my smile was believable enough.

The truth was—I liked being out. Way more than I

should. If I didn't keep a tight handle on myself I knew I could end up like my mother. A young, single mother, working her fingers to the bone for a family of rich people. My grandmother had gotten pregnant with my mom before grandpa had married her and made an honest woman out of her like he always joked.

To me it was no joke.

No way was I winding up in trouble with no husband and most importantly no education.

As soon as I was old enough to cogitate, I promised myself I'd never follow in their footsteps. So far, so good. I'd never even had a boyfriend.

"Time to play Who Would You," Alex announced, setting his martini glass down then slapping his hands on his lap.

I laughed out loud, nearly spilling my drink. Playing this game with Alex was always hilarious. He'd bring it up in the most inappropriate places—school retreats, his cousin's bar mitzvah, or my personal favorite—a homeowners meeting his mom made him—us—go to once when she was out of town.

The full name of the game should be, Who Would You Sleep With. It was a funny way to pass the time especially in mandatory boring situations.

"Hmm, I think that guy over there with the really tight pants is just right for me," he said, raising his eyebrows as he wiggled his body on the stool. "Your turn." His head snapped to me waiting for an answer.

Scoping out the place, my eyes traveled along until they stopped suddenly on a pair of bright blue eyes aimed directly at me. His stare was so intense, I spun around on my seat, leaning on the bar.

"Good, great God up in Heaven, please let that hunk of

perfection whisk our good girl—Paige—up in his very muscular, very strong arms, and carry her away."

Glaring over at Alex, his hands pressed together in prayer, eyes shut tight, I punched him in the arm. "Would you stop? Someone might hear you." My vision searched for the man who'd been staring. A shock went through me when our eyes met again. The side of his handsome mouth quirked up, sending a warmth down to my lower belly.

He looked like trouble.

The kind I knew better than to get involved with.

Also the kind I was very much attracted to.

"Knock me down and call me Susan," Alex said, grasping my arm. "Not once in four years have I ever seen you blush."

Turning around again, I grabbed my barely touched drink. "I'm not blushing," I said, shaking my head at him. "It's the alcohol."

Alex snorted so loud I glared at him. "You've barely had anything." He rolled his eyes as he straightened his shirt. "You've got a thing for Mr. Hotstuff over there. Admit it."

I would do no such thing—to him or to myself. "Whatever."

"All right, girlie. Part deux of Who Would You commences now." He fake shook out his hair like he was some kind of diva—which he was. "Watch and learn, my dear. Watch and learn." Then he strode off as though walking down some kind of imaginary red carpet only he could see.

That made me laugh again so hard I had to put down my drink or risk spilling it. The second half of Who Would You consisted of making some kind of contact with your chosen one. Be it touch or talk it didn't matter. Fail to complete this part of the game and you'd lose.

We didn't play for money or anything. But losing your pride was worse.

As he neared his intended victim, I kept my eyes glued on his progress. A few more yards and he'd be there. My stomach gave a small twist wondering what stunt he was going to pull this time. With Alex you just never knew.

Two more steps and then the show really started. He pretended to trip then both his hands reached for Mr. Tight Pants' arm. Alex ended up on his knees, pulling so hard on the guy's arm that he was nearly bent in half attempting to assist.

The look on Alex's face made me chuckle out loud. He was quite enamored. I had to admit that Mr. Tight Pants was a hottie.

The piece de resistance was yet to come. Struggling to get up, Alex took full advantage by leaning on his new friend, wiping his brow in an exaggerated manner and trying to get as close as he could to him. When Alex finally moved to leave, the tablecloth had other ideas. Like staying attached to Alex's watch.

As he swung his arm up to wave goodbye the drinks on the table went crashing to the floor as though Alex were some kind of mock magician. He looked genuinely shocked —I don't think that was part of his act.

Wait staff from all around zeroed in on the crisis, moving to pick up, clean, and make sure no one was hurt.

The commotion that created made me laugh so hard I doubled over, nearly unable to breathe. My stomach hurt and tears streamed down my face. A few minutes later, the man of the hour glided up to me.

"You're turn now, missy."

That set me off again. "How am I supposed to follow that?" I raised my hands in the air and pretended to bow multiple times. "You win, dude. There's no way I can beat you. You're the master."

Yanking on his collar with his thumbs and index fingers he said, "True. I am the best at this game but it's not truly finished until all participants participate. Now, off you go. Get." His hands pushed me off my stool forcing me forward.

I'd been friends with Alex for years. He would never give up until I at least tried. "Fine, but I don't know who to pick."

Alex shouted, "Ha, yeah right. The guy you're making googly eyes with. Now scoot." One more push and I was on my way. No fooling him.

The rules were really pretty simple. Contact could mean anything. Even just a polite, hello. I could say hi to someone. It wouldn't be the showstopper Alex embarked on. That was okay. One quick greeting then we could leave.

My heart drummed a steady beat as I approached my Who Would You target. I could see the back of him now. His hair wasn't unkept so much as a few weeks past needing a cut. Which made it just the perfect length for me to run my fingers through.

That thought jarred me out of my daydream. I needed to stay focused. Get this done then get home. Wiping my clammy palms on the sides of my dress, I inhaled a deep breath. A few more seconds and this would be over.

My pace slowed now that I was directly behind him. Lollygagging there for a bit I waited in the hope that he'd turn around, halting any further need for me to grab his attention.

Watching the curve of his neck move as he tossed back the amber remnants in his glass caused my skin to heat. Something in me wanted to reach out and stroke the skin there. I bet it was hot—maybe even a bit sweaty.

If I touched my lips—just so—I wondered if—

Just then someone bumped up behind me with so much force I couldn't help but be propelled into the very neck I had been daydreaming about. "Oooff, I'm sorry," I said, genuinely shocked to now be pressed up fully to my target's back.

His skin felt almost scalding through his shirt into my clumsy body. The heat from his back sizzled against my breasts causing my nipples to harden at the contact.

"Well, I'm honored," he said, twisting around placing his hands on my waist. "Thought for a minute I was wrong. But I'm never wrong." That smirk emerged again holding my attention as well as my breath hostage.

I felt almost dizzy being so close to him. My stomach clenched, filling with butterflies. "You're honored for what exactly?" I asked, squinting at him, not comprehending his meaning.

His smile grew. "You and your friend," he said, nodding in Alex's direction. "You're playing, Who Would You. Correct?"

My stomach dropped. How did he—"I've played it many times before. Hell, I practically invented that game." He chuckled, his fingers tightening into my skin.

A blush rose on my cheeks, my legs desperately wanting to give out. "Umm," was all I could say.

"You are the cutest thing I've seen in a very long time." His eyes raked me from head to toe, spending a bit more time on my cleavage than he should have. "By the way, I'm Jake. And you are?" he asked, sticking his hand into mine. His large, warm grasp engulfed my tiny one.

"Umm—Mindy," I replied, not wanting to give him my real name for some reason. Like if I did, maybe it would make this—real. And it couldn't be real.

"Can I tell you a secret?" he asked, lowering his voice a

bit, pulling me closer to whisper in my ear, creating waves of goose bumps. "I already picked you out as my, Who Would You."

≈

CURIOUS ABOUT WHAT kind of trouble Evan's best friend, Jake gets into with Holly's friend, Paige?

I guarantee you're going to love watching this notorious playboy being brought down to his knees—literally.

Grab some popcorn, get a front row seat and hunker down as *Professor Jake Richter* breaks his own iron clad rules in:

Professor Richter's Rules

Pre-order now!!

Don't miss out.

Do you hear wedding bells for Evan and Holly? Because I sure do...

Want the juicy inside scoop on what happens next with our favorite up and coming actress and her vineyard heir? Make sure to pre-order Professor Richter's Rules to find out!!

ACKNOWLEDGMENTS

As always, I have to thank my husband for his patience and love and support. My love for you grows endlessly. My rock and constant to cling to when the waters get rocky. Which they often seem to do.

Carla Kay VanZandt, again...WHAT would I do without your genius to help and guide me? Thank you my dear.

Tina Snider, your help and friendship is as always —invaluable.

Alexis Krobatch and Leslie Wiggins Spraggs—Your input was HUGE. I thank you again for dropping everything and reading a VERY rough draft. Your opinions aid me in all the best ways.

Kristen Theobold—Thank you again for being my beta. Your texting while you read made me smile. Especially the yelly ones.

QB Tyler—Thank you for answering my questions and guiding me in the right direction.

Gywn McNamee—Your advice was direct and spot on with this one. As usual. Thank you.

This book was a joy to write and I had so much fun putting these words down on paper.

What I hadn't expected was how much LIFE was going to get in the way.

It did.

We dealt with it. Then dealt with it again. And yes, once again.

Finally setting this book out in the world is not only a professional accomplishment but also a personal one.

Sometimes it's one step at a time, one foot in front of the other. And that's okay.

Just as long as you keep moving forward.

ABOUT THE AUTHOR

Jessa lives in a very nondescript, unassuming town filled with the best kind of people. Most days, she can be found in the stands of various soccer fields, cheering on her Youngest, or discussing books with her Oldest (who is an English Honors student).

At night, if she's not up burning the midnight oil, Jessa enjoys snuggling up to her real-life-chef hubby and watching his latest cheesy romance movie pick. He always chooses the best ones (after he cooks supper, of course).

Visit her BLOG or drop in and say "hi" on any of the social media links below.

Printed in Great Britain
by Amazon